T0078118

THE TREATY OF I: THE GENESIS

A Novel by

Takeem Ragland

authorHOUSE®

AuthorHouse™
1663 Liberty Drive
Bloomington, IN 47403
www.authorhouse.com
Phone: 833-262-8899

Published by AuthorHouse 10/12/2021

ISBN: 978-1-6655-3477-2 (sc)
ISBN: 978-1-6655-3496-3 (e)

To the thinkers and doers in my life, who continue to break down barriers and encourage me to explore New JourNeYs.

One love

Contents

Hi, I'm Lena

"I have to see what could happen for me. I may not get another chance like this," Terry tells Carla, as he continues to pack up his clothes. "I'm not really happy teaching here and I still need some certifications, before I could get a pay raise. I want to take a chance and see what happens. I want to meet new people, have new adventures, drink at different local bars," he claims.

"Oh boy," she gasps.

"I'm just tired of the mundane type of life. Get up, get dressed, go to work, come home and watch Netflix. And things are spendy here in Portland. I love teaching and I love being in the classroom, but I want something more. I want an adventure that will make me a better man. I want to find my truest self. Should I feel guilty about that?" he says

"You shouldn't feel guilty, and I think you should feel proud that you have the guts and opportunity to do something like this," she says.

"I got that: guts and opportunity," he says as they both share a laugh.

Terry continues to pack and fold up the clothes that he wants to take. The clothes he doesn't want to take, he puts into a box marked, "TERRY'S CLOTHES."

"I just want a new adventure and new friendships," he says. "I understand and who knows, maybe you'll find your wife out there," she says smiling.
"I don't think so," he responds.
"Why not?" she quickly asks.

Terry stuffs his last blue t-shirt into his black suitcase, puts his foot on the top of it, and zips it up. He takes a quick moment to catch his breath and then says, "I'm not really going out there to date anyone, and besides I doubt those girls will be thinking about me."
"Do you not like interracial dating?" she asks.
"I don't have a problem with it. I mean, you know how it is here, usually blacks stay with blacks, whites stay with whites and so on. That's all I've ever known," he states.
"I know, but just keep an open heart, Terry. We can't want to grow if we don't put ourselves under a certain amount of pressure. Anyhow, I'll be up at 8 am so that I can take you to PDX. Make sure your butt is up. I love you Gravy," she says, as she hugs her brother tightly.

"Terry, I just want you to be happy, and if you have to go halfway across the world then I'm with you," she says, taking a drink of water from her eco-friendly water bottle.

"Thanks C, I really appreciate it. I just feel that at 32-years-old, I should have traveled more and seen more of the world. I've never left the country and I think ma and pops would have supported me. I mean a relationship would be nice, but I also want to focus on myself," he says.

"You know I'm here for you and I always will be. You will be the first person in the family to do something like this and I think now is a good time to make a move to China. I want you to do what's best for you on your journey," she says as she walks out of the room and closes the wooden door.

The night before his flight, Terry is in the bedroom at his sister's apartment staring at the ceiling. "Am I making the right decision? Do I need to stay home? What if my life will be better here? What will happen to me? What will happen to my family?" He thinks to himself.

This is a long-awaited journey for Terry, he has been wanting to travel and live overseas ever since he was little and had an opportunity when he was in college. He couldn't afford to pay for all of his visa costs and made a promise to himself that he would one day live and work in China.

Always fascinated by the culture and the country, Terry knew where he wanted to go when he had the chance. Life has a way of doing things in its own time and not the time when we want it. This always helps us to grow and develop further, so when the moment comes, it is the right time for us to supersede expectations.

Knowing that he has to be up early; Terry sets his alarm, turns off the bedroom light, and goes to sleep.

The next morning, Terry wakes up before his alarm clock. When life, purpose, and opportunity are aligned, you won't need to wait for an alarm. Terry and his sister are riding to the airport and he is thinking, "Maybe I should really turn around and go home!"

"No, there's no turning back at this point. I have to go. Don't give yourself a way out," he thinks to himself. It's important to stick with formidable obstacles and not look for a quick way out; there is something greater coming. Want the reward, be willing to suffer and sacrifice for as long as it takes to get there.

Terry and his sister arrive at the airport and he gets his one huge piece of luggage out of Carla's red 2016 Hyundai Sonata trunk. They give each other one final hug and Terry says, "I love you C! Take care of the family for me. I'll be back in a year," he says pulling his luggage onto the sidewalk. "Take care of the family for me, and I'll message you once I get to Beijing. You already downloaded WeChat, right?" he asks.

"Yes, I did," she replies.

He grabs his suitcase, takes out his passport, and checks his ticket. Waving goodbye to his sister, he walks into PDX. Carla gets into her car and drives off, Terry goes to check his luggage and heads towards his gate. "This is going to be the longest flight. What will I do for 20 hours?" he thinks, as he gets to Gate 1 and places his book bag beside him.

The plane begins to board and Terry gets to his seat with no hesitation and he can't wait for the complimentary breakfast; whatever that will be. He didn't eat breakfast, the nerves in his body had tricked him into believing that he wasn't hungry. The nerves began to subside as he sat in his seat, put on his seatbelt and took a couple of deep breaths.

"Good morning everyone, this is your captain speaking; I would like to personally welcome you to Uni World AirLines. This is flight number 6892 heading to Beijing, China with a layover in Vancouver, Canada. Total airtime will be 20 hours. Please fasten your seatbelts and put your phones onto airplane mode. Clear skies today and should be clear skies all the way through. So sit back and relax. We will serve breakfast once we are at cruising altitudes. Thank you again for choosing Uni World Airlines flight 6892 to Beijing by way of Vancouver," the pilot says, as he hangs up the speaker.

This made Terry feel much more comfortable, as he laid his head back and he fell asleep.

A 4-hour layover in Vancouver and a total of 20-hours flight time later, Terry arrives in Beijing and is picked up by a company staff member. The Chinese characters on the wall at the airport, officially let Terry know that he is in China. "Wow, I'm really in Beijing!" Terry thought to himself. Now, this was Terry's first time out of America and he was excited. As Terry stepped outside of the airport to load the van, the warm China sun shone down on his skin. Terry never thought the day would come when he would be in China.

He was dropped off at the hotel and was able to rest once he was in his room. The receptionist spoke English and Terry was happy, because he knew survival Chinese. He studied and taught himself some Mandarin before he came but he was far from fluent. He pays his deposit money for the and gets to his room. After a 20-hour flight, a Vancouver layover, and a heart-pumping van ride through Beijing traffic, Terry passes out on his hotel bed.

He spends a half of the day at the Beijing office and then has to go to his teaching city: Tianjin. It's time for Terry to catch the speed train to Tianjin. Terry has never been on a speed train before and needless to say, he was pretty excited. "I wonder how fast this thing goes?" he thought to himself. The speed train looked fast and it was. "308 kph! What is the conversion to MPH?" he thought.

"It is about 191mph! That's fast!"

Once he gets to the train station in Tianjin he has to find his boss, and head to the bank to set up a bank. "I know she's here somewhere. She has a black jacket, a black bookbag, and long black hair. Wait, I think I saw her over at the Burger King. Yup, that's her." Terry walks over to his boss and says, "Hi, I'm Terry! Nice to finally meet you!"

"Hi Terry, I'm Danielle but you can call me Danni," she says as they walk towards the metro station.

"Thank you for the warm welcome," he responds.

"Oh, you're welcome! Thank you for coming to our center. How are you finding everything so far?" she asks.

"Not too bad. Everything is just going so fast once I stepped off the plane, but I'm adjusting. Is it always this hot in April?" he asks, pulling his luggage behind him.

"Well things will slow down and become easier. The weather usually does warm up around April in the city. Did you get your phone set up?" she asks.

"Yes, the phone is all good. I just need to get the bank account going," he says right as Danni hands him a Tianjin metro card.

"We will get that set up today. I will go to the bank with you," she says as she passes through the silver turnstiles.

He continues his day in Tianjin, sets up his bank account and goes to the office and meets some of his coworkers. Terry couldn't get too comfortable in Tianjin because he had to go back to Beijing for one more day of training.

So, Terry tiredly but excitedly goes from Beijing to Tianjin, back to Beijing, and finally back to Tianjin in about 5 days. "What a first week in China, but this is what I wanted. I need some sleep now," Terry realizes.

Within the first two weeks of arriving in China: he was teaching classes and becoming fully integrated into his new workplace. He became more stable in his teaching, and he was able to find an apartment in a former hotel turned apartment building. Teaching ESL classes to adults was something new for him, but he was a teacher back home. "You're a teacher man! Don't lose what you already know," Terry explains to himself.

One day during his 3rd week in China while Terry is at his desk, he receives an email from Danni that reads:

> Hi all,
>
> I hope you all are having a great week. There will be a new Course Consultant, Lena, starting next week. In order for her to become more acquainted with our products and services, she will be observing some of

7

your classes next week. I will let you know
the time and day that she will observe you.

Best Regards,

Danni Wu
Education Manager

This is nothing new to Terry, he is used to people coming
into his classroom to observe his teaching. Although Terry
is still learning about the products himself, he welcomes the
observations. Really he has no choice but to welcome the
observations as an educator. Whether Terry was teaching at
his old middle schools or teaching in China, observations
were nothing new to him. "I just hope she comes to a class
that I taught before," Terry thought. The curriculum at his
center has many lessons, and he is still trying to familiarize
himself with the content. "But more feedback is useful for
me, especially since I've only just started a month ago," he
thinks to himself.

The following week arrives and Terry finds out that she will
be attending two of his classes. "I have no idea what she
looks like but I'm sure I will figure it out." As Terry walks
up to his classroom, he notices someone in the back of the
classroom with a black blazer and a white-button up shirt.
"Light-brown complexion, blonde and brown short haircut,
nails done, big brown eyes, and just stunning!" Terry says
in his mind. "Good evening class, so we have a special guest
today! Please welcome our new advisor, Lena! Everyone says
hello, Lena," he states.

"Hello Lena!" The class simultaneously says.

"I can't keep my eyes off her. How am I going to teach when I can't even concentrate right now?" he asks himself.

Terry felt that little flutter in his chest every time he looked at Lena. The next class only had one person in it, and Lena was there observing. Terry saw her taking notes and wondered what she wrote down in her notepad so intently.

After class was over, they both walked back to the office. Terry, not knowing what to say, just stays awkwardly quiet. Back in the office, Terry nervously sat down in his chair, and Lena sat at the computers across from him. The advisors and teachers sat across from each other, with 4 computers dividing the two sides.

She lifts her eyes from the computer and asks, "Hi, I'm Lena again. I'm sure you know by now. How long have you been in China?"

"She spoke to me," he thinks in his mind.

Terry swallows before he says, "nice to meet you Lena, my name is Terry. I've only been in China for about a month. Not very long." There were only five people in the office that night, but all the other teachers have left.

"So, why are you still here? You don't have a girlfriend or any friends?" she asks him.

"I know she didn't just call me lonely," he thinks to himself. He quickly chuckles and says, "no I don't have a girlfriend and I do have friends! And I have been staying late to do some extra planning, until I have a good understanding of these lessons," he confidently responds

Lena must have thought that Terry was just some lonely guy who stayed at work, so he didn't have to go home to a lonely apartment. If that's what she thought, then she would actually be correct.

"I was just asking a question," she says.

About 10 minutes later, Terry goes home. "I wonder what she thinks about me? Is she single? Kids?" Terry thought about this all night in his bed. Terry went to bed that night with Lena on his brain, and it wouldn't be the last night he would treasure the thoughts of her.

The next day, Terry secretly couldn't wait to get to work. "I wonder if she is working today," he thought. The advisors had different days off and on than the teachers had. There was a chance that Lena wouldn't be there. Just in case she wasn't there, Terry lays out one of his best outfits. A nice plain-white button-up shirt, with a yellow and blue striped bow tie, and some navy-blue suspenders. As Terry walks to the train station, he can't stop thinking about Lena. "She's stunning. What if she has a boyfriend? What if she has a girlfriend? What if she was just being nice and is not interested?" Terry's mind is doing the 100-meter dash in his mind.

Terry gets to the train station and realizes that he left his bow tie at his apartment. The spring has already started to heat up, and the temperature is already pushing 30 degrees Celsius. To avoid sweating too much and messing up his clothes, he goes to work in regular clothes.

"I look good in my bow tie, but I'm not leaving this train station to go back and get it. But what if she's there? I have to keep making a good impression on her." Terry sprints out of the train station, runs past the Pizza Hut and the

Chinese BBQ restaurant, and hops onto the elevator in his building. He gets to the 27th floor, picks up his yellow bow tie and runs back to the train station. By the time Terry gets onto the train, he is dripping with sweat and out of breath. Luckily the train is pretty cold, so Terry was able to cool off a little.

Terry looks at his gray sports watch as he walks through the door of his office: 11:05 am.

"Hi Kelly," he says to one of the advisors at the front desk.

"Hi Terry. How are you today?" she replies.

"I'm doing ok. Hey, uhhh…is the new advisor here today?" Terry tried to passively ask.

"Oh Lena? No, she's off today. Why? Are you ok? You look a little out of it," Kelly seems to interrogate.

"Who me? I'm ok, I was just wondering because I let her borrow one of my favorite pens," he blurts out.

"Oh, well she's not in today," Kelly states.

Lena has already consumed Terry's thoughts and now she's got him asking about her whereabouts. "Pull yourself together. She's pretty, but she's not all that," he tries to convince himself.

He takes his bow tie out of his bag and thinks, "At least I got my bow tie." This is the same bow tie that was supposed to impress Lena and convince her to go on a date with him. The day goes by uneventfully and he has thought about her all day. "I've never quite seen anybody like her. And the audacity of her to ask me why I'm so lonely. If I wanna be lonely, I'll be lonely," he thinks out loud.

Terry continues to go back and forth in his head as his boss, Danni, walks into the office. "Hi Terry, can I talk to you for a moment? You know about our Dragon Boat Festival holiday coming up, right?" she confidently asks him, standing next to his swivel chair.

"Yes, I've heard about the holiday before, but I don't know what it's about," he responds. "Well, this is a perfect time for you to learn about the holiday. You and Lena are hosting a Dragon Boat Festival Party for our center," she voluntells him.

Terry's mind was doing backflips, but he didn't want to seem too happy. So the only thing that came out of Terry's mouth was a high-pitched, "sure!"

"Ok great! I've already talked to Lena and maybe you two can get together and start planning when she comes in," she explains.

There was only one question on Terry's mind: "What is the Dragon Boat Festival?"

Can I Have Your WeChat?

"Oh, that's a good shot!" The NBA playoffs are on, and Terry is pumped. The time difference causes him to watch the highlights on YouTube the following day. "I bet the Bucks are going to beat the Raptors in 6," he wrongly assumes. Anyway, while Terry was on YouTube, he decided to do some research about the Dragon Boat Festival. In America, Terry would see videos of these illustrious boats flying by on the water, with a Dragon face on the front of the boat. Now it was time to actually see what the boats and the festival was all about. "D-R-A-G-O-N-B-O-A-T F-E-S-T-I-V-A-L," is what he puts into his YouTube search engine. He clicks on the first link that comes up, and it doesn't give him much information.

"That didn't turn out so good," Terry says out loud. Desiring to find out more about this festival, because he wants to impress Lena when it comes time to host the event.

"There has to be something about this festival on YouTube. A song or something," he continues to look and eventually comes across this animation about the Dragon Boat Festival.

"This might work. And it's a little rap about the actual history of the festival," he excitedly thinks to himself. For the rest of the evening, he watches the video and tries to remember as much as he can.

He finds out that the festival is a celebration about the life of a famous Chinese poet: Qu Yuan. "I don't know much about the festival, but the song is nice!" That night Terry falls asleep with the song stuck in his head.

The next day at work, he has a meeting with Lena to plan this event. She brushes her short brown and blonde hair behind her ears and asks, "what do you know about the Dragon Boat Festival?" Terry can barely look away from her big brown eyes, and he loses his thoughts.

Terry's heart starts to do jumping jacks as he says, "I looked up some stuff about it last night," Lena leans her head to the left and continues to look at him.

"I was up late last night trying to look up videos or anything about the festival. I found out that it is about a dead poet named Qu Yuan," Terry is impressed with himself and he believes that Lena is too. He goes on to explain what he briefly researched about the festival. He's hoping this will impress her, and hopefully lead to future conversations. "Just get her WeChat and try to ask her out on a date," he nervously thinks to himself.

On the morning of the office party, Terry is up an hour before the sun. He puts on his pinstriped pants, his navy-blue suspenders and his yellow bow tie. "I may not remember everything, but at least I look good," he declares. On his way to work that morning, the sun was sparkling through clouds like light through a spinning disco ball. This day was quite warm, so

Terry wore one of his favorite navy-blue Nike t-shirts and a pair of gray shorts into work. On the train, Terry is constantly going over the script in his head. "What do I know about the Dragon Boat Festival? Well, I know that…," he practices the script.

"I can't be too loud when I'm hosting this party. They're going to think I don't know what I'm talking about," he continues to go through different scenarios until he arrives at Yingkoudao station. He stops at the Starbucks in the lobby of his office building and orders what is usually a Grande vanilla latte, but today he was feeling different. Something about the sun and the clouds spoke to him on this day.

"Nǐ hǎo ma. What would you like?" says the Starbucks barista with a smiling face. "Nǐ hǎo. Wǒ yào caramel macchiato," Terry replies.

"Hǎo de. Something new today?" says the barista.

"Yeah, I'm feeling a little excited today," he expresses, as he takes out his phone and clicks on the Alipay app to pay for his order.

Terry gets up to the office, changes his clothes and starts his workday. With 3 classes to teach in the morning, he prepares for his lessons and finalizes his notes for the event. For the Dragon Boat Festival, his office has prepared this event for students and their families to attend. They will eat Zongzi, or sticky rice, as well as they will play a trivia game about the history of the Dragon Boat Festival. It's about 3 in the afternoon and Terry and Lena meet in classroom 2, to make the final adjustments for the event.

"Are you ready? Do you remember your script?" Lena winks and asks.

"I'm always ready," he raises his eyebrows and says, as she chuckles.

"I think the families will start to arrive at 4:00 pm. The PowerPoint is all ready to go?" she asks.

"Yes," he says.

"Ok, well I'm going to change. I will see you shortly," she responds.

Music is playing and there are snacks on the main lobby's three tables. Classes are done for the day, as students begin to fill up the main lobby of the office and join the festivities. This is Terry's and Lena's first time hosting an event, so they want it to be perfect. Mainly, Terry wants it to be perfect so that he could hopefully ask her out after the event. Then, it's game time and 4:00pm rolls around and students are fully gathered in the main lobby.

"Welcome to the Dragon Boat Festival Party!"

This is the title displayed on the screen in the lobby. As Terry puts on his navy-blue blazer and fixes his yellow bow tie, he sees Lena out of the corner of his eye. In her form-fitting, dark blue dress, Lena makes Terry's heart stumble. Her light-brown skin shines bright as her brownie colored eyes flatter the room.

"My goodness her booty looks nice in that dress," he thinks in his mind.

"Hey, we match! Just like we planned," she announces to him. In reality, they didn't plan on matching for the event, it just kind of happened. When life corresponds with nature, it always solidifies that things were meant to be.

"It's game time," Terry demands to himself. They go out in front of the students to begin, and he introduces the event as Lena translates.

"So, Terry, what do you know about the Dragon Boat Festival?" she asks with a very scripted tone. He takes a deep breath, looks out the window for a moment and says, "I'll tell you what I know. So the Dragon Boat Festival is about an ancient Chinese Poet, Qu Yuan. He was an advisor to the emperor, but other people were jealous of him. They spoke lies about him, and word got back to the emperor that he was talking bad about him. Qu Yuan left and fled to a nearby river. The emperor's army got to the river and Qu Yuan jumped into the river to avoid capture and drowned. People heard the news and got into boats to try and save him. They didn't want the fish to eat him, so they threw sticky rice in the river so the fish could eat that. And those boisterous drums that you hear; they did that so that body wouldn't be shredded by the boats on the water. So, that is the little bit that I know about Duan Wu Jie." Terry's chest is percolating, as he tries to grab his breath after he says as much as he could remember.

The audience claps and seems happily surprised that Terry knew that much about the Dragon Boat Festival. The rest of the event went perfectly and Terry even impressed himself. They made Zongzi and had a good time. He even found out that he had a particular taste for the red bean ones.

After the event was over, Terry and Lena began to clean up and put everything back into place. Danni walks up to both of them and says, "great job, you two! I think the students had a good time and Terry I'm impressed."

"Me too Terry! I didn't know that you knew all of that about the Dragon Boat Festival. You must've done your homework," Lena says, as she puts a table back in order. As they continue to talk, Danni begins to put some chairs back into the classrooms.

"Yeah, I had to do some YouTube searches over the past week and just did my best to remember," he quickly responds. Knowing that he practiced the script for days, he still missed some information.

"This was a nice event, and we work pretty well together. Maybe I should ask her for her WeChat," he nervously thinks to himself.

"Hey, what do you usually do during the weeknights?" Terry could barely get the sentence out his mouth.

"Nothing much. Usually, I go home and chill or try to get to my gym," she says.

"Well, maybe we could go get together next week and get something to eat, because you like to eat, right? I mean not that I'm calling you fat, I just mean everybody has to eat. It's like a natural thing," he embarrassingly says as he wipes two drops of sweat away from his forehead.

"Are you asking me out on a date mister?" she says, looking down at the table.

Terry's nerves begin to increase, and he starts to sweat even more. "No! Why would I ask you out on a date?" he nervously asks.

"Oh that's a shame because I would've said yes," she says back and seems to blush a little.

"Well in that case, I was asking you out on a date," he quickly changed his response.

"Could I get your WeChat?" he asks, putting the last chair in order, and they exchange WeChats.

I'd Be Careful

The Monday after Terry gets Lena's WeChat, he couldn't control his excitement. Lena was off on Sunday and she took a day off on Monday, so he wouldn't see her smiling face until Thursday. Everyone kept complimenting him on his knowledge of the Dragon Boat Festival, and how well him and Lena did during the event.

"How did you know so much about the Dragon Boat Festival, Terry?" one of his coworkers inquired.

"I just did some research before our party. That's all," he humbly replies. The shine in Terry's smile could've been seen from space.

He was proud of himself for many reasons: reason number one; he thinks Lena was impressed, reason number two; he thinks Lena was impressed, and lastly; he thinks Lena was impressed.

He was happy that his coworkers and colleagues enjoyed themselves and thought that they did a good job, but this was mostly about impressing Lena. Terry finishes up his day and heads to the metro station to go home. Usually around the time Terry leaves his 5th floor office on a Sunday, there are some crowds out enjoying the downtown area. University friends going for bubble tea, couples walking down Nanjing Road, and families shopping at ISETAN. As Terry was walking to the train station, he noticed a young family with a young child. The child is maybe about 3 or 4-years-old, and both parents are holding the young child's hand. As Terry walks by, the child looks up at Terry and smiles. The parents say to the child, "say hi, say hello." Terry smiles and happily says, "Nǐ hǎo," as he waves to the family and the young child.

The young family smiles and seems delighted that Terry acknowledged them and was so nice and warm. Terry gets to the front entrance of the train station and pauses for a second. The spring breeze escapes into Terry's soul and hugs it tight. It reminds him of a conversation he had with one of his childhood friends before he left for China.

Before Terry left for China, he didn't have many close friends. He had a couple acquaintances and only had one best friend from high school who was killed in a car crash. He knew people cared and loved him, but he had to experience more in life.

"I'd be careful, Terry," he could hear his sister explaining.

"What are you talking about, C?" he asks, as he continues to pack up his stuff.

"You know I'm always worried about your safety," she says, wiping a single tear from her left eye.

He goes over to her and wipes the tear from her eye and says, "I know you're worried, C, but I have to try. This is a risk I'm willing to take for something greater," he says, as he sees her ball up of some tissue in her hand. He knew that she was coming from a kind and loving place.

If he was going to expand his knowledge of the world and experience different cultures; become a better and more patient man, he knew that he would have to take greater risk for a greater reward.

Despite the setbacks at the beginning and the culture shock, he felt that things will work out, and he is where he is supposed to be. He gets on the train and heads home for the rest of the evening.

IV

I Miss You

The Tianjin Eye, the Tianjin Television and Radio Tower and the Lion's den. Every night he would hear the Lion's roar, and he could also see his office building from his apartment. Being on the 27th floor affords one these wondrous views of the city. From his window, he could see the whole city and even into the buildings far away from the center city. Terry grew up in Portland, Oregon, in a close-knit neighborhood. His family lived in Northeast Portland, aka "The Soul District." He was proud to be from his neighborhood, and his parents loved the closeness of the community. Terry and his older sister were the only two family members whose attempts to venture out of Oregon were pretty successful. Carla, or "C," was his older sister who was a public relations specialist for a health insurance company in Portland. He talks to his sister every Sunday night and well it's Sunday night for Terry, but Sunday morning for his sister.

"I gotta call, C," he exclaims as he takes a quick peek at his watch. He picks up his phone and goes to his WeChat and clicks her contact. The phone rings twice and then he says, "What up sis?"

"Hey Gravy, call me on video," she demands.

"Ok, give me a second." He quickly hangs up and calls her back on video.

"Hi there! How are you Gravy?" Carla responds.

"I'm good, you know. Just got home and about to eat. And I'm not eating gravy, so don't even ask," Terry responds, as he sits on his beige couch.

Terry and Carla speak for a little bit about formalities, but he knows that his sister is going to ask if he is dating anyone. "So, did you make friends? Are you dating anybody?" she says as he sees her go into her living room with some water.

"Not really. There's this one girl I work with and she is fine! Like she is fine," his eyes widened, as he talked about Lena. "Oh, I see. Tell me about her," she says as she rolls her short-brown hair behind her ear. "Well she's about 5'6."

"So she's about your height," Carla jokingly interjects.

"Whatever. Anyhow, she has this beautiful light-brown skin, big beautiful brown eyes, she's funny, smart. I mean, I get excited and nervous every time I go to work, and I know that I'm going to see her. We haven't gone out on a date yet, but I may ask her out soon," he projects his thoughts into the atmosphere.

"Wow! Is she a local girl?" Carla inquires.

"Yeah, she's a local girl. She's from the city, and she started at the company a little after I did. We actually just hosted an event for our center, and it went well," he states with a slight smile on his face.

"She sounds pretty cool. Don't get out there and fall in love and never come back and have babies. I already miss your face Gravy," she says as she pretends to pinch his cheeks.

"I miss you too," he replies.

"Well, stay safe and we love you. Jared was here, but I think he just went to the store," she says.

"That's ok. I love you sis," he responds.

"I love you too, Gravy baby! Go get some rest," she says, as she drinks her bottled water.

"I will, C, I'll talk to you next week. Tell everybody I said 'hello.' Sleep well," he says.

"Will do," she responds as they both hang up at the same time.

The sweltering Monday afternoon, in June, makes him want water and no coffee on this day. He arrives at the office at noon and heads up to the fifth floor.

Ding! He gets off the elevator and sees his boss, Danni, coming out of the office.

"Hi Terry, really nice job the other week with the Dragon Boat Festival. You and Lena worked really well together and the students and families enjoyed themselves," she says.

"Thanks, Danni! I had fun too and I did a lot of research for my speech about the festival," he humbly says as his eyes land on Lena.

As Terry approaches the office, he sees Lena at the front desk.

"What up bro?" Terry jokingly states.

"Hey bro!" Lena smiles back.

"I gotta get changed, but I'll be back," he says, as he hurries into the office to turn on his computer. Then, he hustles to the bathroom and changes into his bright floral colored shirt and gray slacks. He comes out of the bathroom and sees Lena smiling. "I like that shirt on you. It's like a pink or floral color. It looks really nice on you," she declares.

"Really? I thought you saw me wear it before. I think I wore it a couple of weeks ago," he says.

"You know I don't work on Sundays and Wednesdays, right? Those are my days off, as of right now," she reminds him, taking some notes in her book.

"I knew you didn't work on Sundays, but I didn't know you were off on Wednesdays as well," Terry responds.

"I'm off on Wednesdays as well. Maybe we could go for dinner," he quickly says, as he wipes his forehead and tries to slow his breathing.

"That sounds fun. We can set something up for sure," she replies, flashing a smile at him. "Sounds good. I gotta get ready for class, so I'll talk to you later." Terry breathes a sigh of relief and calmly and slowly walks back to his desk.

As he went back to his desk, he was gleaming from his pores hoping nobody saw him.

"You ok over there, Terry? I see you smiling," Alex asks him. Alex, a 26-year-old UK native, who had been at the center for three years.

"Oh, yeah man, I'm good! I'm just looking at something on YouTube," Terry says, as he pulls his phone out of his right pocket.

"Oh, what are you watching?" Alex asks, fully turning his chair and facing Terry.

"Just some Saturday Night Live sketches," Terry responds.

"What's Saturday Night Live?" Alex intently asks.

"It's a live comedy show that is really popular in the states." Terry says back.

"Oh if you like that, you might like <u>Fry and Laurie</u>," Alex mentions.

"Oh yea? You have to tell me more about it after my class," Terry replies, grabbing his lesson plan for the next class.

It's about 12:20 pm and Terry has 20 minutes before the start of his first class. Terry did his planning and notes the day before and just has to print out the worksheets. The office printer gets stuck at times and today was one of those days. Luckily for Terry it was just a paper jam, and he easily took down the side cover and took the paper out of the printer. Once the jam is fixed, he grabs his lessons, a pen, his notebook and heads to his first lesson of the day. He walks past the front desk and gives Lena a quick head nod, she smiles and gives him a head nod back. Terry crosses the threshold of the classroom and says, "good morning, everyone." "Good morning, teacher," the class responded.

The day races by and it's 8:30 pm, and Lena has left for the day. Terry walks into the office to get some paperwork done, and he checks his classes for the next day. As he's checking his class schedule, he hears his phone *buzz*.

8:30 pm
Lena: What's up? So when will we go to dinner?

Terry decided to answer a question with a question.

8:31 pm

Terry: Do you want to do next Tuesday after I get off?

8:32 pm

Lena: Yeah that sounds good to me.

8:33 pm

Terry: Maybe we can go somewhere close to work.Or on the same metro Line.

8:34 pm

Lena: Ok. What stop are you on the metro?

8:34 pm

Terry: I honestly don't know how to pronounce it. 😂

Terry gets back to finishing up his paperwork. He prints out some work for the week, puts up the lessons from that day, and posts his feedback from the previous class. He turns off his computer and heads to the exit. "How do you say my metro station?"

V

I Think I'm Going to Cry

One week until date

"I wonder where I could take her. I definitely want to go somewhere where we can have a conversation. Maybe we could go to the Hard Rock Cafe. They have good food and maybe a couple of drinks," Terry's up at 2 am thinking and planning, while the blue light vibrates from the TV. He falls asleep with the phone tattooed on his face, from looking at places to eat in his neighborhood. The next day, he is off and he has just signed up for a gym membership. The gym is right across from his building and right next to a new fresh produce store. Terry goes for his typical Wednesday workout that consists of: he does a run for 20 minutes, lifts weights for an hour, and stretches for 10 minutes.

"I need some strawberries, bananas and some oranges," he thinks to himself, as the smell of cool air and fresh fruit enters his nose.

"Nǐ hǎo," he says to the cashier. He gets what he needs and then goes to get some lunch. Terry has been trying to lose weight since he came into China. It could be a little hard with so many food options. Terry has several of his familiar Western food options: McDonald's, Subway, Pizza Hut, Starbucks. He has also found a plethora of traditional local food options: hotpot, Chinese BBQ, Japanese food, Korean food, or jiānbǐng 煎餅. He vowed that when he came to China, he would get himself back into shape and back into a healthy lifestyle. So, having the produce market close to his apartment was an advantage.

Once Terry gets home from the gym on his days off, he usually stays in for the rest of the day, watching CCTV 5 (sports), reading, or watching videos on his phone. His studio apartment had just what he needed, a bed, a couch, a TV, a bathroom, and a microwave.

Terry's two days off speed by, as days off often do, and he is back into the office. Thursdays are usually a full class schedule for Terry, as some of the other teachers are off on this day. Terry comes in around his usual time: 11:25 am. He goes through the day and barely sees Lena. Around 4:30 pm, Terry usually has some planning time before his evening classes start. He comes out of the office and heads to the first desk to see if she is there.

"Hey there. Do you know where you want to go next week?" Lena asks, lifting her head from her phone.

"What do you think about going to more Western restaurants? The Hard Rock Cafe?" Terry asks, leaning over the counter and trying to peek at her phone.

"That's fine with me. There's also a place we can go after if you want to grab a drink," she replies.

"Yeah I'm ok with that," he says with a slight smile on his face.

"I may have to come into the office for about an hour to finish something. Could you meet me here? We could just leave together," she states.

"Of course! Just let me know what time you're going to be done," he responds

"I will let you know," she says, getting up to help a student sign in.

It's about 4:45 and Terry has class at 5:30, so he goes back into the office to finish getting ready. The next couple of days are a blur for him because all he can think about is Lena and this date.

Two Days Until Date

As Terry is deciding what to wear for work that day, he's also thinking about what to wear for the date with Lena. June in Tianjin can be very hot and humid, and it can still be hot at night as well.

"Should I wear my navy-blue Polo, with my denim jeans? Should I wear my maroon t-shirt with my boat shoes?" he thinks to himself. Whatever he decided, he knew that at some point in the night they would be outside, and Terry didn't want to be drenched with sweat. After heavy deliberation, he decides to go with the navy-blue polo and combine it with a pair of navy-blue boat shoes. Even though the date was two days away, he wanted to have his outfit ironed and ready to go.

Terry also checks the Hard Rock Cafe website to see the menu, making sure that he knew what he would order before he got there. Terry did what he had to do to get ready: he has his outfit together, knows the dinner menu, and double checks the time.

As he sits and stares at his mahogany closet, a thought enters his mind, "I can't drink with her. I'm allergic to alcohol."

Day of the Big Date

The day is here and he could hardly sleep the night before. Terry tries to hide his excitement throughout the day, but he can't hide the fact that he is going on a date with the most gorgeous girl he's ever seen. He was excited to get to know her better and have a full conversation with her.

> 6:45 pm
> Lena: Hey there I'm heading to the office now. I will leave the office at 7:30 if you want to meet around then.

As he gets ready, the sun no longer illuminates the sky. He gets a taxi to get to the office faster. Some traffic slows up the trip, but he gets there at 7:20. He walks into the lobby of his office and sees her at the front desk. There she is in her white t-shirt, her denim jeans and stiletto heels. Big beautiful brown eyes, matched with the smile of a lifetime. "How are you?" he asks.

"Hey there, I'm ok! Gotta finish some work and then we can leave," she says, fidgeting through some paperwork.

"Of course I will," he reassures her.

"Do you know what you want to order? Did you look at the menu I sent you?" he asks.

"I looked at it quickly, but I didn't pick anything. I will pick something once we get there. Train or DiDi? she inquires.

"Let's take the train tonight. It shouldn't be too crowded around this time, even though there's still some traffic out there," he replies.

"Great!" She gets out of her chair and walks out of the office. Her stiletto heels pound the floor, with the sound echoing in the hall.

Ten minutes later she comes back in and says, "I'm ready." They left the center. "How was your day?" he asks.

"It was fine. Stayed in bed until I went to the gym. Then, I went to my family business to do interviews," she says.

"Your business?" he interrogates.

"Yes, my parents own a coffee shop. I help with interviews and basic upkeep of the place," she responds.

"I understand and I love coffee! How were the interviews?" he inquires, as he pushes the button for the elevator.

"It was ok. The girl was cute."

The elevator promptly arrives and they both get on as he says, "so is that all you look for when you hire people? Attractiveness?" he says this, with a smirk on his face.

"Not the only thing," she replies.

They continue on with the conversation until they reach the metro station. They head down to the platform and wait for the train to their destination, The Hard Rock Cafe Tianjin.

"So, what stop do you live at?" she asks.

"I couldn't say it if my life depended on it. I could show you the name of it." Terry shows her the name of his train stop, as their train quickly arrives.

"You live by the zoo and the water park. Your train stop is called, Shuishanggongyuandonglu. That's a pretty long name for a metro stop," she states.

"Say what now?" he says. She laughed, as he struggled to say the name of his metro stop.

"Well, we can work on it at dinner, because we are about to get off," she says, as they get off the train.

They take the escalator to the exit. As they get close to the exit, the stifling June air squeezes his nose.

"It's so hot in Tianjin! I'm like sweating through my shirt, and I've only been outside for like 10 seconds," he breathlessly says.

"Welcome to the Tianjin summers. It gets quite hot out here in the summer and of course the winters can be really cold," she responds.

They walked about 15 meters to the restaurant and walked into the cool building.

"Ahhh, finally some relief!" he shouts.

"Welcome to Hard Cafe Tianjin! Would you like a table or a booth?" the waitress asks.

"Doesn't matter to me," Lena says.

"Could we get a table?" he responds to Summer. He caught a glimpse of her name tag when she walked over.

This night there was a live band playing to an almost empty crowd. Some folks were sprinkled throughout the restaurant.

Terry and Lena are given a booth in the front of the restaurant, and they both begin looking through the menu as the live band continues to play.

"Do you know what you want to eat?" she asks.

"I think I'm going to get one of my favorite Western foods!" he says, flipping the menu over.

"What would that be?" she replies.

"Well, since I've been in China, I haven't had Macaroni and Cheese. So, I'm thinking about that one," he responds.

"That's a really good option. My mom can make some really good Mac and Cheese. I don't know what I want," she says.

As they both look through the menu and finally order, the band continues to play. There were some people adjacent to Terry and Lena, who were loving the band. Maybe they had too much to drink, but the band brought out their enjoyment.

After Summer comes and takes their order, he takes a sip of water and his necklace slightly shows in front of his shirt.

"What kind of necklace is that?" she asks.

"Do you really want to know?" he responds.

"Why else would I ask?" she says back.

"It's an Eye of Horus necklace that my parents gave me," he hesitantly replies.

"What is the purpose of it?" she asks.

He takes another sip of water, looks at her, and says, "Well, a few years ago my parents passed away. Before they passed, they gave it to me. I have two necklaces from them, but this is my favorite. They never had a chance to travel, and I thought it would be special to have them with me in China.

So, I can say that they had a chance to travel the world," he softly says.

He notices her eyes starting to water up a little bit.

"Are you serious? I think I'm going to cry," she says.

"Please don't, but I do appreciate you asking about it. I used to run track in college and I always wore it. I wore it during my college graduation as well. Typically, I always wear it," he says, as he takes a napkin and wipes her eye.

He feels like she might really care, and she's the first girl to show some genuine interest in him in quite some time. He's only been away from home for a couple of months, but he felt good about having her attention.

Their food comes and he finishes his meal in record time, but she doesn't finish her meal.

"Are you not hungry?" he asks.

"No, I just eat too fast and get full really quick. Give me like a minute and I'll finish," she says, as she holds her stomach.

Terry thought it was cute.

Lena eventually finishes her Shrimp Alfredo and doesn't have any room for dessert. They both continue to enjoy the live band and finally, they prepare to leave.

They both get up to head out, as Terry goes to the cashier counter.

"Thank you for paying. Usually, we could just split it," she says.

"No worries. I believe I asked you out, so I'll pay for this one. The next time we go out, you can pay," he suggests.

"For sure. Do you want to grab a drink?" she asks.

"Ummm…about that. Usually, my face puffs up and I get hives on my arms when I drink. It's not a pretty sight. So, I can drink, but not that much," he says.

"That's weird. Usually, we're the only ones who have what's known as, 'Asian Flush.' It's quite rare that you find it in other people," she explains.

"Ummm….what is 'Asian Flush,' because it sounds super offensive," he says.

"It obviously occurs in people of Asian descent. Basically, it means your body has trouble breaking down alcohol, and it causes a toxic reaction in your body. Some of my friends have it," she explains, as they walk onto the street.

"So, this 'flush,' does it go away?" he asks.

"Some people take antihistamine while they're drinking if they want to drink that bad," she says. "It started for me right after college, and I just stopped drinking for a little while. But maybe we could have another night with drinks," he suggests.

"But thank you for that medical lesson, Dr. Lena," he chuckles, as they walk down the street. The summer heat is unforgiving and he is starting to sweat through his shirt. It's a little past midnight and they both need to get home.

"How will you get home?" he asks. "I'll call a DiDi," she says.

"Ok, I'll wait with you until your DiDi comes," he says. Her DiDi comes in five minutes and they give each other a hug. Her car pulls off, as he takes a stroll home that night. Walking home that night, he saw the Tianjin Eye shining off in the short distance.

VI

I'm Into Her

The next day, Terry was elated just thinking about how the date went. He went back to work and couldn't keep the excitement off his face, like a kid waiting for Christmas morning. Working quietly in the office Terry's coworker, Barry, slowly turns to him and says, "Hey Terry, I see you got a big smile on your face."

"I'm doing ok, Barry. Just thinking about something," he replies to Barry's observations.
"Thinking about something or thinking about someone?" Barry replies.
"He's good," Terry thinks to himself.
"Reminds me of growing up as a young lad in Manchester. That's the look I used to have on my face whenever I saw my crush," Barry says with a smile on his face.
"I'll tell you a little later. Maybe when we get off work," Terry responds.

Barry helped Terry when he first started at their center. Barry was a major part of Terry's teacher training and would come to observe Terry's classes. As well as, he gave feedback and tips to help with Terry's instruction. At times, they would also co-teach, which Terry quite liked. This helped to develop a nice expat bond between the two of them. Not only could he learn from Barry in the classroom, but he could also learn from him in life. The silver fox was present in Barry, along with a world of wisdom.

"How many classes do you have today?" Terry asks.
"Only three and I don't think I have any classes this evening," Barry responds.
"Maybe you can spend that last hour getting ready for future lessons," Terry suggests.

"Alright, well I have to run off to my first class of the day. I will see you all later," Barry says.
That was Barry's usual sign-off before he would go to class.

"I guess I should print all my documents out for my next one," Terry thinks to himself.
He goes to class and the day speeds by.
"Good evening, everyone," he addresses the class as he walks in.
"Good morning, teacher," the class responds.
After the class is over, he goes to the office and sees Barry chatting with another coworker.

"Hey guys," Terry expresses to all in the room.
"Hey. How was your class?" Barry asks.

"Not bad man. It went by really quick and I'm exhausted, to be honest," Terry replies. Terry puts up his paperwork from the class and quickly checks his emails before he leaves the office.

"Are you ready?" Barry asks.
"Yeah, just let me finish up my feedback and then we can leave," Terry responds. The āyí begins to turn off the lights in the center and to make sure everyone has left for the evening. The āyí in the center would always say "hello," to Terry. Even though that's really all they could say; neither Terry nor the āyí spoke both English and Mandarin. Terry and Barry both grab their belongings and head for the exit. As they got into the elevator, the blast from the cold air struck Terry's face.

"Man this air feels good because it's going to be burning up outside," Terry says, as the elevator doors close slowly. "It is quite hot and humid, isn't it? I've lived in quite a few places and haven't felt heat particularly like this," Barry replies.

"I've lived in Canada, Japan, and now in China. I was born and raised in Manchester and am a proper Mancunian," Barry says, as the elevator reaches the bottom floor.
Terry has a puzzled look on his face.
"All those words mean that I'm from Manchester. Like a New Yorker is from New York," he replies.

They head outside into the dome of heat and begin walking down Nanjing road.
"You know at one point in my life, I wanted to be a full-time fisherman and take some time off to travel and sail. Just sailing the ocean, relaxing and listening to the water crash

up against the side of my boat," Barry says, breathing in the hot summer air.

"My part-time life as a fisherman was fun, but it was sporadic with work. Sometimes you could find jobs and get a good catch, but it depends on many things. It's also time-consuming to take care of a boat," Barry explains.

"I didn't know that. I just thought it was all about relaxing and enjoying being on a boat," Terry replies.

Barry laughs for a quick moment, as they are stopped by a red walking signal.

"It can be, but there's a lot of moving pieces right. And there are things you can't control, but you still put your best foot forward in hopes that it works out," Barry says, stepping into the clear walkway first.

"There are many things you can't control, and you go out to hopefully get the big catch. Oftentimes, we take what we can get, but you know that there's something else better out there. The fisherman's life wasn't fun, and it just wasn't for me," Barry adds.

"So, you know that I'm into Lena, right? Like, really into her. She's absolutely amazing and I can't stop thinking about her," Terry confesses.

"I think she has been the first girl that I've met that actually made me feel like she gives a damn. It's like she was kind of just sent into my life at this moment. It can get a little lonely here, and it's nice that a beautiful woman is attracted to you. Or at least cares enough to want to know about the necklace you wear," Terry explains.

"I knew it mate," Barry chuckles.

"I think a couple of people in the office knew that you two have something for each other," Barry continues.

"Really? How did you know?" Terry tries to act surprised.

They continue to walk down the street, passing quite a few restaurants.

"Well, let's think about it: you two are very playful in the office, always joking and laughing with each other. You two are always smiling at each other. And I see you two looking at each other from across your desk. I could tell when people are genuinely into each other. It just shows on their faces," Barry says.

"I guess I couldn't hide it at all. I tend to wear my emotions on my sleeve. I did try to hide it, but after our date last night, she just absolutely made my mind go into overdrive. I really can't stop thinking about her and I don't want to," Terry exclaims.

"I could tell mate. Don't be ashamed. You don't need to hide your feelings. Plus you do a shit job at it anyway mate," Barry says and slightly laughs.

They continue to walk down the semi-crowded street and Terry says, "She is a cute girl, and she seems like she has a good head on her shoulders. Do you know how old she is?" Barry asks.

"I believe she's 25," Terry responds.

"Ok, and I'm guessing you're 21?" Barry smiles and says.

"That's flattering, but I'm 32," Terry replies and smiles back.

"Not too significant of an age gap. Sometimes a slight age gap could be beneficial for a couple. I think you two seem to work really well together. Just always keep in mind that there may be things that you can't control or understand," Barry says.

Terry stops in front of a Chinese BBQ restaurant and asks, "What do you mean by that?"
"She's a young beautiful woman, who I assume may not be in a relationship. You just may not want to get your expectations up too high, just in case there's an unforeseen storm coming," Barry says.
"I understand that, but that is a very negative way to look at it. Obviously, I'm not saying that she's the one, but I do think we work pretty well together. She is single as far as I know. She may have other guys trying to talk to her," Terry expresses.

"Or other women," Barry interjects.
"I think you two should take it slow and see where it goes. You two seem to make each other smile, and that's always important," Barry responds.

Terry looks down the street and continues walking. "What about you?" he asks.
"Am I single? I'm quite single and this is the way I like it. I was engaged to a young lady a long time ago and it didn't work out," Barry responds.
"Oh, what happened?" Terry asks, as he readjusted his book bag on his back.

"Sometimes the world just isn't too kind to you," Barry says. Terry could see the strain in Barry's eyes and wondered if he should ask any further questions, but decided against it. Terry feels a sense of sorrow, as he feels that Barry may have still been heartbroken. Terry decides to bring the conversation back around to him.

"I think dating as an expat is difficult. Especially, when we both know that I probably won't be here long term. I think that could make her a little hesitant about the whole thing. At some point, somebody will go home," Terry says.

"What do you mean by that?" Barry asks.

"I mean that at some point, I will go back home and she will be here. She did mention that she eventually wanted to move to Canada, but I don't know when that's going to be," Terry responds

"Would you stay if things worked out?" Barry asks him.

"I think she would be worth thinking about," Terry says.

"Well, I think we tarried all the way down the street and passed your station a while ago. I think I'll be making my exit here," Barry says.

"No worries, I can just get on the metro station up the street," Terry says, as he points to where he thinks the metro station is.

They exchange a quick handshake, as Terry goes down to the metro and Barry vanishes into the semi-crowd of shoppers on the street.

VII

Can I Kiss You?

The music is blasting as red, blue, green, and yellow neon lights are glaring all around the room. There's some sort of techno music playing and Terry can barely see the person in front of him; the fog from the cigarette smoke is too thick.

"Do you like me?" she asks.

"Do I like you? Like a boyfriend should like his girlfriend?" he responds.

The young lady leans over and whispers into the young man's ear, "I want you so bad!"

He takes a quick sip of his beer, as he inhales the unfiltered smoke.

"I want you too," he says. "Do you want to leave?" he asks.

She slowly bites her bottom lip and nods her head.

"Let me take my last sip of beer and we can get outta here," he states.

The beautiful young woman slightly grips his right index finger. They begin to walk out of the club, and he sees a dark shadow in the corner of the club.

He stops and stares at the shadow, and then rubs his eyes. "What's wrong?" she asks. "Do you see something in the corner over there?" he asks. She laughs and says, "Are you ok? There is nothing over there. Well, other than some people dancing,"

He shakes it off as they continue to walk out of the nightclub.

"Is everything ok? Did you have too much to drink?" she asks.

"No, I'm not drunk, I just, I just...never mind," he stutters. "I think you might need to lay down," she replies. They continue up the stairs of the club, and the young lady holds his hand really tight like she's going through a haunted hayride.

They reach the top of the stairs and exit the nightclub.

"I guess we have to wait for a DiDi," the beautiful young lady states.

"I guess so, but maybe we could walk a little bit and catch one up the street," he suggests.

They begin to walk down the street, but can't keep their hands off of each other. The streets are empty, and you could hear the water rushing down the drain, as it had down poured earlier. At this point, the two of them are in the middle of the street face-to-face.

He confidently asks, "Can I kiss you?" The beautiful young lady nods her head and licks her lips. As he begins to go in for a kiss, he sees flashing lights coming in fast. The bright lights get closer and closer and closer, and they both hear the sound of a blaring horn and...

Terry jumps up out of his sleep, drenched in sweat and struggling to catch his breath like he's just participated in a marathon. "What just happened? Was I dreaming the whole time?" he asks himself. This dream seemed very real to him and he decided to get out of bed to gather himself together.

He goes into the bathroom, turns the light on, and glances at himself in the mirror. He takes his towel and slightly dampens it with warm water to wipe his face off. "This girl has my mind!" After he finishes in the bathroom, he grabs his water bottle out of the small compact refrigerator in his studio apartment. Terry puts the water back in the fridge and walks over to the panoramic-view window. He loves that his apartment has a view of the city.

It's 2 am, so the city's shouts have turned down to whispers as lights were turned off and minds were turned on. Terry looks down at the city zoo and can hear the lions roaring. Usually, this doesn't bother him, but tonight Terry wasn't in the mood to hear them. (It's not like he could go down to the zoo and tell them to be quiet). Terry keeps his curtain slightly open, enough to see the clouds walking by the night sky.

"I really have to get it together. What was that all about?" The dream perplexes him, but he tries to lay back down. Ten minutes go by, and he still can't fall asleep. He looks at the back of his phone but doesn't pick it up. Terry has done quite the research on how the light from the phone can keep you up throughout the night. Five more minutes go by, and he starts to wonder what Lena is doing.

"I've never texted her this late. What if she's with somebody else and I interrupt her?" Terry contemplates his thoughts out loud. "But what if she's up and not doing anything." He finally gives in after much debate and looks at his phone. A couple of messages, but none from the person that he is really checking for. He taps on the WeChat app and looks for the last conversation he had with Lena.

> 2:02 am
> Terry: I really did have a nice time at dinner with you.

> 2:04 am
> Lena: Yea me too. We have to do it again soon.

> 2:06 am
> Lena: I know this bar that we can go to. I know you can't really drink like that, but it's a cool place with a nice vibe.

> 2:08 am
> Terry: That sounds good to me!

> 2:09 am
> Lena: Cool, maybe we can go this weekend? After work on Saturday?

> 2:10 am
> Terry: We can leave straight from work.

2:11 am

Lena: I like that plan! ☺

2:12 am

Terry: Then it's set. How far is it?

2:13 am

Lena: It's a surprise 😉

2:14 am

Terry: I'm always up for a surprise.

2:15 am

Lena: I'm full of surprises. 😉

2:16 am

Terry: I'm looking forward to it. ☺

Terry lays down and just stares at the white ceiling. He knows he woke up in a panic, but doesn't remember what happened. All he remembered was that Lena was in his dream and he almost kissed her. Outside of that, his memory is blank. "It couldn't have been that good if I woke up in a panic," he thought. Terry sits there for a couple of minutes and just looks out his window. Even though most of the lights in the city are off, the city is still illuminated.

A few more minutes went by and he got up to get some more water.

"I knew that was a risky time to text," he thinks to himself. Just as he goes to grab a cup, he hears his phone vibrate.

He sprints towards his bed so fast that he hits his toe on the coffee table in his living area. He jumps on his bed and looks at his phone.

He unlocks the phone and looks at his messages, and it's an advertisement from his Alipay app. "Well that was uneventful," he thought. "It's also weird that I'm getting this message now. I know my phone has not been acting right since I've been here." His phone has been moving quite slow and has trouble working in some places.

After he gets up and wobbles to get his charger, he lays back down and turns off the television. He will be asleep within the next 15 minutes.

> **9:30 am**
> Lena: Good morning, I fell asleep last night. I'm on my way to the center. Message me when you wake up. ☺

The sun is bursting through Terry's thick brown curtains and into his room. Shining right on his face, the sun is his alarm clock today. As Terry turns to the side of the bed his phone is on, he takes a quick look at his sports watch: 10:00 am.

"Guess I should get out of bed." He reaches for his phone and unplugs it. He sees Lena's message and a slight smile crosses his face.

> **10:19 am**
> Terry: Hey there! I just woke up and I'm still in bed right now.

> I guess you have an early shift today. How's your day going?

As he awaits her response, he shuffles to the bathroom and then to his small kitchen. "What do I want for breakfast?" He's been trying to get back to eating healthy and going to the gym regularly. This summer morning, he chose a banana and some oatmeal for breakfast.

He begins to cut up his banana when he hears it. He briskly walks over to the phone on his bed and fumbles it as he tries to tame his excitement. He presses his thumb to the phone, slides down his notification bar, and clicks on her message.

> **10:26 am**
> Lena: You texted me kinda late last night. What kind of girl do you think of me?

> **10:28 am**
> Terry: The kind of girl that texts at 2 in the morning...haha. Anyway, how was your night?

Terry sits on the edge of his bed and starts to lay back on his royal blue comforter, as he is off today.

> **10:31 am**
> Lena: It was ok. I tried to sleep because I had an early shift this morning. You must have a busy day off, right?

10:32 am

Terry: Not really. I will just go to the gym and come home and eat.

10:34 am

Lena: What were you doing yesterday? I thought you were single.

10:36 am

Terry: I am single. I guess I was just thinking about you. Anyway, did you eat anything today?

10:40 am

Lena: Not yet, I'm just at the front desk doing some paperwork. What are you doing later?

10:43 am

Terry: Being lazy I see! But I'm not doing anything. I'll be home. What are you up to?

10:45 am

Lena: Nothing much. Want to do dinner again and then I can show you the surprise.

10:49 am

Terry: Yeah that's fine with me. What time are you off?

10:51 am

Lena: I'm done at 6 today so I will go home to change. Just meet me at my apartment. I'll send you the address.

10:53 am

Terry: Sounds like a plan to me. Enjoy the rest of your day. I'm going to eat and then head to the gym.

10:56 am

Lena: 😊

Terry lies on his bed for a moment and closes his eyes. He thinks of Lena's big beautiful brown eyes, her glowing light-brown skin, her ruby red lips, and how he would love to just kiss her one time. He jumps up out of bed and lands awkwardly on his right foot.

"That hurt!" he exclaims. He hops over to his closet to decide what to wear. Now, it's still hot in the city, so Terry decides on some jean shorts and a navy-blue polo shirt. That way he can feel comfortable no matter where they go and hopefully not sweat too much. He takes out his clothes for the evening and gently lays them on the bed. Some of his clothes still have wrinkles on them. He hasn't picked up an iron yet, but he will put the clothes in the bathroom while he showers to help flatten out the wrinkles.

Terry finishes eating and he gets ready to go to his gym. As he walks to the door, he grabs his water bottle and his black and gray Under Armour weightlifting gloves. Terry walks to the elevator and sees his next-door neighbor. They passed by each other quite a few times, but have never spoken to each other. Usually, they would give the typical manly head nod. On this day, Terry sees him at the elevator, and for some reason on this day, he actually spoke to his neighbor while waiting for the elevator.

"Hey man! How's it going?" Terry asks.

"I'm good bro. I see you live right across the hall. What's your name, man?" Terry sees that the elevator has stopped on the tenth floor.

Terry turns and points at his apartment. "Yeah man, I live right in 2703. I'm Terry, it's nice to meet you!"

"That's actually my old apartment, bro. My wife and I used to live there before we moved to the bigger spot down the hall. My name is Matt. Where are you from?" Matt inquires.

"I'm from America," Terry says.

"Really dude! I know you're from America," Matt responds. Terry doesn't know why he said it. He does get asked that question all the time, and he always just says America. He went into cruise control with that answer.

"My bad bro. I'm originally from Stumptown aka the City of Roses," Terry responds, as the elevator finally arrives on the 27th floor. Two people step off the elevator. Terry and Matt get on and the elevator slowly descends through the building.

"Oh, Portland is a cool city. I'm from Emerald City. I haven't meant another person here who is from the Northwest part of the States," Matt explains.

"Yeah, I was born and raised in Portland. I went to the University of Oregon for Track & Field. And I see that there's not a lot of Pacific Northwesterners out here," Terry states.

"That's cool man! I went to the University of Washington," Matt happily replies. The elevator declines to the first floor and they both step off. They turn the corner, pass the bǎo'ān in the building, and step into the oven of the city. "Hey man, feel free to stop over one day if you're free," Matt says. "For sure bro. I'm sure I'll see you around," Terry responds. They walk down the steps and go about their business for the day.

Terry gets to his gym in a flash. The gym is on the 3rd floor of the mall, and Terry gets on another elevator. There's a big mirror in the elevator, and out of the corner of his eye, Terry sees the outline of a shadow in the corner of the elevator. He quickly turns his head but nothing is there.
"I need to get it together," he says out loud, as he is the only one on the elevator. The doors open, he shakes his head and walks to the welcome counter.

"Nǐ hǎo," the attendant says to him. Terry waves as he hands her his smartwatch for entrance. She gives him his smartwatch back and he enters his fitness haven. Today is Terry's arms and chest day which consists of bench press, curls, shoulder press, and lateral pull down. He always starts his workout with a quick 20-minute run on the treadmill. "Can't forget to do my cardio for the day," he thinks to himself.

This particular day, there are some very pretty girls in the gym. Although, none of them seem to catch his eye quite like Lena has. Terry daydreams about Lena and how badly he wants to be with her. He refocuses and puts in his headphones to finish his workout. At the end of his workout, he always works on his abs or his back.

"Six sets of ten sit-ups and then I'm finished." Terry pushes through the final part of his workout, and he's finished. By the end of his workout, he can barely lift his arms above his head. There is an area to stretch by the boxing ring in his gym. He goes over to the area to begin stretching when he sees a beautiful girl. She is looking at her phone and is absolutely stunning. Long black hair down to her waist, sun-kissed skin, she's fit and has some raspberry-colored lips.

They locked eyes for a second, and she slightly smiles as she walks by Terry. When she walks by, he notices that she also has these beautiful brown eyes that captivate his attention instantly. She keeps walking and goes to the water fountain, as he continues to stretch his arms and legs. This young lady was quite pretty and enticing, but he still was thinking about Lena. "I mean, Lena looks way better than her," he thinks. Done stretching, he begins walking to the locker room to change and wash his hands. The young lady is running around the indoor track in the gym. She passes him one more time, and they smile at each other and keep on about their business.

Terry gets into the locker room and stares at the gray lockers for a moment. "Where is my locker?" he says out loud. "110, where is locker 110?" Terry always has this problem finding his locker. "Oh, there it is." He puts his smartwatch to lock and the door opens. His book bag falls out slightly, but he manages to grab it before it spills onto the gym floor. Terry puts his Under Armour weight lifting gloves into the bag and wraps his brown towel around his neck.

The locker rooms are particularly hot, so he begins to sweat just from standing. He walks to the sink to wash his hands and wipe his face. It's around 1 pm, and he knows he will see Lena later on tonight.

> 1:06 pm (to Lena)
> Terry: What's up big head? How's your day going?

Terry puts his phone into his right pocket and begins to leave the gym. He fills up his water bottle one more time to help him battle this summer onslaught of heat. The pretty lady that he previously saw is at the water station, and she looks like she may be leaving too. She finishes and then turns to Terry as he approaches the station. "Nǐ hǎo," she says, as she smiles and walks by Terry.

"Hi," he says back.

> 1:08 pm
> Lena: Big head?? I think you're the one with the big head. But it's ok. I'm ready to leave already... hahaha.

Terry feels his phone vibrate and immediately puts his attention to Lena and her message.

> **1:09 pm**
> Terry: First of all I don't have a big head. I'm sure you are ready to leave.

Terry walks out of the gym and gets onto the elevator. This time there are two other gym goers in the elevator with him. He checks the corner of the mirror, just to make sure that the shadow isn't there.

> **1:10 pm**
> Lena: How was the gym? Working on your arms today?

> **1:11 pm**
> Terry: Yeah, and just did a lot of cardio today. So what time did you want me to meet you at your apartment?

Terry gets off the elevator and goes into his favorite local fruit store to get some strawberries, oranges, nuts, and any other fruits that caught his eye.

> **1:12 pm**
> Lena: Yes. Can we meet at like 7? This gives me enough time to change and shower real quick.

> **1:13 pm**
> Terry: Yea that sounds good to me. Just send me your address.

1:15 pm
Lena: I'll send it to you. What are you about to do?

1:17 pm
Terry: Gonna go get some fruit and then get some lunch.

1:18 pm
Lena: Yuuummm fruit? What kind of fruits are you buying?

As Terry begins to answer the text from Lena, he walks into his favorite fruit stand in the city. He greets the cashier, and he continues to walk through the single aisles of fruits and nuts.

1:19 pm
Terry: Today I'm just buying some mangoes and some nuts. I really want pomegranates, but I have to wait until fall for them. So I think I'll get some strawberries for now.

1:21 pm
Lena: I love fruit, strawberries, and especially pomegranates.

Pomegranate juice is the best. ☺

1:23 pm
Terry: I agree. I'm about to check out and then grab some

lunch. Don't forget to text me
your address and I'll leave my
apartment around 6:15.

1:25pm
Lena: Ok big head! Talk later! 😊

Terry pays for his strawberries and mangoes and decides to pass on the nuts and come back in another week or so. As he pays, he takes a quick glance outside and notices these big fluffy gray clouds.

"I hope it doesn't rain tonight," he thinks to himself.

"Zàijiàn," he says as he waves goodbye to the cashier. Then, he immediately goes to his favorite sandwich shop.

His usual was a turkey club sandwich that included: "with a little bit of mayonnaise, bacon, pepper, lettuce, and tomato." The perfect healthy snack for him after the gym. While waiting for his sandwich to be made, he continues to look out of the window. The clouds are moving fast, as if it's a race to see which cloud could make it rain the fastest. Before he turns his head to ask for a drink, he sees the same exact pretty lady from the gym walk by again. This time she has a faster pace to her step and goes by the sandwich shop in a blink.

Terry notices her because she had on bright pink sneakers. He turns his attention back to his order and pays for his food. He pulls out his Alipay code and the cashier scans it for him. Walking out of the sandwich shop, he notices a couple drops of water on his phone. "Heavy rain tonight," he reads out loud, as he looks at the weather report on his phone. This seems like it's going to be one of those intense summer rains that comes after the earth has been scorched by the sun. The Earth needs some relief, and it seems that tonight the rain will arrive with force.

He rushes back to his apartment and just as he arrives back at his building, he hears the thunder clash. Terry sits in front of his building as he watches the rain quickly run in and soak everything on the street. As he sits underneath the entrance, he takes a moment to just look around. He sees a Chinese restaurant, a delivery man on his motorbike speeding by, the people running for protection from the downpour, and the rain hitting the ground and joining the rest of the puddles.

"I'm really living and working in China," he says to himself. This is something that he's always wanted to do. When he was in college, he had an opportunity to go to Beijing during the 2008 Olympics. Sadly, he didn't have the money to make the trip and to cover all the visa costs. Finally, about a decade later, he found an opportunity to come to China to live and work.

He takes a couple more moments to enjoy the sound of the rain connecting to the city, and he takes a quick photo on his phone.

He goes inside and gets on the elevator to ascend to the 27th floor. Terry looks at the time on his watch: 2:08 pm. Terry notices that Lena has sent him the address for her apartment. He does a quick Google search and finds out that she is very close to their office.

2:10 pm
Terry: Thanks for the address! Still good for 7?

Terry takes off his bag and puts his fruit on the small island in his apartment. He goes to wash his hands, as he hears the wind and rain colliding with his window. His stomach starts to talk as he is hungry, and has only eaten his oatmeal breakfast today. Grabbing his strawberries and plate, he plops on his couch. "Time to grub," he says to himself.

2:12 pm
Lena: Yeah 7 is still good!!

2:14 pm
Terry: Ok. I'll text you when I leave.

2:15 pm
Lena: 👍

Before he dives into his snack, he opens up his blinds to see the view of the rain encompassing the city. He proceeds to go back to his couch and finish his food. Five minutes later, the fruit disappears and he starts to clean up his apartment. Even though he will go out later, he still wants to clean up and keep his place as spotless as possible. He puts up his fruits, cleans his bathroom, and does a little stretching because he didn't stretch before he left the gym.

Once again, he checks the life timer: 3:15 pm. He feels his eyes getting heavy and belts out a lustrous yawn. "Maybe I can just lay down until about 5:30, and get up and start getting dressed. That still gives me an hour to get ready and then I can leave around 6:30." Terry stretches out on the couch. "I need a pillow." He gets up and grabs a pillow and then lays back down.

He plugs his phone up to the wall and then takes one more glance at his watch: 3:16pm. An alarm is set on his phone for 5:30 pm. After a couple of quick blinks, Terry is fast asleep on his couch.

> **6:45 pm**
> **Lena: Hey there! Are you ready?**
>
> **6:55 pm**
> **Lena: Where are you? Are you awake?**
>
> **7:00 pm**
> **Lena: Is everything ok?**
>
> **7:10 pm**
> **Lena: ???**

The television remote falls and hits the floor with a *bang*. The sudden noise wakes Terry up out of his slumber. He quickly stretches, thinking that it's about 5:30 pm. Then, he notices that the sun has retired for the day. He sits up and begins to breathe deeply and shoves his hand into the couch. "Where's my phone?" he thinks. Frantically looking for his phone, he finds it in between the two soft cushions.

He quickly presses his finger against the screen to unlock it, and he sees the 4 missed messages from Lena. He looks at the time on his phone: 7:45 pm. "Oh shit!" Terry exclaims.

> **7:45 pm**
> Terry: Hey Lena, I'm so sorry, but I overslept. I thought I set my alarm, but I guess I didn't. Hopefully you're not mad and you haven't been waiting too long.

He nervously rubs his knees and waits for a response from her. He can't believe that he overslept and didn't hear his alarm. Looking at his phone, Terry realizes that he never turned on his alarm and it was never set.

"Why do I even try sometimes?" he says to himself. He's never quite had the best luck in the relationship department, and he thinks that this situation with Lena will be no different. His hands cover his face in embarrassment and disappointment, and then he hears his phone *ding*.

> **7:46pm**
> Lena: I'm just sitting at home having a drink. So, you took a nap...hahaha.

> **7:47 pm**
> Terry: Yeah, I'm sorry. I thought I could set my alarm and get up and still have time to get dressed and meet you.

> **7:48 pm**
> Lena: That's ok, but I think we may have to forget about dinner. Or we can get something to eat real quick and then go to the bar.

7:49 pm
Terry: We can get something fast
and then go to your bar. I'm going
to hurry up and get dressed and
then I will meet you. Is that ok?

7:50pm
Lena: Yes!

Terry drops his phone and runs into the bathroom to turn on the shower. After his speedy shower, he quickly throws on his preplanned outfit. He ties his navy-blue boat shoes up, puts on his brown belt, and turns off his television. Terry comes out of his room and his neighbor, Matt, is going into his apartment.

"Hey man, how's it going? If you're going out, it's still raining a little bit so take an umbrella," Matt advises.
"Hey bro, I'm good and it's a good idea that I should take an umbrella," Terry replies.
He goes inside and quickly grabs his small gray umbrella. "I'll talk to you soon, bro. Have a good night," Terry says to Matt.
"Thanks bro, you too. Talk soon," Matt says.

Terry gets on the elevator; he sees the same girl from the gym. He notices her same pink shoes, long black hair down to her waist, sun-kissed skin, and has those same voluptuous raspberry-red lips. They end up locking eyes again, and he provides a half-smile for her. She gives the smile right back. "I've never seen this girl in my building before. Even though I've only been here for a couple of months," he thinks to himself.

As the elevator subtracts to the first floor, he can't help but still think about Lena. "There's a beautiful woman who just smiled and nodded at you, and you're still thinking about Lena," he thinks to himself. The elevator comes to a complete stop and they both exit into the lobby. She gives him one more smile, and she goes off into the mysteries of the city.

The rain has slowed to an annoying sprinkle, so Terry decided that he didn't need any protection from it. Dodging puddles on the sidewalk, he walks to the metro station. He wipes the sweat from his brow because the humidity still encompasses his body. He takes a quick look at his phone: 8:20 pm.

"I can't believe that I overslept. Lena must be upset." She didn't seem upset to him. It seemed as though she was just waiting for him. The train station isn't full, and he is able to get a seat. The doors close, and he sits back slightly in preparation for the 15-minute train ride. The ride is going smoothly and comes to the first stop. The doors open and close, and he looks at the window and sees a dark silhouette in the reflection.

He quickly looks behind him at the other windows and doesn't see anything. "What is happening to me," he thinks to himself. The train continues to Terry's destination. He gets off and looks at the directions that she sent him:

> Lena: Once you get out of the train station, go to exit 4. Walk up the stairs and when you come out cross the street. Walk past

> the mall by work and there'll be a
> KFC on the corner. Text me when
> you're at the KFC.

He follows her directions to the very last detail. He still has his umbrella, just in case the sky decides to open up again and let the world know how it felt. "Where is this KFC at?" There are quite a few tall apartment buildings by his office, and they all looked the same to him.

Crossing the street, he takes a quick look at the time: 8:40 pm. He passes the mall and sees the KFC on the corner.

> **8:40 pm**
> Terry: I'm by the KFC.

As he waits for her response, he takes a look around the neighborhood. "I've never been over here, and it's right across the street from my job," he thinks to himself. He looks at the promotions on the KFC window and realizes that he is a little hungry. No sound from his stomach, but it does feel empty to him. "I could definitely go for a chicken sandwich and some fries right now."

> **8:42 pm**
> Lena: Ok, coming down now.

> **8:44 pm**
> Terry: See you shortly.

"I'm almost two hours late, and I forgot to put on deodorant!" He was in such a rush to leave after he got out of the shower, and he forgot to put on deodorant. "Well, maybe she won't notice. I did put on some cologne, though." It was hot and humid outside, and he had already begun to sweat through his navy-blue polo.

He sees her coming out of her building, he slightly tugs his shirt down, and pulls his pants up. Her big brown eyes came rushing up to him, "Well, it's nice to see you," she says.

Terry cracks a slight smile, "I fell asleep by accident," he tells her.

"I thought you were napping and forgot to set your alarm," she corrects his untruth.

"Oh yeah, that's what happened," he stutters.

"Why did you lie right there? You wanted to nap and just forgot to set your alarm. I'm not mad, just tell me the truth," she states.

His eyebrows raise a little. He didn't understand why he had lied about something so trivial, especially when he told her the truth moments ago.

"You're right. I apologize," he responds.

"For?" she asks.

He looks at her and says, "For lying about what happened and for falling asleep?"

"That sounds better. So, I think it's too late to go to the restaurant I was thinking about. We can grab something from KFC and then go to the bar," she suggests.

"I think that sounds good to me. I was looking at the promotions on the window anyway," he responds.

He notices that she has on a dark red and flowy long-skirt and yellow short-sleeve t-shirt. She had her makeup done, her hair was in a short ponytail and her lips were a metallic red. Terry is taken back at her glow and can't take his eyes off her.

"You look amazing tonight," he says.

She tilts her head to the side, blushes through her makeup, smiles, and says, "Thank you!" She takes another moment and says, "You're looking good yourself!"

Terry holds the door for her as she walks into the KFC, and they order two KFC Famous Bowls and two Cokes. As they finished eating their dinner, the sky decided to let the world know how it felt. It went from a drizzle and directly to a downpour within a single breath. "I think we should call a DiDi to get to the bar," she proposes.

"I think that would be the best idea, and I have an umbrella since you forgot yours," he remarks.

"That's a very smart idea," she responds.

She orders a DiDi, and it's seven minutes away. "So, you know I can't drink much, right?" he asks.

"I know, I will have a couple, but I think you will like the atmosphere of this place," she responds. "Ok cool. Shall I put our trays up?" he asks. She nods her head and looks to check how far the car is from them. "We still have about four minutes."

He comes and sits down with corn, mashed potatoes, and chicken grease dancing in his stomach. "So, what's your favorite drink at this place? Or just in general, what's your favorite drink?" he asks.

"Well, I don't drink beer. I mean, it's ok, but I just don't have a taste for it. So, I would say that a Gin and Tonic is what I typically drink," she responds with a smile.

"How do you feel about sweet drinks?" he asks.

"No, I don't really like those sweet drinks, they make me sick," she says. *Ding!*" The notification lets them know that the car isn't far from them.

"I think our car is outside," she says.

They both get up and begin to walk out. The rain has begun to sprint down to the ground, so he reaches for his umbrella. The car is a couple of feet in front of them, but he didn't want her to get wet. He pushes open the door and opens his umbrella as they get out. "Thank you," she states. "You are welcome. This rain is coming down." He responds by making sure to cover her head. They reach the doors of the DiDi, a black Toyota Camry, and Terry opens the door. She slides into the car, he quickly shakes some of the water off the umbrella and flops into the car.

As he closes the door, he hears the driver say something in Mandarin. "What did he say?" Terry asks.

"Hahaha. You need to learn some Mandarin! He just says hello, and he says the last couple digits of your phone number. He also reminds you to put on your seatbelt," she says.

"So, every time you get into a Taxi or a DiDi you don't know what the driver is saying?" she asks.

"I mean, I just assume that the driver says something about putting on my seatbelt, and I do it anyway," he chuckles and puts on his seatbelt.

The bar is about 10 minutes away; with the rain it will take 15. They're in no rush to get there, and Terry is just enjoying being next to Lena. The driver goes over a bump in the road and Terry feels his stomach do a front flip. He grabs his stomach with his right hand and slightly leans over.

"What's wrong?" she asks.

"I'm ok! I think maybe the chicken and corn may be sitting wrong in my stomach, but I'll be ok," he responds.

"Do you have to use the bathroom?" she asks.

"No, I'm fine. I'll get some water when we get to the bar," he says. He wasn't planning on drinking much anyway, so water was always the original plan. Although, he was thinking about getting one beer.

Since he graduated from college, he found out that he is allergic to alcohol. One mild Portland summer night after graduation, Terry and Carla went out for a night of drinking and partying to celebrate his graduation. He remembers going into a bar and drinking enough whiskey shots to knock out a sailor for weeks. Terry started to feel hot, and he started sweating when he saw Carla's face. "Hey bro, is your face swollen?" Carla asks. "What are you talking about?" Terry says, and goes into the bathroom and sees what he thought was his face. He finds his lips were puffed out, his eyelids swollen and hives formed on his neck.

He ran out of the bar with Carla not too far behind him. There was a local pharmacy close to the bar and Terry darted in, almost hitting the sliding doors. Carla bumped into the sliding door and spun around halfway. Terry runs straight to the allergy section and looks for something he can take and work very quickly. He finds some Benadryl, grape-flavored, and goes to the counter to pay. They both sit outside while he sips on the medicine.

"Damn dude, what happened back there?" Carla asks.

"I have no idea!" Terry could barely mutter it out.

"I don't know what brought this on," he responds.

"I could barely keep up chasing you. I don't think we paid our tab either," she realizes.

He didn't know that he had an allergy to alcohol, but a trip to his doctor two weeks later would confirm it. "You have an allergy to alcohol Mr. Jones," his doctor says.

"I was fine in college, Dr. Daniels. All four years of college and maybe a little bit in high school, I was fine." Terry reluctantly states.

"Well, Mr. Jones, sometimes these things can come on without warning and happen at the most inconvenient times," Dr. Daniels replies.

"What can I do?" Terry asks.

"This might be the end of your drinking days. Which may not be a bad thing. You may be able to have a small glass of wine, and if things flare-up you can take an antihistamine pill. But I doubt you would want to go through that every time you drink," suggests Dr. Daniels.

"I'll do whatever it takes!" he says.

As Terry drove home after the doctor visit, he knew his life would completely change after that experience. Thinking about this instance, while he was in the DiDi with Lena, didn't help his stomach feel better. They finally reached the bar, as the rain became a marathon more than a sprint.

"We're here!" Lena excitedly says.

"That just looks like the side of a building. There's no bar here," Terry suspiciously says.

"Just get out of the car and I will show you," she says, pushing him out of the car.

They thank the driver, say goodbye, and exit.

"There is only a soda machine here. I don't see anything that would resemble a bar," his intuition is getting to him.

Lena comes up to what looks like a soda machine and puts her hand behind a lever. As she lifts her hand up, the soda machine opens up. To Terry's surprise, the doors slowly open and show a set of stairs leading to a bar. "What did you just do, and what kind of speakeasy is this?" He asks, as he begins to follow Lena into the basement bar. He can hear music playing and people talking. The smell of cigarette smoke stuffs his lungs, as he inhales the cloudy air. Carefully making his way down, the smells get stronger and the lights brighter. There's a young lady wearing a black vest with a white t-shirt greeting people, as they come into the main area. Lena asks for a table for two and the greeter walks them to a corner of the bar.

"This place smells like an ashtray," he says, as he grips his stomach while he sits down.

"Stop complaining and sit down," she tells him.

"How's your stomach?" she asks, sitting in her chair. Gripping his belly, he says, "It will be alright." The waiter comes over and asks Lena what they want to drink. She ordered a Gin and Tonic, and he was suggested to order some hot water.

"What will hot water do for me?" he wonders.

"It will make you feel better. Hot water makes everything better," she responds. Their drinks come and he begins to sip on his hot water as she sips her Gin and Tonic.

"So, why are you single? she asks, putting her drink on the clear glass table.

"Why are you single? Since you want to ask questions," he answers a question with a question.

"These guys don't interest me. Now you?" she quickly responds.

"Well, that was quick. I was in a relationship before I came over, I thought it could've gone somewhere far but it didn't." He pushes his hot water close to the candle on the table.

"What happened?" she asks.

"It's not that important but long story short, we ended up splitting," he says, just as the waiter comes back to the table to check on them; Lena tells her that they are ok. His stomach continues to do backflips, and it feels like someone is punching the inside of his stomach.

"Are you sure you are ok? I mean we can leave if you don't feel well," she suggests.

"I'm ok. I think I'm going to have a beer and then we can leave," he confidently says.

"I don't really think that's a good idea. Being that you can't really drink, and your stomach seems to be hurting quite badly." He is taken aback at how much she seems to care. Unfortunately, he is not in the mood to listen. "Maybe the beer will make me feel better," he says

"That sounds like a bad idea, Terry." The waitress comes back and Terry orders a beer. He downs the beer quite quickly and to his surprise, it didn't help. By this time, Lena has had three Gin and Tonics and is dancing to the song playing in the bar.

Terry looks at his watch: 12:55 am.
He gets another glass of hot water and he starts to yawn.
"I know you are not tired when you sleep all afternoon," she says.
"I think this is my last drink," he replies, gripping his stomach.
"Well, I'm not too far from here. You can walk me home," she says.
"That sounds fine with me. Let me go use the bathroom and then we can leave." He goes to use the bathroom and feels the pain in his stomach increasing. In the bathroom, he leans over the toilet and begins to sweat a little bit. He looks in the mirror, splashes some water on his face, and walks out. "Did you pay for the beer? I can send you the money back," he said.
"It was only like 70 RMB for you so don't stress," she says.

They begin to walk up the stairs and Terry bends over in pain. She doesn't see him, as she continues to leave the bar. Outside the bar, she spins around and hugs him. He squeezes her tight and puts his hands around her hips. He looks at her in her big brown eyes, leans in, and proceeds to say, "Can I kiss...can I..." he can barely get the words out. Darting over to a nearby bush, he sees that it has some wet tissue on it. Terry doesn't care. He is letting out his stomach issues, as she slowly walks over to rub his back and hold him slightly up. "I told you that the beer wasn't a good idea if your stomach was hurting," she says. Terry lifts his head out of the bush and begins to laugh uncontrollably. "You're right. But I do feel instantly better now though," he responds. Lena gives Terry a napkin out of her purse, and they begin to walk down the street to her apartment.

"You know, before I ended up in the bush, I was going to ask if I could kiss you?" he says.

"You were going to ask what?" she asks.

"Can I kiss you?" he states.

"Not now!" she says, vehemently shaking her head.

They both laugh as they walk in the middle of the street. She gives him some of her passion fruit hand sanitizer, then she gently holds his right hand.

"You still have to tell me what happened between you and your ex, ex-fiancé, or whatever you two were?" she insists.

"I will soon enough," he replies.

Walking down the street, he looks down an alleyway between a pharmacy and an apartment building. He notices a small shadow in the distance and quickly shakes his head a little bit.

"What's wrong, Terry?" she asks, gripping his hand tighter.

"Nothing, I just thought I saw something over by the pharmacy," he replies.

"You must be having a rough night. Poor baby," she smirks, as she takes a look at the alleyway. "I think I may need to lay down for a quick minute when I get to your house. If you don't mind, I can lay down on your couch," he suggests.

"That's ok. I have some hot water that should make you feel better," she says.

"You and this hot water. Is that the only remedy you have?" he asks.

"Yup, and it works. You just have to believe it. You don't have one thing that cures all remedies?" she asks.

"Ginger ale," he says.

Ginger ale? Like the soda?" she asks.

"Yes, like the soda. In the black community, it's used to be a remedy for a lot of things: stomachaches, headaches, hiccups, or even heartburns. People may not use it so often, because it's a little old school. Does it fix everything? I don't think so, but it tastes good and could make you forget about your pain." He says.

"Well, your ginger ale for Black people, is hot water for Chinese people. Except, we can make hot water right at home and don't need to go to a store," she says.

"Neither do we," he says.

"I live right up here," she says, as she points to her skyscraper of a building.

"That was a quick walk," he thought. The rain had finished the race, but there were still puddles everywhere. They arrive at Lena's apartment building and go up to the 30th floor. Entering her apartment, he instantly starts sweating.

"Could you turn on the air when you get a chance?" he asks.

"Ok, Mr. Boss!" she replies and gives him a salute.

"While you are doing all of that, I'm going to lay on your couch," he states. "Be my guest," she says.

Lena turns on the bulky air conditioner; then, she goes into the kitchen to get some hot water. Upon her return to the living room, she finds him sleeping with his mouth wide open. She puts the warm water next to him, puts a small red blanket over him, and goes to her room for the night.

VIII

Missed Messages

Terry covers his face with his right hand, to protect his eyes from the glaring sun. Then, he feels something licking his face. Slowly opening his eyes, he sees a brown and white puppy on top of him. "When did she get a dog? I don't remember a dog from last night and I wasn't even that drunk," he thought. He sneezes a couple of times, as he checks his watch for the time: 9:31 am. Terry knows that he has to work today, as his days off have changed. Not having to be at work until noon, he knows has enough time to go home and change clothes. He slowly gets off the couch and the dog follows him, trying to get his attention. The dog is right behind Terry, but then is stopped by the bathroom door.

Grabbing his nose to stop him from sneezing uncontrollably, he notices that his shirt has a tiny branch on it. "What really happened last night?" All he remembers is leaving the bar and not much of anything else. He splashes some water on his face and swishes hot water from the bathroom sink around in his mouth. He hears the dog move around the bathroom door as the door opens up. Continuing to sniff Terry's leg, the dog runs back into the bedroom through a little opening in the door. Terry sits down for a minute and checks his phone; he sees that he has 15 missed messages. Just as he begins to check the messages, he hears Lena moving around in her bed. Her feet stomp on the hardwood floors and one-by-one make their way into the living room.

Stretching and walking at the same time, Lena belts out a "Good morning, sunshine!" She comes and sits next to Terry, with the dog close behind. "How are you this close to me with your morning breath?" Terry jokingly states.

"You shut up," she says and smiles.

"I have a question. Ummm...since when did you get a dog?" he inquires.

"You don't remember seeing her last night? Her name is Riley." she says.

Terry rubs his eyes as he really can't remember. "No I don't remember meeting Riley and I don't remember seeing her," he says

"I adopted her a couple of weeks ago. Are you allergic to dogs or something?" she asks.

"I have a tiny allergy to dogs. So if you could've told me that before, I could've taken some allergy medicine beforehand," he says.

"Oh, I'm sorry. I really thought I told you. Your allergies must get really bad around dogs?" she asks.

"Not really, it seems to only be when I first meet them, but it gets better with time. It's weird, I know," he replies.

"It's not weird, I have a friend who is like that around cats. The longer she stays around a cat, I guess the better her allergies adjust," she says.

"Well, nice to meet you, Riley," Terry looks at the beagle, and then starts to gather himself. "I have to work today but not until later," he tells her.

"I know your days off are switched, just like mine. What will you do on your day off?" Terry asks. "Nothing much, maybe just meet up with a friend and go to the gym," she replies.

"Sounds like an eventful day. Could I get a toothbrush really quick?" he asks.

She goes and comes back with a small travel-size toothbrush and toothpaste for him.

After he brushes his teeth, he picks up his phone to put it into his packet. Quickly glancing at his phone, he notices that he now has 21 missed messages and an unread message on Instagram.

"Last night before you ended up in the bushes, I think you were going to ask me a question," she says.

"Oh, is that what happened? Anyway, yeah, I think I was going to ask if I could kiss…" just as he was finishing his sentence, Lena squeezed his cheeks, pulled him close, and shared a kiss. His heart goes into high gear, and he feels a sense of calmness come over him. They spend about 12 seconds locked in paradise and then they part. With her eyes halfway open and blushing a little, she licks her lips. "I hope it was everything that you wanted it to be. And I hope you have a good day at the office," she says.

"It was perfect Lena," he responds.

They stand next to each other, stuck in a moment, but knowing that it won't last forever. "I have to go," Terry says, as he kisses Lena on the lips one more time. They hug, and he slowly pulls away, as Riley is still at his leg.

"Bye Riley, I'll see you soon. Enjoy your day. I'll text you once I get to the center," he says. They kiss one last time, as he opens the door to walk out. She comes up to the door and they both wave goodbye. On his way to the elevator, he can't believe what just happened.

"Is she the one? Does she really care about me? Could this really turn out to be something?" His mind is racing, and he is blocking the path to the elevator. An older gentleman is trying to walk around Terry as he is still thinking about Lena. "I'm sorry. Ummm….duì bùqǐ," he says to the older man. The older gentleman smiles and walks past Terry to the elevator.

As he puts his hands on his hips, he feels his phone in his front pocket. Terry remembered that he had quite a few missed messages. He rips his phone out of his pocket and begins to look at the messages. His cousins, Naomi and Jared, have been sending him messages all morning. He even received a message from his Uncle Jeremy, who lives in Seattle.

5:00 am
Naomi: Hey cuz, are you free?

5:01 am
Jared: Yo you up?

5:01 am
Naomi: Hey??

> **5:02 am**
> Jared: Yo bro have you spoken to Carla?

> **5:04 am**
> Naomi: Have you heard from C?

> **5:06 am**
> Uncle J: Hey man, when you get a chance message or call us.

> **5:08 am**
> Jared: Hey man, call me or message me when you get the chance.

Terry knows that he is sixteen hours ahead of his family back home. He texts his cousins while he is waiting for his taxi.

> **10:04 am (To Jared)**
> Terry: Hey cuz, I'm just about to get ready for work. What's going on?

Summer is still in full swing, and he has begun to sweat through his polo shirt. The taxi comes fairly quick, but he has yet to receive a response from Jared.

> **10:10am (To Naomi)**
> Terry: Hey Nay, is everything ok?

Jared and Naomi are Terry's two closest cousins. They grew up together, played sports together, went to school together, and still have a close bond. They are two of Terry's biggest supporters. Growing up in the same neighborhood, they relied on each other for much-needed support. They may not have had much money and resources growing up, but they had all they needed: love and each other. Terry graduated from high school first, then Naomi, and finally Jared. After high school, they went on to pursue their own dreams. Terry went to school in Oregon for track and field, Naomi went to the University of Washington, and Jared stayed in Portland after landing a job with a construction company. After a while, they lost touch and didn't keep up with each other, but life has a way of bringing people back together.

Naomi went to the University of Washington on an academic scholarship and was working on her degree in Hydrology and Water Management. Her goal was to help find ways to provide clean and sustainable water production to the world, but sometimes life doesn't follow the path we want it to. She ended up having to return to Portland, because she got pregnant with her daughter in her sophomore year. Two months after she came home her mom got sick. She started working as a secretary in a law office in downtown Portland. She eventually went on to become a paralegal, and she would go to Eugene to watch Terry's track events.

Jared would always come to Terry's track & field events. Jared was so proud of his cousin and would always be in the stands with a sign that read: "TERRY WINS AGAIN AT OREGON!" A little corny, but Jared liked it and Terry appreciated it. Jared thought Terry would be fast enough to qualify for the Olympics and he was almost right. Terry was a top athlete for his university, and he was fast. Winning the Men's 100 and 200-meter dash races, at both the indoor and outdoor college track and field championships. When Terry graduated, he went to the Olympic trials, but missed his qualifying times for both the 100 and 200-meter dashes. He was crushed, but Jared was there with him the entire way. Even helping Terry to get a job with the construction company Jared worked for. Terry would also help Jared with his application to get into Clackamas Community College, so Jared could study engineering. The bond between the cousins was strong and only getting stronger as they got older.

10:15 am
Naomi: Hey Gravy, are you free?

It's so hot in the taxi," he thought to himself. He rolls down the back window to get some extra air. The cold air was on in the taxi, but it was barely reaching him in the backseat.

10:16 am
Terry: Yeah I'm free. I have to work but not until later. What's going on?

10:17 am
Naomi: It's C.

His heart starts to do front flips, as he thought it was something going on with his sister.

10:18 am
Terry: What about her? Is she ok?

He approaches his apartment and grabs his stomach. "Not my stomach again," he says under his breath. He is patiently waiting for the next text to arrive, as he thinks about different things that could be wrong with his sister. "She's never had any type of disease, and she hasn't been sick lately. At least, I don't think she is sick. What could be wrong?" he thinks.

> **10:19 am**
> Naomi: She's missing! We don't know where she is.

The taxi stops in front of Terry's apartment building and he slowly gets out. He gets a notification that he's paid for the taxi, but he doesn't see it pop up on his phone. He notices someone walking by him very slowly, and he is having trouble hearing the morning traffic. Everything appears as if he has just opened his eyes from a night's rest.

> **10:20 am**
> Terry: What do you mean she's missing?

Slowly walking into the building, he goes to the elevator with his eyes glued to the phone. He is still sweating, and his clothes have begun to stick to his body.

> **10:21 am**
> Naomi: We haven't heard from her or her boyfriend for almost 2 days.

> **10:22 am**
> Terry: Have you talked to Tim?

10:23 am
Naomi: We haven't heard from him either. We informed the police and we filed a missing persons report. We called her, tried reaching out to her on Instagram and Facebook and no response.

10:23 am
Terry: What did the police say? How long has she been missing?

10:24 am
Naomi: They are looking into it but we're scared, Terry. We noticed a couple days ago that it was dead silence from her.

Tim was Carla's on and off again boyfriend, and Terry was not the biggest fan of him. The couple had been "dating" for about two years, and Terry noticed that Carla was changing. Her attitude wasn't as positive and upbeat, and she wasn't as focused as she used to be. For their parents' birthday, they would always have a barbecue. Usually, they would do this at Naomi's apartment. On one occasion, Carla totally missed the dinner because she was arguing with Tim. "But would Tim really hurt his sister? Does he know anything?" Terry turns on his VPN and goes onto Instagram and Facebook to see what's going on. Times have changed when social media has become our top source of family information. Terry scrolls up and down his Facebook feed and doesn't see anything. He goes to Tim's page and sees that he hasn't posted anything for a couple of weeks. Most of the people

Terry knows post on Facebook at least twice a week, and maybe more for some of his friends and family. Carla hasn't posted anything in weeks, either.

> 10:30 am
> Terry: I just checked their Facebook and Instagram and I didn't see anything. Are you guys looking for her?

He sits on the edge of his bed and turns the air conditioner on to help combat his sweltering apartment. A feeling of helplessness is spreading through his emotions. This was one of his biggest fears about moving overseas. "What if something happens and I can't be there?" This thought plagued his mind for months before he left the U.S.

> 10:31 am
> Naomi: We went to her apartment and called her job and nobody has seen her. We about to hit the streets and go down Belmont and Hawthorne and see if anybody has seen her. We printed out some flyers to pass out. I'm so scared Terry. I've been crying all night.

> 10:33 am
> Lena: Hey are you home?

> 10:33 am
> Terry: I know Nay! Could you send me the flyer? It's not like I can

hang them up here but I would like to see it. I can't believe this. I hope Tim didn't do anything to her.

10:34 am
Naomi: I hope he didn't either. Did you talk to Jared?

10:35 am
Terry: Not yet. I have to work in a few so I'm about to get ready.

10:36 am
Naomi: Ok Gravy! I love you and I'll keep you updated.

10:37 am
Terry: I love you too Nay! Speak to you soon.

Terry slowly lays his phone next to him and puts his head on his pillow. Thousands of thoughts are clashing in his head; he tries to prepare himself for the workday. A tear slowly climbs down his left cheek as he grabs his pillow. He hears his phone *ding* and picks it up to see if there were any instant updates.

10:39 am
Jared: Did you hear about C?

10:40 am
Terry: Yeah, Nay just told me.

10:41 am
Jared: Do you think you can come
home? The family is in a panic.

Terry knew that this was his biggest fear come true. He had a conversation with Carla about it before he left the states. They were sitting in Carla's living room, and she had on her favorite Portland Trail Blazers hoodie, as it was chilly that day. "What if something happened to Uncle Rick and Aunt Pam? Or Uncle Jeremy? Or me for that fact? Would you be able to get home fast enough?" Carla asks, as she sits on her maroon and black couch. This was in February, a couple of months before he was set to venture to China. "I'm sure I can get back home if I need to. It would take about 18 hours depending on how long my layover is," he replies.

"I'm just worried that something will happen and you won't get back in time. I mean I still want you to go and take this adventure on, but I'm just worried about you Gravy," she says.

"I know C, but if something happens, I'll do my best to get back home. I'll be over for a year, and then I'll be back. How much could happen in one year?" he naively thought. They hugged and went back to watching the Trail Blazers game.

Terry has to start getting ready for work, and he begins to pick his clothes. His family has supported him even when he felt that he didn't deserve it. How could he abandon his family in their time of need? There was no way he was going to get off work this soon after he just started. He didn't even know how long he would be home. This move was for his family and more importantly: himself. A pact, made to himself to become the best version of himself, no matter the circumstance. He would have to stay and support his family from the other side of the world.

Terry picks out one of his favorite shirts, and it was a shirt that Carla also liked. It was a black and red plaid button-up shirt. "I like that shirt, baby bro!" Carla's voice echoed in his fragile mind. "Thanks, big sis!" he replies. Terry does his best to pull himself together, takes a shower, brushes his teeth, and continues to get ready for the workday. He takes about 5 minutes to cry in the shower. The warm water feels refreshing bouncing off his skin.

11:03 am
Naomi: image attached

Terry looks at the flyer that Naomi created, and he begins to tear up.

"Last seen Monday leaving her job. She has curly brown hair, she's 5'8, brown skin, brown eyes, has a nose ring in her left nostril, and has a rose tattoo on her upper left shoulder. She also wears an apple necklace. If you've seen her or know anything please contact Naomi Jenkins at 503-555-4321."

Terry sees the picture that they used for the flyer. It was a picture of Carla at her 30th birthday party. She was smiling from ear to ear that day and was so happy. They didn't have a huge celebration, just a backyard BBQ with some family and friends. He continued to get ready for work, and he decided to take a taxi to work on this day. Terry just didn't feel like being social at the moment. Sometimes, when thoughts are heavy, being around people doesn't always make the load lighter. Alone time can be the best time.

11:05 am
Terry: Thanks for the flyer. Keep me updated, I'm about to go to work.

11:06 am
Naomi: I will.❤

He calls a Didi and leaves his apartment to go downstairs. Once he gets on the elevator, he sees the girl from the gym again. This time she is wearing all black. Black Nike t-shirt, black Nike yoga pants, and black tennis shoes. This time, he smiles and waves at her. She lifts her black Louis Vuitton shades and winks at him with her right eye. He winks back with his right eye as the elevator begins to descend to base. He feels his phone vibrate and looks to see that the Didi driver is outside.

He steps out into the omniscient heat and gets into the red Toyota. There is very little traffic in the city around this time, as it is right before the daily lunchtime rush. He gets into the office 30 minutes before his first-class starts. As he sits in his chair, he barely sees Barry waving at him.

"Hey Terry. You ok?" Barry asks.

"Ummm...not really man. I have some stuff from back home that I'm dealing with," Terry reluctantly says. He felt that he could trust Barry, even though he's only known him for a couple of months. There was something warm and comforting about Barry, and he knew that was something rare to find. Kindred souls often connect in the most turbulent times. Barry was of course in his 50s and a native of the UK. He was well-traveled and well-versed in the songs of life. Terry was in his 30s and trying to get on the same page as life. Terry needed something at that moment and wasn't quite sure what it was, but he felt more than comfortable expressing himself to Barry.

"Yeah, I've been in contact with my family all morning. Apparently, my sister has gone missing and nobody knows where she is," Terry says.

"I'm so sorry to hear that, mate. That's bloody awful," Barry responds. They continue to chat as they both get ready for their classes. "I had some missed messages from my cousins on WeChat and when I woke up I texted them back. They told me that my sister, Carla, had been missing for a couple of days," he states.

"I'm sorry mate! If you want to talk about it, we can go for a bevy after work. I'm done at 8:30," Barry offers.

Initially, Terry wanted to be alone, but he felt that Barry really cared. "Yeah sure, I would like that bro. I will get off a little late tonight," Terry just realizes.

"That's ok, mate. I'll wait for you," Barry replies. Terry is at the printer and a slight smile comes over his face.

"That would be great," he says. They finish getting ready for their respective classes and then head to class. Terry needed some coffee before class started, so he went to the coffee machine. Usually, he pushes the one-cup button, but on this day he decided to press the icon with the two coffee cups on it. A student walks up to Terry and drops a paper cup in the trash. "Hi Teacher," the student says.

"Hi, Jess. I'm ok today, and how are you?" Terry asks. Jess was one of Terry's newer students. She was a 24-year-old young professional, who wanted to improve her English-speaking skills.

"Are you ok, Teacher?" She asks. When Terry had a lot on his mind, he tended to wear his emotions on his sleeve. "I'm ok Jess, just a little tired, that's all. But thank you for asking," he responds. "You're welcome, Teacher! Do you have class now?" she asks.

"Yes, I'm going now. I will see you later if you come to our group discussion later," he says, as he walks into his classroom. He pushes through his first three classes with help from one of his best friends: coffee.

The afternoon and evening sprint by, and it's time for his evening classes. He checks his messages in between classes and doesn't see any new information from his family. Thoughts began wrestling his mind again: "I hope her boyfriend didn't do anything. What if she's scared or lonely? What if she's…." his thoughts began to become darker. "Don't go to the dark side, Terry. Think happy and positive thoughts. Your mind and thoughts have power." He keeps repeating this sentence to himself. The rest of the day goes by with the help of coffee. After his final class, he walks into the office and sees Barry finishing up some paperwork.

9:31 pm
Lena: Hey are you ok? Haven't heard from you.

"Hey mate. How were your classes tonight?" Barry asks.

"They were pretty good. Being in the classroom makes me forget about the ills in the world. It's partly what made me want to stick with teaching and to keep pursuing growth in education," Terry expresses.

"It is a wonderful thing to know that you are helping people and there can be an instant benefit from what we do every day," Barry replies.

"I could certainly use a drink, man. I have to work tomorrow, but not until later on. Are you off tomorrow?" Terry asks.

"Yeah, I'm off for the next two days. I'm going to relax and study some more Japanese," he tells Terry. They both finish up with some paperwork and begin to shut down their Dell desktops. "Let me get my book bag," Terry states. He grabs his bag and whips it around his back. "Is there a place that you usually go to, Barry?" he curiously asks.

Ben takes his brown computer bag and puts it under his left shoulder, and they walk out the center. "There's a pub right around the corner from here. It's about a 10-minute walk from the office," he states.

"That sounds good to me," Terry replies. Walking out of the building, the āyí shuts off all the lights and sets the alarm. The elevator adds up to the 5th floor and Terry and Barry get on. "How are you feeling?" Barry asks. Terry's mind was in a sprint and wasn't slowing up anytime soon. "It's been a little bit of a struggle. I've been trying to think about work and keep my mind off of it, but it hasn't worked," Terry states. "It's ok to not be distracted from reality. That gives you time to process your most pressing emotions. If you're always distracted and occupied, how can you truly know how you feel?" Barry says.

"I hear you. But we are going to a bar to de-stress and drink," Terry responds.

"This is true, but through this process, you will be able to work through your emotions and understand what you're feeling," Barry offers back. Although Terry would prefer to be by himself when he was going through something, he wanted to seek Barry's advice and guidance on this. They begin to walk towards the bar and the Earth sends cool breezes to help calm Terry's thoughts. "It's not too bad out tonight. It's almost August and I thought it would still be hot out," Terry says.

"This is an unusually cool night, at the end of July. Particularly, that cool breeze that seems to be coming from the shores," Barry replies.

The streets aren't too crowded, and they make it to the bar within a few minutes. Terry's has never been to this pub. It kind of reminds him of a bar that he went to when he was visiting one of his college friends in New York. The lights were dim, there was some jazz playing on the bar stereo and the bartenders were in a black vest and tie. "When you said 'pub' this isn't what first came to my mind," Terry jokingly says.

"What did you think?" Barry asks.

"I'm not sure what I thought. Maybe guys playing pool or watching football, house music playing, and a bartender that looks sad," Terry laughed as he replied.

"On the contrary, that's not all bars in the UK mate," Barry laughs back, as they both sat at the edge of the bar. Terry takes a quick look around and scans the room. One thing his sister always told him was to scan a place before and after he walked in. "Read the room, Terry." This was one of Terry's skills that he felt personally proud of, because his older sister taught it to him. He sees mostly shirts and ties in the bar and some dresses, but nothing too fancy. Automatically, Terry thinks that the drinks shouldn't be too expensive based on what people were wearing in the bar. He took a look at the drink menu, and he was wrong.

"These prices are high. Although, I definitely like the music in this place. It reminds me of a Manhattan-type bar that I went to a long time ago. It's pretty chill and laid back" Terry says.

Barry sees the bartender and begins to say something, as he extends his right hand. "Hi mate, how are ya?" he smiles and says. The young bartender, a young gentleman with bouncy brown hair and slim blue-trimmed glasses, walks up to Barry and gives him a hug.

"How are you Barry?" the bartender says.

"I'm doing well, mate. This is my mate from America, Terry. Terry, this is Bobby." Barry introduces the two gentlemen. They shake hands and quickly introduce themselves.

While Barry is talking to Bobby, Terry takes out his phone and looks at the lock screen. A picture of the flyer for Carla. He looks for any sign of hope from back home, but no luck. Deciding to look at his sister's Instagram, he grabs the menu to continue looking for a drink.

"Hi, Bobby, what drinks would you recommend?" Terry asks.

"Well of course we do have the classic Moscow Mule, and we do our version of the Dark and Stormy," Bobby responds. "Dark and Stormy sound like my life," Terry thinks to himself. He orders the Dark and Stormy and looks at his phone again. As he scrolls through, he notices that he had a missed message from Lena. "Oh my goodness, how did I miss that message?" Terry's face froze like it was stuck in time. He completely missed her message and went a whole day without responding to her.

> **10:10 pm(to Lena)**
> **Terry: Hey I made it home, I was just dealing with something? What are you doing now?**

Terry slightly lifts his face, and he sees a Captain Morgan Rum bottle in the air. Bobby is right there to catch it. He takes another look at his phone to see if Lena responded. "What is she doing?" He thought. Terry can hear something out of the corner of his ear, but he also feels like he just got off a rollercoaster.

"Hey mate, you alright?" Barry asks.

"Not really, man," Terry responds.

"Well, your drink should be up soon. What do you think about Bobby? He's a fine young lad, isn't he?" Barry says.

"Yeah, he seems pretty cool, I guess," Terry says, as Bobby comes back with a Dark and Stormy and a Moscow Mule. "Thanks mate!" Barry exclaims.

Terry begins to put his phone back in his pocket, but he feels it vibrate. He races it out and places his finger on the screen to unlock it. He pulls the notification bar down, only to see it was an email.

"So tell me, mate, what's been rackin' your brain?" Barry says.

"Well, you remember earlier when I told you that my sister was missing? They still haven't found her. They still haven't heard anything from her. It's been on my mind all day." Terry pours his emotions and feelings out to Barry.

"I'm so sorry to hear that, mate. Was she older?" Barry asks.

"Yeah, she was born on December 21, and we always considered her a Christmas baby. To me she was just my big sis who always had my back," Terry says.

"I'm sure they were concerned about you leaving the country. What was your life like before moving abroad?" Barry asks.

Terry grabs his drink, and they clink their glasses together for a 'cheers,' as he begins to spill his heart out.

IX

Growing Up

Terry's life back home was full of love, but it wasn't without its share of troubles. There were some rough times growing up in Portland. The Albina neighborhood of Portland, is where Terry grew up. Terry's father was a mechanic at Daimler Trucks North America and his mother was a stay-at-home mom. He lost his parents while he was still in college. He and Carla have been depending on each other ever since. Ready to drop out of college to go back home, Carla convinced him to stay.

"Do you think mom and dad would want you to quit? You're so close to graduating. You can't quit now, Gravy. You have to finish strong." Carla's words still echoed in his dreams. After the death of his parents, he went home to be with his family and missed a couple of races. When he returned to school, he had a newly crafted tattoo on his right forearm with his parents' name on it. Terry's coach told him that if he needed to have some time, he could take time for himself. He thought about it, and his teammates at the University of Oregon were very supportive. They bought him cards and a new book bag with his parents' initials on them. The emotional support he needed came from his closest bonds. Even though the guys on the team came together as friends, running track together glued them as brothers.

"You must've been pretty fast," Barry states.

"Ehhh, I was ok. Not fast enough to get into the Olympics and represent my country, but that's another story for another bar," Terry explains.

"After the whole thing with my parents, I finished college and then went back to Portland. My sister was living with her friends, and we had decided to stay in Portland. Although, I considered moving to Seattle with my uncle at one point." Terry puts his phone on the bar and looks up. Terry turns his attention back to Barry; he sees this shadow in the corner of the bar. This time, the shadow steps a little closer to Terry, but he still can't get a good look at it. He quickly does a double-take and blinks a couple of times.

"You alright?" Barry asks.

"Yeah, I'm fine. It's just that. It's just that...sometimes I see this shadow out of the corner of my eye. Almost like something is following me. But it only shows up when something bad is going to happen, or I'm thinking too hard. I know it sounds wild, but I'm telling the truth," Terry says, as his voice increases.

"No, mate, I don't think that's wild. Same thing used to happen to me. Except for me, it wasn't a shadow, it was a bird," Barry states.

"A bird? What kind of bird?" Terry asks, as he takes a sip of his Dark and Stormy.

"It was a Nightingale. One would always seem to find me. Whether I would be sitting on a bench, or walking to the grocery store. Or getting ready for a night out, one would always seem to show itself. The subconscious has a way of manifesting itself differently, to tell us something that our conscious brain is missing. That's why the subconscious is there, to help us store information we need when our number one source is preoccupied," Barry says.

"Well, what's the significance behind the hummingbird?" Terry intently asks.

"Well, there are many verdicts out on the Nightingale, but there's one that resonates with me. The Nightingale is said to be the cry of a poor soul that is stuck. Asking for help and guidance, but doesn't know how to quite seek it out. It's also said that the Nightingale represents virtue and purity, but that's too fluffy for me," they both share a light chuckle. "So, tell me about what you did after graduating from school," Barry insists. "Oh right! Well, I stayed around the Portland area and started doing some substitute teaching. It was kind of hard to get a job out of school. I was so focused on track & field and thought I had a good shot at the Olympics. I didn't qualify for my time in the 1 and the 2, so subbing was the best thing for me at the time. I stayed with one of my friends for about a year, and it was a tough time for me." Terry takes a look down and quickly presses the side button of his phone to wake it up. Still no messages from anybody.

"Sounds like some trying times. I think the important part was that you finished school and were able to be back with your family," Barry replies.

"I didn't think that my sis and I could get any closer, but we got closer. She was staying with some of our cousins at the time; she moved out and got her own place in the Alphabet District. Eventually, she got a job working for a health insurance company as a public relations specialist. She was always super smart and talented." Terry explains from his deepest feelings; then, turns his head to the bartender to request another drink.

"You downing those quickly aren't ya mate?" Barry asks.
"I'm a little thirsty tonight, bro. But she ended up helping me to get my first car. She helped co-sign for the loan. She actually put Terry "Gravy" Jones on the loan application," He says.
"Who is gravy and why would she call you this?" Barry asks.
"Oh, it's a long story. It's something that she and the rest of my family have called me since I was a young child. When I was younger, for reasons still unknown to this day, I always wanted gravy on my food. I just loved the taste of it. I would put it on everything: things like pizza, hot dogs, and pancakes were always covered in gravy. Weird right? Well, my parents would let me have it sometimes and I would just eat it. Sometimes I would just drink it straight out of the bowl. One night, before dinner, my mom had finished making her homemade gravy. As my mom went into the kitchen to get the chicken she baked, I snuck into the dining room and started drinking the gravy. For me, it was like Gatorade, and I was fresh out of basketball practice. She came back into the room and just stared at me. Ever since then, my nickname in the family has always been gravy. I know people love gravy, and I just took it to a whole other level," Terry explains.

"So, there are other black people who love gravy just as much as you, right? That's what you're saying," Berry chuckles.

"No, I think I took the cake on that one, and I put gravy on it," they both cheerfully laugh, as the bartender brings over another drink for Terry. At this point, Terry notices that his skin is starting to feel quite hot, like someone is taking a hot iron and rubbing it across his body. He ignores the feeling and continues to enjoy the conversation with Barry. "Now, my whole family calls me 'Gravy,' or 'G.' She helped me get my gravy fix in as well. When my parents got tired of me asking for gravy, they would hide it or just not make it. My sister would sneak out of her room at night, pour the gravy in a cup and bring me the cup. I would drink it before I went to bed like It was warm milk," he describes.

"That's bloody mental, mate!" Barry laughs and takes a long sip of his drink. "That's quite a cool way to get a nickname. In the UK, we do our own take on gravy. I just never met someone with the nickname 'gravy.' But it seems that your sister had a huge influence on your life," Barry implies.

"Of course. She was the whole reason why I went to college and was able to get a scholarship. Even before I started running track, she always thought I was superfast. We would always race the other kids in the neighborhood and I would always win. There was one kid, James, who lived up the street, and for the longest time he was known as, 'the Michael Johnson of the hood.' I knew I could beat him, but we never raced," Terry says.

"Who is Michael Johnson?" Barry inquires.

"Really?" Terry says, as he blinks quickly.

"Michael Johnson was an Olympic athlete, who was once the fastest man in the world. Before Usain Bolt came along, Michael Johnson won gold in the 1996 Olympics. He wore these cool gold-plated shoes on his way to victory," Terry explains.

"They were real gold?" Barry asks, putting his drink on the bar top.

"I think so. And he was like my favorite athlete at the time. I liked him more than Michael Jordan. You know Jordan, right?" Terry gives Barry the side-eye.

"Of course, I know Magic Jordan. He was quite popular in the UK." Barry laughs and looks at Terry.

"Anyhow, James was quick, and I mean really quick. One day, my sister was talking to his sister and bragged that I was faster than James. Carla came and got me out of my room and told me that James wanted to race me. Of course, I told her that she was wild and that there was no way I was beating James. She somehow talked me into it and I went outside and James was waiting for me. We always raced from the stop sign to the next block, which may have been about 120 meters. My sister was the one who counted us down. I'll never forget it. 'On your marks…set…go," James took off and I was trailing behind him, but I heard my sister in the background cheering me on. I started to catch up. Now, James' sister was at the finish line waiting to see who won and I caught up to him, as we both came across the finish line. We all ran up to his sister to see who won, and she hesitated for a moment and finally said that I won." Terry says downing his second Dark and Stormy and his body feels like it's on fire. The shadow suddenly appears in the corner again. He decides to ignore how his body is feeling and the shadow in the corner of the bar. Terry checks his phone and sees a message from Lena.

> **11:08 pm**
> **Lena: I'm out with a friend. Are you ok?**

> **11:09 pm**
> **Terry: What friend?**

"It's interesting how one person can make us feel that we can take on this cold world. It seems that your sister was that person for you. It's very similar to the relationship I had with my sister. But I don't think we are as close as you and your sister," Barry explains.

"Why do you say that?" Terry thought that most siblings were close like him and Carla, but maybe he was a little naive in that sense. "Well, I'm a few years older than my sister, and I was a little bit of a rebel. I did my own thing, went where I wanted to go and did what I wanted to do. I went to school and left and came back. I worked in a theater for a little bit, lived on a boat, went into teaching, and I'm now living in China. She was more straightforward: she went to uni, graduated, met someone, got married, had kids, has a good job, and seems to be quite settled." Barry takes a sip of his beer after talking. "Well, maybe that fits her and not you. That more traditional path isn't for everyone, right?" Terry suggests. "I believe so. Things have changed and people want to travel more and focus more on their careers. There is nothing wrong with either option, but it should be solely up to the individual," Barry blinks a couple of times, and takes another sip of his beer.

"My parents sure thought that her path was perfect and mine was unstable. 'Barry, why can't you be more like your sister? She's settled down and raising a family.' My mom would always say that to me. I never wanted to follow that status quo. She doesn't believe me, but I'm quite happy. I think no matter what choice people make, they have to be happy about it. Whether that is getting married and having kids early on, or waiting and deciding to pursue personal and career goals. Maybe someone doesn't want to get married or have kids at all. There's pros and cons with every decision and people have to be at peace with whatever decision they make," Barry finishes his beer and asks for one more.

Terry excuses himself to the bathroom; he stands up, but his leg almost collapses under him. "You alright, mate?" Barry asks.
"Yeah, I'm ok. I haven't had that much to drink." Terry stumbles through his words, as he feels like there are 100 fire ants on him. He goes into the bathroom and splashes some water on his face and checks his messages. Nothing from his family back home, and nothing from Lena. He realizes that he hasn't really talked to Lena all day and wonders what she's doing. "But she is not your girlfriend. She can do whatever she wants," Terry thinks. He still wants to see what she is up to.

11:15 pm(to Lena)
Terry: What friend are you with?

He feels a little better, but his body still feels like it's on fire. He does want one more drink. Getting back to the bar, he orders one more Dark and Stormy.

"I think after this I may go home," he informs Barry.

"That's fine mate. I think I'm almost finished here myself," Barry agrees

"You know, Barry, one of my biggest fears about coming over here was that something would happen and I'm not there to help or support. It's not like I'm around the corner. So it just makes me nervous and scared," Terry states.

By this time, hives have blanketed Terry's arm, and he has started sweating. "Even if you can't physically be there, you're spiritually there. Your presence is still felt and wherever your sister is, I'm sure that she can feel you guys in her spirit. There's a difference between the soul and spirit. Soul you can educate with books and knowledge, but your spirit is in your intuition. It's that gut feeling that you have when you know something is wrong, and it's that thing you can't teach. Sometimes your soul can get you in trouble, because it can tune out your spirit. Sometimes your soul can become too indoctrinated, and you stop listening to your heart. Trust in your spirit and your inner voice, and I'm sure you will find peace with this situation," Barry says.

Barry's words hit Terry like a heavyweight punch. He's always felt that he and his sister had a deeper connection with each other. "I appreciate that man," Terry says.

"I hope you and Lena workout too." Terry's face is surprised, because he didn't mention Lena all night.

"How did you know?" Terry asks.

"I just knew that somewhere in your mind, you were thinking about Lena," Barry says. They both pay for their tabs and get ready to leave the bar.

"I'm going to walk home, mate. I don't live too far from here," Barry insists.

"That's fine. I'm going to call a DiDi, since I'm a little bit further out," Terry says, as they walk out of the bar and into the grasp of the summer night heat.

"Thanks for taking the time to hang out tonight. I needed it," Terry explains.

"No worries mate. Anytime! Are you sure you're alright?" Barry's concern seems to have grown. "Yeah, I think I'm just hot, you know. This summer heat has gotten to me a little, especially with the drinking. I'm going to go home and get some rest," Terry tells him.

"Sounds good. Well, enjoy your night and I will see you soon," Barry says, as he begins to turn his back.

"Hey Barry, I have one question for you. Whatever happened to the Nightingale you used to see?" Terry shouts, as Barry pauses for a moment and looks up at the crescent moon in the sky. "The Nightingale disappeared once I decided to stop talking and start listening. Have a good night, Terry." Barry says, and starts walking to his apartment.

Terry brings out his phone to call for a DiDi, but he starts feeling even dizzier. He felt as though his head was on a Ferris wheel and he couldn't stop it. His phone falls to the concrete, as his body slowly follows his phone to the hot city ground.

X

Talk to Me

"Where were you all day?" Terry asks Lena.

"I was just hanging out with a friend, but I was trying to get in contact with you. Are you ok?" she asks.

"Yeah, it's just been such a long day and week. Things have just been out of sorts lately." He puts his head in his hands and begins to softly cry. "Hey, hey, I'm here for you, ok. I care about you and I want to be there for you. You're one of the best men I've ever met," Lena smiles as she finishes her statement. "Really? You think that highly of me?" he softly smiles.

Lena puts both of her soft hands on his cheeks and pulls him in closer. He slightly misses her lips and kisses the side of her mouth. He chuckles in his mind, because he doesn't want to spoil the moment. They begin to kiss, and he opens his eyes and looks at her. Her eyes are open as well.

"What are you staring at?" she belts out.

"What are you looking at?" his best rebuttal falls short, as they both start to laugh. Lena stands up and reaches back with her right hand, for him to follow her to his bedroom. She sits down on the right edge of his bed and pulls his hips closer; she helps him take off his shirt and pulls him close. They continue to kiss, and he strokes her short brown hair, as she slightly moans in his left ear, "I want you so bad Terry."

He slides his left hand slowly up her right thigh, and his fingertips start to get wet. They both pull off Lena's pants, as she begins to put her short brown hair in a tight bun. He grabs her by her hips and helps her get on top of him. He reaches for his wallet to look for a condom, and Lena pushes his wallet away.

"I want it badly," she whispers in his left ear. He sits up to kiss her, as his body goes limp. He tries to move his arms and legs, but everything has gone stiff.

"Terry! Terry, are you ok?" Lena shouts. She tries to shake him on his shoulders and wake him up, but he doesn't budge. "Terry! Talk to me! Talk to me!"

"Terry! Terry! Talk to me! Hey, wake up, mate!" Barry shouts at Terry.

Terry slowly starts to open his eyes, and he realizes where he is. "Terry, are you ok? Talk to me!" Barry shouts at him. Terry lifts his head from the couch pillow, confused and very dazed. After a couple of slow blinks and an extended yawn, he says, "Where am I?" Barry power walks into his kitchen and grabs a bottle of water for him.

"You're at my apartment, mate. Are you bloody alright? Bobby ran down the street to get me, because he saw you collapse on the pavement. How are you feeling?" Barry says, handing him the lukewarm bottle of water.

"I don't remember much of anything, man. I just remember coming out of the bar, talking to you, and then everything went blank after that." Terry tries to run his memory, but it's out of gas.

"Did you have that much to drink? I didn't think that you did," Barry states.

"No, I'm ok. Apparently, I'm allergic to alcohol and if I drink too much my body starts to get hives. But when it happened before, I just got some allergy medicine, and I was ok. I'm not sure what happened tonight," Terry says, sitting up on Barry's wool couch.

"Why didn't you tell me, mate? Maybe we could have fancied somewhere else?" he says.

"It's ok. How did you get me up to your apartment? This seems like a journey," Terry asks, uncapping the water and gulping quickly.

"Bobby came and got me, and he helped me carry you to my apartment. It's not that far from the pub, so we didn't walk very far. We got you into the building, onto the elevator, and into my apartment. He went back and I stayed here with you. I heard you breathing, so I figured you were ok and just drunk," Barry says. Terry wipes his face with his left hand and continues to drink the water that Barry brought to him.

"Where's my phone?" Terry asks.

"I didn't see it. It might be at the bar. Let me message Bobby to see if he has it with him. I reckon it can't be very far," Barry explains.

"I appreciate that man. And for literally picking me up off the street. And for bringing me to your apartment. I know I'm not the lightest guy." Terry tries to let his gratitude show.

"No worries mate. I'm glad Bobby was able to see you fall and then able to chase me down." Barry says.

"How are things with you and Lena?" Terry's eyes widened in response to Barry's question. "Come on, mate. I know there is something deeper going on with you two. You both bicker with one another all the time and the flirting is obvious. I'm sure your sister is on your mind, but I'm also sure Lena is in there somewhere," Barry's insight, requires Terry to put his emotional defenses down.

"It's quite a lot, you know? I'm infatuated with her. I didn't really expect to come here to meet someone, especially not someone who is as beautiful and smart as she is. And on top of that, she genuinely seems interested in who I am as a black man. She asks questions, she asks how I feel, she genuinely wants to understand everything about me and why I am the way I am. She...she...she sees me." Terry again pours his heart out to Barry. Although Terry knows he should get going and find his phone, he spends a few more minutes with Barry.

"Love can come from the most unexpected places and people. I had a situation like that with the woman I was engaged to. She was in the UK going to school, but she was from Germany. We met when I was in college. This dislike really came from our parents who remember the 'The Good War' which is a weird name for a war. But it also went back to The Treaty of London from 1839, when Britain agreed to defend Belgium from being invaded. Our parents can place a lot of their prejudices on us. This is what their parents did, and their parents before them. No need to be upset, but you have to be aware of this at some point. Otherwise, you're not thinking with your own mind, but the mind of the past. The mind of your parents, or somebody who lived during a different era. I had to break away from those thought processes and think for myself. Long story short, we made it up until our wedding and then split. But why did you come here? To China?" Barry asks.

"I wanted a new adventure and to meet new people. Most importantly, I wanted to do something for myself. So, what happened to you two? What did she end up doing?" Terry asks.

"She got cold feet at the altar. She bailed on me at the last-minute, mate." Terry can see Barry's eyes begin to tighten up a little.

"I'm so sorry, bro. That's devastating." Terry provides some sympathy to the situation.

"I appreciate that. I tried reaching back out to her, and she said she wasn't ready." Barry starts to choke up a little.

"What did you do? Like, how did you get past that?" Terry asks.

"Honestly, I let go. One of the greatest powers in life is learning how to let things go. Let people go, let things go, and let situations go. You can't control everything that people will do to you, but you can control your reactions to those things. Was I heartbroken? Of course! It took many months of therapy and counseling to be at peace with what happened. I still care about her as a person and I hope she is well. I just had to let it go and do my best to understand." A tear rolls down Barry's left eye as he continues to tell his story. "Letting go is hard. What if the person never comes back?" Terry asks.

"Then you have to accept it. If you stay stuck in the past, you will completely miss your future. Life is giving you opportunities to move forward, but many people want to stay stuck in the past. It took me a long time to understand this. Life is about movement, you see; change is inevitable, and comfortability is a trap." Barry's words are really making Terry sober up now.

"What do you mean, 'comfortability is a trap?' I don't understand," Terry asks in his state of confusion.

"When you hear scientists talk about the environment, you'll never hear them talk about a comfortable environment. You'll always hear them talk about a sustainable environment. This makes more sense," Barry says.

"What's the difference between both of them?" Terry asks.

"Comfortability can be broken quite quickly. It lulls you to sleep and breaks down your defenses, so when something goes wrong, it really goes wrong. Sustainability, on the other hand, is the bend but don't break option. When something goes wrong, the whole system won't go to shit," Barry responds.

"What if things need to be completely broken down to be built back up? What if your comfortability needs to be broken to develop something more sustainable?" Terry asks.

"That's fine, as long as you can come back from that broken place," Barry says, wiping another tear from his left eye.

Terry takes another sip of water and looks at his watch: 12:15 am. "I need to head out, find my phone, and then get home. I do have to work tomorrow." He finishes his water and stands up off of the couch. "Bobby does have your phone, it's back at the bar. He said you can come over now and pick it up." Barry puts his phone down and picks up Terry's water bottle to place it with the rest of the recyclables. "Thanks so much! I gotta be more careful with this alcohol allergy thing. Just got a lot on my mind." Terry begins to walk to the door. "No problem mate. Take care of yourself and if you still feel dizzy, please let me know. You can stay the night here if you need," Barry offers.

"Thanks, I should be ok. I'll send you a message once I get home." Terry opens the door and heads back out to the wonders of the night.

"Where's my sister? I hope she is ok? Where is Lena? Well, maybe she did text me again, but I don't have my phone, so I don't know." He leaves Barry's apartment and gets on the elevator to go down. As the doors are closing, someone sticks their hand through the door to stop them from closing. He lifts his head and sees that it's the woman from his gym, the same woman that he sees on the elevator in his building. She has on the same workout outfit from before.

She looks up at Terry, as they both reach to push the close button for the elevator. As the elevator doors combine, Terry catches a quick glimpse of her. He notices that she has a scar on the right side of her face. It goes from the bottom of her right eye to the middle of her right cheek. He can tell that she has tried to cover it, because of the rosy red blush that she put on. He can still notice it, and he sees that she is staring at the shoe marks on the elevator floor. She has both her arms crossed in front of her chest, and she hasn't blinked since she has been on the elevator. He can tell that something may have just happened, and she may be in some sort of uncomfortable situation. Terry turns from her for a second and then turns back. He notices that there is a single tear coming down her left eye, so he decides to speak to her.

"Nǐ hǎo ma?" Terry's spotty tones try to express his emotions as best as he can. She slowly looks up at him and gives him a little smile. As the elevator detracts to the first floor, he gets a glimpse of a necklace that she has on. It's a gold necklace of the Eye of Horus. This ancient Egyptian symbol has always stood out to him. The elevator reaches its temporary destination and the doors slowly open. When the doors open, the young lady sprints out of the elevator and out of the building.

He steps out of the elevator quickly and shouts, "Wait! Wait! Are you ok?" She runs off into the darkness with only her pink shoes showing her path. Terry has had quite the night, and just wants to get his phone and go home. He begins to walk down the street towards the bar.

He takes another look at his watch: 12:26 am. By this time of night, the streets are calm in the city. Just the taxi cab drivers, the bǎo'ān smoking a cigarette outside his building, some late-night partiers, some food vendors, and the women of the city are out now. He wipes the sweat from his eyebrows, as he can't continue to allow it to drip right onto his cheek.

He is about three minutes away from the bar, when he hears a familiar voice to the right of him.

"That sounds like Lena," he thinks. Terry turns a little bit to his right and sees this young lady with short brown hair, and these ruby red lips. "There's no way that's who I think it is." He was confused at this point, and took a closer look at the two ladies to his right.

"That is Lena!" His whole body is encompassed immediately with goosebumps, and he is at a standstill. He locks eyes with her, as she walks by with another girl.

"They are holding hands!" Terry wants to say something, but he can't. His mouth and face can't move. He is emotionally stuck, and it has made it unbearable for him to want to walk any faster. "Who is that girl? Why is Lena with her?" Thoughts are running through his mind, but he knows that he still needs to get his phone from the bar.

He gathers up enough courage to continue walking, but he takes another look around him. All the stores and restaurants are closed, and all the workers have gone home for the evening. While Terry is still wandering the streets, trying to figure things out. He approaches the bar and sees Bobby waiting for him.

"Hey, you alright?" Bobby asks.

"Yeah, I'm ok. Thanks for asking, bro. I wasn't drunk or anything, I'm just allergic to alcohol. Tonight I decided to ignore all of that rationale for some reason," Terry responds.

"Dude, if you have an allergy, why do you drink?" Bobby asks.

"I'm ok! Thank you for getting help," Terry responds.

"I saw you come out of the bar and collapse. Me and another bartender ran out here to check on you. I remember you were with Barry, so I ran to him and got him to come back and help. We checked to make sure you were still breathing, then we carried you to his apartment. We both thought you just had too much to drink and needed to rest." Terry just wants his phone at this point, because he is still thinking about Lena and the girl he saw her with. "Well, I definitely appreciate that. But could I just grab my phone?" Terry's impatience has started to grow. "Yea, let me just go inside and grab it." Bobby goes back inside to get the phone, as Terry follows his fast-paced footsteps. Terry takes a couple of steps inside the bar. He does a quick look around the bar, and he hardly remembers leaving.

"Here is your phone. Take care of yourself. If you need anything, you can let me know. What's your WeChat?" They both exchange information and Terry leaves the bar.

12:59 am
Terry: Who were you with?

After he messages Lena, he calls for a DiDi so that he can get home. "I still have to work tomorrow and I need to get some sleep," he thinks. As he awaits Lena's response, the DiDi app says his ride is about three minutes away. He walks back into the bar and asks Bobby for a small cup of water. "Hey Bobby, could I get some water before my Didi comes?" Bobby agrees and goes behind the bar stand. He pours Terry some warm water in a small clear plastic cup.

"Here you go." Terry takes the cup from Bobby's hand, "xièxiè nǐ," Terry responds. As he finishes his cup of water, he hears his phone *ding*.

1:01 am
Lena: Why?

This message makes Terry a little angry.

1:02 am
Terry: What do you...

Just as Terry is about to finish his angry text, his DiDi shows up. "I think your taxi has arrived," says Bobby.

"Thanks again Bobby," Terry puts his plastic cup on the table and then gets into the White Geely GE 11 and they take off. He grabs the seat belt with his left hand and picks up his phone with his right hand.

> **1:03 am (To Lena)**
> Terry: What do you mean, 'why?'
> I saw you walking with that girl?
> Who was she?

Terry rubs his temple with his left hand and sighs briefly. "What a day?" He checks his phone to see if there are any updates on his sister. "Nothing." He reaches back out to his cousins.

> **1:08 am (To Naomi)**
> Terry: Hey cuzzo, any word about C?

The trip will take a couple of minutes; Terry lays his head slightly back in his seat. The sizzling summer air beats up on Terry's face in the back seat. He hears his phone *ding*, and he temporarily drops it on the floor.

> **1:09 am**
> Lena: I haven't heard from you all day. And are you my boyfriend?

He puts the phone down for a second, as he has learned it's better to think before sending an angry text. He doesn't know what to say, because he is feeling embarrassed. The feeling of admiration is also present in his soul.

1:10 am
Naomi: We just went through her apartment. And her wallet was gone. So the police are still investigating.

1:10 am
Terry: Ok cuzzo. Just keep me updated, please.

1:10 am
Naomi: I will. I love you!

1:11 am
Terry: I love you too!

The driver pulls up to Terry's neighborhood: he opens the door, re-enters the world. He immediately begins to start sweating again, as he walks up the stairs to his building. Before he walks into the building, he takes a look at the sky and sees the moon. It's a crescent moon tonight. The light from the crescent moon guides his pathway into his building through the revolving glass door. Terry gets onto the elevator and begins to ascend up the building.

1:13 am
Terry: No, I'm not your boyfriend. I was just asking a question.

He gets to the 27th floor and walks down the dimly lit hallway to his apartment. Fumbling with his keys, he drops them on the floor by his apartment door. He scratches the door handle trying to put the key in correctly. The door unlocks loudly, and he gently walks into his apartment. "It's so hot in here. And I left the window open," he says to himself. Walking over to close the door, he stubs his left big toe on the edge of his bed. Curling in pain, he sits on the bed for a moment and hears his phone *ding*.

> 1:15 am
> Lena: Ok, so if you're not my boyfriend, why do you want to know?

> 1:16 am
> Terry: No reason, you can do whatever you want Lena. I don't care.

Terry heads into the bathroom to wash his face and brush his teeth. He quickly checks his schedule for the next day and notices that he has to be at work by 11 am. "Still got some time to sleep in," he thinks.

> 1:17 am
> Lena: Ok then! I didn't hear from you all day and I went out with a friend.

He gets some water from the cooler in his room, and sits on his beige loveseat sofa for a moment.

> 1:18 am
> Terry: I saw you kiss her on the cheek. And I've been dealing with family stuff all day.

1:19 am
Lena: So what if I kissed her on the cheek? And how come you couldn't respond to me all day? Even if you were dealing with family stuff, you could let me know you are ok.

1:19 am
Terry: Well I also had to work you know. And I went out with Barry for a quick drink.

Terry decided to go lay down, as his room went from an oven to a refrigerator. He gets under his royal blue sheets and grabs his phone charger. After plugging in his phone, he goes back to his chess match with Lena.

1:21 am
Terry: And I didn't know you were dating someone.

1:21 am
Lena: So you could go out with Barry, but you couldn't message me back? And you know you have an allergy to alcohol. Why would you go out drinking?

1:22 am
Terry: I had like 2 drinks and I just needed to talk to Barry. I didn't know that was a problem. And I did text you back earlier.

1:23 am
Lena: Look I have a friend over,
so I will talk to you another time.

1:24 am
Terry: Instead of solving this, you
are going to blow me off and go
hang out with your new friend.
Whatever Lena. I hope you have
a good night!

1:25 am
Lena: Thanks!

He knew that when he received the one-word replies, that she wasn't interested in him at the moment. Terry puts the phone down next to his pillow and slowly drifts off to a night's slumber.

XI

I Like You

It's about three weeks away from Halloween, and the center is planning a party for the students and staff. The two people in charge of this party are Lena and Terry. Over the past couple of months, they haven't really been talking to each other. Terry still hasn't heard much of anything about his sister. Lena has a girlfriend and Terry has been living the single life. Not much luck for him, but he's tried dating other girls; it just hasn't been working out for him. He's tried Tinder, Bumble, Badoo and everything in between. He's even tried Tantan, which is a specifically Chinese dating app. And there hasn't been much luck on that app either. Well, maybe some success, but Terry speaks very little Chinese. No luck there! It's been quite a trying couple of months for him. He's been checking up on his family to see if there is any word about his sister, and trying to get Lena off his mind. Both operations have been unsuccessful.

At work, he and Lena keep it cordial. Terry has seen Lena's girlfriend because sometimes she meets Lena outside the office. One time her girlfriend came into the office and Lena introduced her to everyone. Of course, he was fuming, but he tried his best not to show it.

"That is why you don't date people that you work with." Terry can hear Carla telling him this like it was yesterday. This was a conversation she had with him, when he was dating one of his coworkers. She was already working for her public relations firm, and he had just started substituting at his old high school in Portland.

His former high school track & field coach got in contact with him and asked him if he would be interested in doing some substitute teaching. Terry didn't study education in college, he was an engineering major. His dream was to work for NASA one day, and help people explore some of the most mysterious places of the world. It was tough for him to get a job out of college, as he came out of school and ran smack into a national recession. Jobs were at a standstill, and he had to do something. Parents gone, and living with friends and family, Terry decided to give substitute teaching a try. He tried it and fell in love with teaching and coaching. Terry got a chance to be an assistant coach for the basketball, and the track and field teams. While he was working at his old high school, he met Jessica. She was a 10th grade Math teacher, who just graduated from Oregon State University. His rival school, but this was a talking point for him.

He saw Jessica the first week he started working at Jefferson High School. He saw Jessica walking down the hallway, and they both gave each other a quick smile and said, "hello." They wouldn't properly introduce themselves until a basketball prep rally in November. He was taken aback by her beautiful brown skin, long black hair, billion dollar smile, and her black and red glasses. He always thought girls with glasses were the cutest. They exchanged numbers and slowly started talking to each other. The occasional, "Hey, how are you?" "How's your day going?" "Can I buy you some coffee?" The typical early-stage messages, that are sent between assuming couples trying to get to know each other. About one month after they started talking to each other, Terry told Carla about the possible special woman in his life.

"What's her name?" Carla asks.

"Beauty is what her name really should be. But I think her parents liked the name, Jessica," he smiles, as he sits down for dinner with Carla. They went to their favorite spot, The Blue Room Bar, and just got some food and a quick drink. This was Terry and his dad's favorite place to go on a Saturday afternoon.

"How long have you two been talking?" Carla raises her right eyebrow a little bit.

"We've just been talking for a little over a month. Is that ok with you, Dwayne "The Rock" Johnson!" Terry jokingly says back.

"All I'm saying is be careful," she responds.

"Be careful of what? We haven't even been on a real date yet. It's just been a lot of messages back and forth," he refutes.

"It could be a bad idea to date someone that you work with. There's always the potential that things could go wrong," she says, taking a sip of her water.

"That's very true, but there is always the chance that things could go well. And you end up with your future partner. Gotta stop thinking so negatively, C!" Terry's optimism shines through his grin. Her face squeezes up like she just tasted a lemon for the first time.

"Workplace romances are dangerous. They could be catastrophic. I had a coworker who started dating someone in another department. The guy worked in finance and the girl worked with me. They thought they were in love and were ready to get married, and at the last minute they broke off the wedding. Needless to say, they still worked together after their breakup, but it was very awkward in the office after. Everybody knew that they were together and had an ugly breakup. Now, even when we all hang out after work, there are like little cliques of people who agree with him and people who agree with her. It's just a mess." Carla's tone increases slightly.

Terry scratches his head as he tries to process what Carla has just told him. But he was ready for her argument.

"I hear you and understand you C, but..." she stops him mid-sentence.

"There's always a 'but' with you." she says, taking a sip of her vodka and cranberry.

"Just listen," he calmly replies. "It makes sense that dating in the workplace is a risk, right? Of course, if it doesn't work out, then you have to deal with that. Statistically speaking, if you meet someone at work, you are more likely to stay together and get married. I mean, think about the ways that people can meet once they get out of school: online, through friends, they are already friends, or they work together. Of those, people who meet at work are more likely to go the distance than people who meet in other ways. I think if you set boundaries about how you will act at work, and you don't let your relationship get in the way of your work, I think it's ok. Two mature adults could meet at work and even if it doesn't work, they could still do their jobs and not be super awkward," Terry inhales his breath, as he finishes his thoughts.

Carla looks at him, smiles, and says,"You must really like this Jessica girl? How much research did you do on all that before you said it?" They both chuckle, as he takes a sip of his Heineken.

"I did quite a bit of research, because I knew you would say something like that. So, I had to prepare for my debate and make sure I had my points correct," he states.

"Look, I'm sure she is a nice girl. I'm just saying be careful and aware of your actions. Don't allow that relationship to compromise your future." Carla was always the prototypical bigger protective sister, especially when it came to Terry's relationships.

Terry and Jessica dated for about a year, but the relationship went sour. Everything Carla said came true, and Terry was devastated. That conversation played over and over in his head like his favorite song lyric. Fortunately for Terry and Jessica, they were understanding and were still able to get along at work.

This situation was different with Lena. Unexpectedly, Terry fell for her, and he fell hard. Although they haven't been speaking much lately, he still thinks about her every day. "What's she doing? Who's she with? Is she ok? How's the coffee shop? Did she go to the gym today?" These thoughts swarm through his mind on many crescent moon nights.

During one Sunday at work, he sees an email from Danielle:

Hi Terry,

I hope you are well and enjoying fall in Tianjin! We will be hosting a Halloween Party for our students on Saturday, October 29. You and Lena will be the hosts for the party and will be in charge of coordinating the activities. Be sure to meet with Lena this week and begin planning the activities and structure of the event. Lena already has some ideas that you two can discuss. Let me know if you need anything, and we can talk about the budget later this week.

Happy Halloween,

Danielle Wu.

Terry wasn't asked to do this event, he was more so volun-told to host this event. He was ok with it because he enjoyed hosting events for the students, but he wasn't looking forward to hosting with Lena again. Terry also wasn't a big costume guy. He enjoyed scary movies and Halloween, but didn't spend money on costumes. For this event, he would have to spend some money on a costume. He leaves the office and goes to look for Lena. When he gets into the lobby area, he remembers that she is off. He goes back into the office to send her an email.

Hi Lena,

I hope you are well. I see that we will be hosting the Halloween party and will have to organize activities for our students. Will you be able to meet Monday at 2 pm?

Regards,

Terry Jones

Whenever he just puts 'Regards' at the end of his emails, he is being very passive-aggressive. It took everything out of him just to type, "I hope you are well." He gets done teaching for the day and goes home for the evening. The weather has started to change in the city. It's becoming the cool and temperamental weather that many people love. Leaves are turning colors, the cool autumn breeze is comfortable and refreshing, it's officially jacket weather for Terry. For him, he can wear his favorite blue and black Under Armour track jacket and feel comfortable.

He wants to text Lena just to see how she's been, but he's hesitant.

> **7:04 pm (to Lena)**
> **Terry: Hey there! How have you been?**

He types the message into his phone, but he doesn't press the send button. He puts the phone down on the table in his living room and stares at it as if it's going to start dancing. It's been about a month since he and Lena last talked. Being hesitant to message her, his right thumb slightly shakes as he hits the send button and waits for a response from Lena. He puts his phone down, as he hears a knock on his door. Looking through the peephole, he sees that it's Matt. He unlocks his door and greets Matt with a handshake.

"What's up, bro?" Terry says to Matt.

"Nothing much man. Wanted to see what you were up to. Me and a couple of friends are going for a couple drinks and some food if you want to join." Terry doesn't feel like going out tonight.

"I appreciate that bro, but I just ate and I think I'm just gonna chill tonight," he responds. Matt gives him a little bit of a side-eye.

"You sure bro? This place has some pretty good food and drinks. It's a nice Korean BBQ place." Matt continues to try to convince Terry to join.

"Yeah, I'm good. I appreciate the invite though. Maybe the next time you guys go, I'll join," he says, as he hears his phone *ding*.

7:08 pm
Lena: I'm ok.

"No problem. We might get together next weekend. If you're free, you're more than welcome to join us. Do you work on the weekends?" Matt asks.

"Yea, I'm usually working Saturdays and Sundays. I'm done around 6 or 6:30 though," Terry responds, as he continues to look back at his phone.

"Well, I hope you enjoy your night. We'll catch up soon." Matt begins to walk off as Terry responds.

"For sure bro. Enjoy your night." He closes the door and rushes over to his phone. In his fast travels, he hits his left foot on the edge of his living room table.

"Ahhh shit!" he shouts, as instant pain introduces itself to his left foot.

He reaches for his phone and sees the message from her. "Another short and to the point answer," he thinks. Pondering his answer for a minute, he gets up and gets a drink of water. "Responding to a text message shouldn't be this hard." He sits back on the couch, and decides to send a message back.

7:14 pm
Terry: That's good. Are we working on the Halloween party together?

"On the bright side, she did respond quickly. If she really didn't care she wouldn't respond at all. It's short, but she did respond." Terry tries to rationalize the situation in his mind. He lays down on his couch and watches some basketball highlights. "This team from Guangdong is pretty good," he looks at the highlights, and he hears his phone *ding* again.

7:16 pm
Lena: Yes.

7:17 pm
Terry: Ok, sounds good. I sent you an email but would you want to meet tomorrow in the afternoon sometime?

7:18 pm
Lena: That's fine. What time will you be free?

"Ok, there's more than one word in that message. I think we're getting somewhere. Even though it's all about work," he thinks out loud.

> **7:19 pm**
> Terry: I have two classes early in the afternoon. I'll be free @ 2. Is that cool with you?

> **7:20 pm**
> Lena: I have a meeting at 2. Can we do 2:30?

> **7:21 pm**
> Terry: That's good. I'll see you tomorrow.

Terry is ecstatic that she has responded, even if it was just for work stuff. He wants to continue the conversation and see how she's been. "She has to be thinking about me as well, right? Maybe she still cares," he thought.

> **7:23 pm**
> Terry: Is everything else ok?

> **7:24 pm**
> Lena: Yes.

> **7:25 pm**
> Terry: When can we hang out again?

He knows that she is in a relationship, or that's the way it seems. Deep down in his thoughts, he knew that it was none of his business. The feelings he had for her could not be erased that easily. Again, Carla's words of wisdom pop into his head in an instant. "Don't let that relationship compromise your future." He could hear her loud and clear and even see her shaking her head when she said it. "Is it such a bad thing to compromise for a relationship? Life is about compromising and coming to an agreement. If there are going to be two people involved in a relationship, there has to be some sort of middle ground," he thinks.

> **7:29 pm**
> Lena: I don't know if that would be a good idea.

> **7:30 pm**
> Terry: Why is that?

"This must be more serious than I thought. She must be in love with this girl. And I can't blame the girl that she is with. Lena is beautiful, and I'm sure women and men want her," Terry continues with these thoughts in his mind.

> **7:31 pm**
> Lena: I'm kinda in a relationship right now.

His heart sinks to his knees. Every negative thought he had about the situation was true, and he doesn't want it to be. He knew the truth, but he didn't want to accept it and deal with it. The mind can be a powerful indicator of the future.

7:32 pm
Terry: What do you mean kinda?
Is she your girlfriend or not?

7:33 pm
Lena: I mean like we are dating
and trying to work on something.

To him, it sounded like she didn't quite know what she
wanted to do. She was seven years younger than him. Terry,
32-years-young and Lena, 26-years-young.

7:34 pm
Terry: Oh. I didn't know that you
were talking to her. It seemed
like it happened pretty quick. I
mean, we were just hanging out
a couple of months ago.

7:36 pm
Lena: Yeah. I met her around the
same time I met you, but we've
been talking more lately.

7:38 pm
Terry: Oh I see. You could've told
me that. Just so I don't step on
anybody's shoes.

7:39 pm
Lena: And you could've told me
about what was going on with
your family back home.

Terry realizes that she has made a good point. The communication between the both of them appears to be off, and he knows it.

> 7:41 pm
> Terry: That's true. Could you agree that our communication has been off at times?

> 7:42 pm
> Lena: I can agree with that. I apologize.

> 7:43 pm
> Terry: I accept your apology and I apologize as well. If we need time to ourselves let's just tell each other.

> 7:44 pm
> Lena: That sounds good. ☺

> 7:45 pm
> Terry: Could we still message though?

> 7:46 pm
> Lena: That's fine. I think Riley misses you. ☺

> 7:47 pm
> Terry: I think we bonded that day..haha. So, I'm sure she does.

7:49 pm
Lena: I can agree with that. But I
do have to go. We can talk later.

7:50 pm
Terry: I hope you have a good
night.

7:51 pm
Lena: You too!

Terry lies on the couch for another hour watching basketball highlights. His phone slowly falls out of his left hand, as his body and mind retire for the evening.

Through his slumber, he hears his phone *ding*. He jumps out of his sleep and frantically looks for his phone. Inside the creases of the couch, behind the couch cushions, and he looks down and stops. "It's on the floor." He reaches down for it, as he wipes his eyes with his right hand. "I slept forever, is what it feels like. I must've been tired." He was tired, but more emotionally drained than tired. He sees that it's a text from his family back in Portland.

6:44 am
Jared: Hey cuzzo, the authorities
found Carla's car and purse out
by The Columbia River crossing.
They still haven't found her body
though.

He is struck by the information, but wonders why his cousin said, "They haven't found her body." He wipes his eyes again and looks at the message. "Why would there be a body to find?" Terry thinks out loud.

> **6:49 am**
> Terry: What else did they find in the car?

> **6:50 am**
> Jared: Just her purse I think. They are still looking at the car for any more evidence. How are things going with you?

He thought that Jared was acting a little strange, but Jared was known for acting strange sometimes. This was the same cousin he wouldn't hear from for months, and he would just randomly pop up. One day he's in college, the next day he's not and working on trading Bitcoin. The next minute he wants to open up his own car wash, and an hour later he wants to be an attorney. Terry would always support him in whatever strange and quirky ideas Jared had.

> **6:55 am**
> Terry: Ok man. Well, just let me know if I can do anything. I know I'm on the other side of the world, but I can do something. I'm ok bro, I don't have to be at work until 11, so I'm going to chill for a little bit.

> **6:57 am**
> Jared: I will bro! I love you!

6:58 am
Terry: I love you too!

Barefoot, Terry walks into his bathroom. The floor instantly freezes his feet as he continues to the toilet. "It's going to get cold soon. I need to get a full winter jacket." He turns the light on in the bathroom, which impairs him momentarily. After his eyes adjust to the light, he pours some water on his face. "They found her car by the Columbia River." There have been many people who have disappeared in the Oregon wilderness and never came back. Terry's fears grew larger, because he hopes his sister hasn't become one of these cases. She is missing, but it hasn't been confirmed that she has fully disappeared. He is trying to stay positive about the whole situation. Between the circumstances with his sister, and trying to figure out his standing with Lena, he has found it impossible to be fully present in his life.

Oftentimes, he would zone out at work, he would have trouble sleeping, he wouldn't eat for days, and wouldn't go out of his apartment. He leaves the bathroom and gets into his bed, grabbing his back. "This couch is always hurting my back," he says. He resets the alarm on his phone from 9 am to 10 am. "That should be enough time to get a little more sleep."

Before he plugs up his phone to the charger, he can't get the conversation with Jared out of his mind. He decides to text Naomi to see if she knows or has heard anything.

7:10 am (to Naomi)
Terry: Hey cuz, I heard they found C's car. Did they find anything else?

144

He puts his phone down on the right side of his pillow and instantly falls back to sleep.

Ding! Ding! Ding! Ding! His alarm wakes him up at 10 am. He stretches out and takes in a deep yawn. Taking a look outside, he sees the sun trying to peek through the autumn clouds. He reaches over to his phone and sees that he has a couple of messages.

> **8:30 am**
> Naomi: Hey gravy, they found her Apple necklace. You remember the one that your parents gave her?

"I've forgotten all about that necklace," he thought to himself. Terry and Carla both received the necklace from their parents when they were in junior high school. He put his necklace away after his parents passed away. To their parents, the apple represented knowledge and learning. Their parents always wanted Terry and Carla to seek knowledge and truth for themselves.

> **8:32 am**
> Naomi: Still nothing on where she is, but we have her car, purse, and the necklace. I still think this slime ball had something to do with it. He went a little MIA for a moment but now he's back and helping. How are things over in Tianjin?

10:06 am

Terry: I remember those necklaces. I put mine up a while ago. I couldn't bear to look at it after the accident. But I knew C wore her necklace faithfully. I'm doing ok, about to get up, eat, and get ready for work. I really feel bad and guilty, you know?

He left his apple necklace with his Uncle Jeremy in Seattle. He visited his Uncle before he moved to China, and he left some stuff with him. Terry also left his silver necklace with a red apple on it; he left a class ring that his dad brought him. The gold University of Oregon class ring had his initials on it: TJ. It also had a green track shoe on it with yellow wings. Although these were special to Terry, and he cherished them, he couldn't bring them with him to China. Every time he looked at them, they would always bring him back old painful memories.

10:08 am

Naomi: Why do you feel bad?

10:09 am

Terry: I just feel like I should be with you guys out in the sticks looking for C. I just don't feel right being out here with all that's going on back home.

10:11 am

Naomi: Don't feel guilty, Gravy. We love you and we understand that you are doing what you need to do. We got you, you just continue to handle your business and we'll do our best until you get back to Stumptown. We love you!

10:12 am
Terry: I love you guys too! I'm about to get breakfast. Maybe we can do a call this weekend if you're free.

10:14 am
Naomi: Let's do it. Just let me know.

10:15 am
Terry: I will.

He heads into his kitchen and begins to make some oatmeal and cut up some apples and strawberries. Opening up the blinds, he sees the sun break through the clouds and illuminate the sky. Leaving from his window, he heads to his closet to pick out his dress shirt and pants for the day. "I think I'll wear my salmon-colored shirt with some gray pants. I'll also wear these brown shoes with it." This is one of Terry's favorite shirts that he used to always wear when he was home.

He eats his breakfast, and gets dressed for work. He calls for a Didi, as he doesn't feel like taking the train today. The DiDi comes within 5 minutes, and he leaves his apartment. Terry is waiting for the elevator, and he sees Matt getting off the elevator.

"Hey bro! Off to work?" Matt says, stepping off the elevator with grocery bags attached to his wrists.

"Yeah, I'm about to head in. You're off today, bro?" Terry asks.

"Yup, I'm off the whole week. If you're not doing anything on your days off, we can go for lunch if you want," Matt says, walking towards his apartment.

"For sure bro maybe we can go for a drink," Terry says, as he was holding the door open with his right hand.

"Yeah, I'm down for that. I'll message you later. Have a good day at work," Matt encourages him.

"Thanks man! I'll catch up with you later," Terry says.

Terry gets to the lobby of his building and receives a message from the Didi driver that he is outside. The weather is starting to turn, as it has a hint of Siberian winds on its way back for the season. A breeze rushes through the opening of his jacket, as a chill shoots down his body like he just stepped out of a steamy shower into a wintry bedroom. He decides it would be a good idea to zip up his jacket, then he gets into his ride for the afternoon.

He arrives at work around 11:15 am, and stops in Starbucks to grab a quick coffee.

"Nǐ hǎo ma?" the barista says.

"Wǒ hěn hǎo," Terry responds, as he attempts using his limited Mandarin skills.

"Vanilla latte today, right?" the barista asks.

"Yes! Xièxiè nǐ," he responds.

"One moment," the barista states, grabbing a latte cup for Terry.

Terry checks his phone to make sure he has enough time to print out the handouts he will need for class. "11:17. I still have time to print out what I need," he thinks to himself. Just after he puts his phone into the back of his gray slacks he feels it vibrate; he pulls it back out.

11:18 am
Lena: Are you at the center?

He is shocked that she texted him first. It's been a long time since she texted him first, but he knows that it's probably for work. "At least she is acknowledging me," he thought.

11:19 am
Terry: Not yet, I'm at Starbucks and then I'll be there.

"Vanilla latte sir! Here you go." The barista passes him a hot vanilla latte.

"Xièxiè nǐ. Zàijiàn." He picks up his latte with his right hand, and walks out of the Starbucks towards the elevator.

11:20 am
Lena: Ok. I'm here. It's so cold in the office.

11:20 am
Terry: You're always cold. Everywhere you go.😎

11:21 am

Lena: Whatever! Hey could you bring me a venti caramel macchiato.

11:22 am

Terry: Sure, I got you since you took care of me that one night. I'll see you soon.

11:22 am

Lena: 🕯️

This little exchange between them made his day just slightly brighter. He scans the I.D. code on his phone to get into the elevator lobby. Terry gets onto the elevator with the rest of the financial and sales professionals, as he proceeds to the fifth floor. *Ding*, the elevator doors open up, and he gets off the elevator with someone he's never seen before.

Terry takes a quick glimpse at her; notices that she looks a little bit like the women he's seen on the elevators every so often. He sees that she is wearing the Eye of Horus necklace, just like the girl from the elevator. They both walk into the office and the woman sits down in the waiting area. Terry walks into the center and instantly feels a chill, as his deep breath feels like he has ice cubes in his nose.

"Hi Terry," Danni says to him, as she flips through some paperwork. "This is weird." Terry says to himself, because Danni is never at the front desk.

"Hi Danni. I didn't know you had a new desk?" He jokes with her.

"Not at all," she chuckles.

"I'm just covering for Lena, until she comes back from the restroom. Are you two meeting today?" She asks.

"Oh, I see. Yeah, we are going to meet after my first two classes. I have some ideas for a couple of games and activities that the students might like," he says, putting the coffees on the front counter.

"Sounds good. Let me know if you need anything from me," she says, as she continues to look down at her paperwork.

"Will do," he responds.

Terry appreciated the relationship that he had with his manager. She allowed him to be himself at work and fostered his creativity and imagination. It's part of the reason why he enjoyed teaching his ESL adult students. He goes into the office and sees Barry and Alex.

"Hey guys. How are you two doing? Terry asks.

"Doing alright, mate," they both responded simultaneously.

"How are you, Terry?" Alex asks.

"I'm ok. Just had to stop by Starbucks and grab some coffee," Terry responds.

"Oh, nice mate! You should invest in a coffee maker or a French press," Barry suggests, as he sat back in his roller chair," Danni said, as she swiftly walked into the room.

Terry wraps his book bag around his chair and powers on his computer.

"I had a French press before I left home, and it was literally one of my best investments," Terry says.

"It saves you some money, and it's nothing like a fresh cup of French pressed coffee in the morning," Barry adds.

"That's very true. I put it up in my family's storage bin before I left," Terry states.

"My parents bought me one right after I graduated from uni a couple of years ago. It's good you didn't give it away. That way you will still have it when you get home. Well, as long as nobody goes into storage to get it," Alex slightly chuckles.

"Nobody will go in there. It's just storage that I share with my sister and two cousins," Terry's eyes get lower, and he becomes still.

"Carla, where are you?" he thinks to himself.

"You ok, Terry?" Alex asks.

It takes Terry a moment to come back from space. "Yeah, I'm ok. Umm...I'm just trying to think about what I need to print out for class," he mumbles out.

"Well, long story short, French presses are a worldwide treasure!" Alex exclaims.

Just as Terry's papers are printing out, Lena walks into the office. "Hey there!" She looks at him and gives him a half-smile.

"Hey there. Are we still good for this afternoon?" he responds.

"Yup, just come get me. I'll be at the front," she says, rushing out of the office with papers in her hand. "Sounds good to me," he says, rushing out of the door as well.

They both leave the office, with Terry one step behind Lena. He takes a right to go towards his classroom, and she makes a left to go towards the front desk area.

As he walks to class, he sees the women who got off the elevator walking by with the sales manager. "She must be a new sales rep," he thought.

He finishes his two classes and walks back into the office and sees Kelly, another consultant, sitting at her desk.

"Hey Kelly, have you seen Lena?" he asks.

"Hi Terry. She should be at the front desk. You two planning the Halloween party? she responds.

"Yes we are. We're going to meet about it now and decide on some activities," he replies.

"I'm so excited! I get to dress up and be my favorite character!" she says, with a sparkle in her eye.

"And what character would that be?" he asks.

"The werewolf." Kelly acts out being a werewolf for a moment; she moves swiftly over to Terry with her hands shaped as claws.

"The werewolf will be out all night and shape-shifts when there's a full moon. That's when its natural instincts kick in. The werewolf can be a protector or guardian, but it's also a werewolf so don't mess with it," she says in a very low-pitch type voice.

"Well, I think that you will have a chance to be your best werewolf at our Halloween party," He says, moving around her claw-shaped hands.

"I better be!" She responds, as she jumps at him with her claws.

He walks out of the office with a laugh on his face, and sees Lena with her head down behind the front desk.

"Are you ready to meet?" he prompts.

"Yes, sure. Where shall we go?" she said, as she stood up.

"I think there is a classroom open in the back of the office," he suggests.

They gather their things for their meeting: a pen, a brown notebook, a laptop and their imaginations are what they need to plan this party.

"I think this one is free," he says, as they both walk into an empty Classroom 8.

"So, I've been thinking about some events we could do," she says, as she opens up her brown notebook.

"What is that? I have some ideas as well," he states.

"Well, I was thinking we could split them up into groups when they get here and have them compete against other groups. We can do a couple of games and maybe include a Halloween trivia. We can also give an award for the best Halloween costume," she says, as she reads off of her notes.

"You read my mind. I was thinking that I could lead the trivia, and we can have them do some sort of arts and craft. Maybe a mask painting contest? They could spend 10 or 15 minutes at each station. I think our center is big enough for it." He agrees to her thoughts and ideas.

"Great! I will put together a rough rundown of the events. We can start around 4:30 and make sure that everybody is in the lobby. Then, we can start with introductions and get them into their teams," she says.

"How will we get them into their teams?" he asks.

"Hmm...maybe we could give them bracelets when they come in. Then, halfway through the intro, we can have them stand and find their groups," she proposes.

"That sounds like a really good idea. Where can we get them from?" he responds.

"We can just order some from Taobao," she says.

"I like the way that sounds. When you finish the rundown, let me know and we can get together later this week and make sure we are still on the same page," he states.

"That's fine with me." Lena pauses for a minute and looks down at the floor. Terry notices her blonde and black hair swivel from left to right. She takes a deep breath and slowly starts to lift her head.

"Hey, are you ok, Lena?" Terry reaches his left hand out for her right hand.

"I'm ok I guess," she said, as she reached her right hand out for Terry's.

"What's wrong? You look stressed." He knew that something was going on with Lena. This is the most that they have talked to each other since the end of summer. He was happy that she was paying attention to him again, but she didn't seem like the same person.

"Yea I'm ok. Just tired, I guess. What's up with you? I haven't really seen you around," she probes.

"Me? Oh, just out doing my own thing. Hanging out and relaxing," he nonchalantly responds.

"Dating?" she shortly asks.

"Yes, a couple," Terry lies right through his teeth. He had only been on one date since Lena, and it was a disaster. He really didn't want to go out on other dates and meet other women, because he just wanted to be with her.

"Why haven't you talked to me lately? You even ignore me at work?" Her eyes widened a little bit, as she finished her sentences.

"I thought you were dating the girl and I didn't want to impose. You seemed super distant and I just wanted to give you your space," he says.

"Did I ask for space?" she swiftly responds.

He was slightly taken aback by her sharp words, but he didn't take it personally. He knew something was up with her.

"No, you didn't ask for space, but you also didn't respond. I didn't want to keep messaging you," he says.

"Oh," she says back, pulling her right hand away.

They sit there for a moment in silence; he mumbles something under his breath. "What did you say?" she asks.

"I said, what's wrong with you?" his voice goes up.

"What do you mean?" she slightly raises her eyebrows.

"You know, when I first got here I wasn't expecting to meet anybody that would really understand me. I was going through a lot, and of course, I was nervous about moving to China. I was overweight and struggling mentally to keep myself together. Then, we started working together and instantly clicked. We hang out and get to know each other. You saw me throw up in the bushes and everything. You know my sister is still missing and things have been tough," Terry sits back in his chair and takes a deep breath.

"So what are you saying, Terry?" she says, folding her arms.

"I like you! Ok, I like you! A lot! Like a lot a lot," his voice decreases, as he sees Danni walking by the classroom.

"Look, I didn't mean to say that so abruptly. I just like you. And it's been hard to keep my feelings inside. I hope you can understand. Just be sure to send me the rundown once you're finished." Terry gets up, opens the door, and walks down the hallway back to the office.

XII

She's Mine!

"Police officer, doctor, werewolf, firefighter, sexy nurse. I don't want any of these. I just want something simple that I can wear to this thing," Terry thinks to himself, while scrolling through Halloween costumes online. "I just want something that is still a classic and will never get old. I'll just look some more," he says to himself.

"Hey mate! What are you going to be at the Halloween party?" Barry asks Terry, when he walks into the office.

"I'm not sure. I'm still deciding. I want to be something simple and to the point," Terry says.

"I totally understand that. I think I may go as a drifter," Barry responds.

"How? Why would you go as a drifter?" Terry asks him.

"It's something simple and to the point," Barry smiles and says.

"It's not, though," Terry says back.

The Halloween party is quickly approaching, and Terry and Lena have spoken about it. They never really addressed him telling her, "I like you!" While cordial at work, they only message outside of work about the Halloween party. The schedule is set, and they know what they will be doing:

4:40 pm-Introduction-Terry & Lena
4:45 pm-Break into teams-Terry
5:10 pm-Break out games-Trivia -Terry

Terry was only concerned about the events that he had to lead and organize. Although he is still emotionally clouded, he is excited and has prepared quite a few questions for the Halloween trivia. Halloween has always been one of his favorite days. Like any child, he loved dressing up and going trick-or-treating. As a child, he dressed up as Jason from the "Friday the 13th" movies.

"Wait wait! That's it! I'll do a classic Jason mask. The Jason mask never gets old, and I don't have to do the full outfit," he thinks to himself. He does a quick search for a Jason mask and plenty of them come up.
"I think I found out what I'm going to be," he says to the rest of the staff in the office.
"What's that?" Danni requests.
"I'm doing the Jason thing. You know? From the old Jason horror movies of the 80s and 90s. It's classic and never really gets old. If somebody walked up to you with a Jason mask, you would still be a little frightened," he says to his colleagues.

"That is pretty classic, mate!" agrees Alex.
"What's that movie you just said?" asks Danni.

"I'm assuming horror movies just aren't your thing?" Terry states.

"Not at all. I mean I know the mask, I just don't know if I've ever seen the movie," Danni responds.

"It's a slasher, gory, type of horror movie. It used to scare me as a kid, but I think life has screwed me up, so I just laugh at the gore. It's sick, I know," he laughs and smiles.

"Do you know the story behind the mask?" asks Barry.

"No, I don't. Enlighten us, Barry." Terry smiles and turns his entire chair towards Barry. The office knew that Barry was always good for random but interesting facts. Every office has at least one person like this. Just as Barry is about to start talking, he sees the girl from the elevator walk into the office.

"Excuse me guys. You might not have seen the email, but this is the new sales rep, Melissa!" Danni stands up and says.

"Hi, Melissa!" All of them say simultaneously.

"Hi, Melissa, my name is Terry!" he says, as they both shake hands.

"Hi, Terry! I like your shirt. It looks very handsome on you," she says, as they continue shaking hands. "This old thing? Well, thank you very much. Welcome to the center! If you need help with anything, let me know," he says, as he straightens out his salmon-colored dress shirt. Melissa continued greeting everyone and eventually went to the front office.

"So, what's the story behind the mask?" Alex says, getting everyone back on track with the initial story.

"Yes! So you know in the first two movies he didn't have the infamous hockey mask? He wore a burlap sack with the eyes cut out. Well, it wasn't until the third movie in the collection that he got the face mask," Barry says, as he crosses his hands together.

"So, why did they change it to a hockey mask?" Danni asks.

"Well, rumor has it that they wanted to get rid of the burlap sack and come up with something that would have a long-lasting effect. In the first film, they found ways to hide his face and in the second one it was decided that he would wear the burlap sack. While planning for the third movie, one of the directors who had a background in hockey, made a suggestion about the hockey mask. The suggestion was put out there and the crew and producers decided to run with it, and now we know the iconic mask we see today," Barry states.

"That's quite interesting. But what was the point of it all?" Alex softly laughs.

"Well mate, it's a story of the origin of the mask and also how what may have seemed as a minor suggestion turned out to change pop culture forever. No idea is too big or too small, right? It's more of a matter of trusting yourself and keeping things simple," Barry says, as he explains one of his random interesting facts.

"That's it then! The final decision has been made, and the jury has decided, I will go with Jason mask," Terry declares, as he looks at all of his colleagues.

He orders the mask and another coworker helps him to get it delivered to the office. He knew that he would have to meet with Lena, to just go over the rundown. Terry walks up to the fairly empty front desk and sees Melissa sitting there. "Hey Melissa! How's it going?" Terry inquires.

"I'm doing ok. Still getting used to everything here and still going through training," she smiles, as she looks up from her paperwork.

"I'm sure it's a lot to learn in a short time. It was for teachers and I could only imagine how it is for a sales rep," he empathizes.

"Yes, it's quite a lot. How long have you been in China?" she asks.

"About 5 and a half months," he responds.

"That's really cool. I'm glad you're here. How do you like it?" She says, swinging her long black hair behind her back.

"I really like it here. I'm enjoying myself, and I'm learning a lot. I didn't know much Mandarin before I came here, and I still don't know much. But I know more than what I did before I came if that makes sense," his hands move up and down in confusion, as he tries to get his point across.

"I get what you mean," she says, as she slightly laughs.

"Is Lena here today?" he asks.

"No, she is off today," she responds. He knew that Lena was off, but he wanted to spark up a conversation with Melissa. "Oh, that's right," he confirms.

"You two are hosting the Halloween event, right? I have to find my outfit," Melissa says.

"I think the whole office has been talking about Halloween outfits this week. Hey, could I ask you two questions?" he says.

"I see what you did there," she says, as she smiles.

"My second question is about your necklace: The Eye of Horus. That's a really nice necklace. Where have you seen that symbol before?" he asks.

"Oh, thank you! My dad gave it to me before he passed. I remember seeing it as a child at a museum and I always talked about it. After I graduated from university, my dad gave me this necklace," Melissa responds, as she touches her necklace.

"Oh, I'm sorry about your dad," he says.

"Thank you," she responds.

"What do you know about the symbol? Like the meaning?" he asks.

"Well, I thought it just looked cool. Then, I did some more research on it, and it made me love it even more. It's all about having a deeper understanding of someone. That third eye, right? Not the physical but the metaphysical; learning how to understand someone beyond the physical. I learned all about the story of Horus and Osiris from Ancient Egypt," she says.

This highly impressed Terry, because he knew all about the symbolism behind the Eye of Horus and the different meanings. He didn't expect to meet someone in his center who had an appreciation and understanding for the symbol. "Not only was she smart and beautiful, she knew about this particular symbol," he thought to himself.

"That's so cool that your dad gave that to you. I hope I didn't dive too deep into things for you. I hope I wasn't all in your business. I enjoy learning about symbols and the meanings behind them, and I saw you on the elevator before and noticed your necklace," he replies.

"I noticed you too," she responds.

"Really?" his voice cracks a little bit in shock.

"I was thinking, 'Who is this handsome guy on the elevator?' I was secretly looking at you," she blushes slightly, as her cheeks turn a light bubblegum color.

"Well, thank you. Look, I have to get ready for my class, but we could chat later," he highly suggests.

"Sure! What's your WeChat?" she asks him.

"Let me grab my phone real quick." He briskly walks back into the office to grab his phone off his desk and returns to the front desk. They unlock their phones and exchange information. "Have a good class," she encourages.

"Thank you! I hope you have a good rest of your day and if you need help with anything just let me know," he states.

"I sure will," she says, as she goes back to working on her laptop.

Terry walks back into the office and sees a piece of paper on his desk.

"Your mask has been ordered and should be here by Wednesday," Shelley says. She was the new teacher that was brought on two weeks ago, and she sat directly behind Terry.

"Thank you so much, Shelley. How much do I owe you?" he asks.

"No worries. Just buy me bubble tea one day," she responds.

"Sounds like a plan to me." Terry grabs his papers and heads down to his class.

His teaching day has concluded, and he is in the office finishing up some paperwork. He checks his phone and sees that he has an unread message.

7:00 pm
Melissa: Hey there! ☺

7:02 pm
Terry: Hey Melissa. How are you?

7:03 pm
Melissa: I'm doing ok.
I'm off for the day. ☺

7:04 pm
Melissa: Going to eat something soon. How's your day been?

7:06 pm
Terry: It's been ok. Just finishing up some paperwork.

7:08 pm
Melissa: ok. Thanks for complimenting my necklace. Sometimes I don't even think about it. I never really take it off unless I'm doing something really important.

7:10 pm
Terry: Yeah, I thought it was pretty cool. Especially, because you know the meaning behind it. What will you have for dinner?

7:12 pm
Melissa: I research symbols and the meanings of them, so I can try to understand. Some of the stuff is too deep...lol.

7:13 pm
Melissa: I'm going to eat hot pot. Have you ever had hot pot?

7:14 pm
Terry: No, I haven't. I know what it is, I just never had the pleasure of trying it.

7:15 pm
Melissa: Maybe we can go one day. 😉

7:15 pm
Terry: I would like that!

7:16 pm
Melissa: Ok well I'm meeting my friend now.
Talk later?

7:17 pm
Terry: Yeah, sure! Enjoy your dinner!

7:18 pm
Melissa: 谢谢你

7:19 pm
Terry: I guess that means, "thank you."

7:20 pm
Melissa: 👍

Terry goes back to finishing up his paperwork and Shelley walks into the office. He turns his chair towards her, as he sees her wiggle her mouse to wake her computer up.

"Hey Shelley. How are your classes going? You're teaching beginner classes, right?" he asks.

"They're ok. Just getting to know the students and becoming familiar with the curriculum," she responds.

"That's good. Where were you teaching before?" he requests.

"I was at a kindergarten for a year and then decided to transition to teaching adults. The kids are really cute, but it's a lot of work," she insists.

"I could imagine. I substituted for a first-grade class before. It was that day that I knew I wanted to teach adults. Super cute, but a lot to handle," he says.

"Who are the kids or adults?" she says, as they both laughed.

"Well, if you need anything, let me know. I haven't taught many beginner classes, but I could help you navigate through the materials we have," he offers.

7:25 pm

Lena: Hey! What are you doing?

"Will do, Terry. I have a quick meeting, so I'll catch up with you later," she says, as she gets out her chair and walks into the hallway. "Talk to you later," he says, turning his attention back to his desk. He looks down at his phone and sees he has a notification from WeChat.

7:26 pm

Terry: Hey there! I'm still at work finishing up some things. What are you doing?

"I wonder what she wants. Maybe she just wants to see what I'm doing," he thinks to himself.

> **7:27 pm**
> Lena: You should meet me at the café shop for a catch up.

Terry wants to play hard to get, but he won't. It's hard to lie or even play hard to get when your crush wants your attention. He really wants to see her, and it appears that she wants to see him.

> **7:28 pm**
> Terry: Why? Do you miss me or something?

"That line will get her thinking," Terry thinks.

> **7:29 pm**
> Lena: No! Just wanted to talk to you and catch up. I can give you the address. It's not far from the office. You could catch a taxi there or walk.

> **7:30 pm**
> Terry: You don't have to beg.

> **7:31 pm**
> Lena: Whatever!

> **7:32 pm**
> Terry: Send me the address, and I'll catch a taxi over there. I'm

almost done here, so give me like 15 minutes.

7:33 pm
Lena: Great, I'll send the location in a moment.

7:34 pm
Terry: 😎

"That's kind of random. She ghosted me for a couple months and now, all of a sudden, she wants to talk. Something is up with her," he thinks. He is still going, but he knows that she is thinking about something or someone.

He finishes up his work, grabs his jacket, shuts off his computer, pushes in his chair, and heads out of the door. "See you guys tomorrow," he says, as he walks out of the office.

7:40 pm
Terry: Send me the location. I just left the office.

He is about to step on the elevator and hears heels heavily stomping towards him. He turns around and sees Kelly's face, as the elevator doors stay open long enough for her to enter.

7:41 pm
Lena: I'm about to send the location.

"Hey Kelly," he says.

"Hi Terry, I hope I didn't scare you," she says.

"No problem. I didn't even realize that you were behind me, but did hear your footsteps," he says to her.

"I understand. Any plans for the remainder of the evening?" she investigates.

"I'm going to meet Lena for a cup of coffee," he says.

"Oh, I see. You two like each other, no?" she continues to investigate.

"Not really. We are just friends, and she just asked me to come for a late coffee," he says, trying to blanket his obvious feelings for Lena.

"I thought she was dating that girl from the coffee shop," she responds.

"What girl from the coffee shop?" he asks.

Ding! The elevator reaches the bottom floor and they both proceed to the exit.

"Well, I was in the coffee shop one day and I saw her girlfriend in there. I thought she worked there, but I'm not sure. Anyway, enjoy your coffee time!" she says.

"Yeah, thanks," he replies.

"I knew she was with this girl, but I didn't know the girl worked at the coffee shop," he thought.

Putting his phone to the scanner, the lobby doors open up, and he walks out. He checks his phone and sees the notification for a new message. His eyes widened, and his heart began to race a little faster.

7:43 pm

Terry: Ok, I'm about to put it into my map.

He copies the address and puts it into his Tencent map. "Oh, it's only a 10-minute walk from West Binshui Road," he thinks to himself.

> **7:44 pm**
> Terry: Hey, it's only about a 10-minute walk. I should be there shortly.

> **7:45 pm**
> Lena: Ok. ☺

> **7:46 pm**
> Lena: Did you bring a jacket to work today? It's a little cold outside tonight.

> **7:46 pm**
> Terry: You worried about me now? Hahaha!

> **7:47 pm**
> Lena: Now, I hope you didn't bring a jacket.

> **7:48 pm**
> Terry: lol. I'll see you soon.

As he leaves the office building, he takes a look at the sky. "It's a crescent moon tonight," he says. The late autumn air infiltrates his skin and into his bones, making him slightly shiver. He buttons up his jacket and pulls his blue baseball cap down, so that it hugs his head a little closer.

Following the directions on his phone, he still notices the crescent moon getting bigger. "Seems like it is following me tonight."

He gets to a crosswalk and the light is red, and he looks down the street for a moment. He looks between the office buildings and into the restaurants and sees nothing. The light turns green, and he continues to walk across the street. "I should be there shortly. Just a couple more meters," he notices on his map.

He picks up his pace and the wind picks up its strength. The winter is on its way, and Terry can certainly feel it.

8:00 pm
Terry: Almost there.

8:00 pm
Lena: Ok. I'm sitting down in the corner.

He walks through the door and sees a couple sitting down working on their laptops. The coffee shop smell hugs his nose and shakes his stomach. "Kind of late for coffee. I drink coffee late as well," he thinks. He sees Lena sitting in the corner of the shop by herself.

"Hey there. How are you tonight?" he asks.

"I'm ok. You got here pretty quick," she says.

"I did, because it wasn't that far away. So, why was it so important for me to meet you tonight?" he interrogates, as he takes off his jacket and sits down.

"Can I just see my friend?" she says.

Terry lifts his chin and face in suspicion. "You just wanted to see your friend? You haven't wanted to see your friend for a couple of months. Why now?" he asks.

"Why are you asking so many questions? Can we just enjoy each other's company?" she asks and looks out the window.

"If you say so. Well, since I'm here, could I get a cup of coffee?" he proposes.

"Sure," she responds.

"Discount?" he asks and shrugs his shoulders.

"No discount," she says and laughs out.

"That's a ripoff! Anyway, let me get a medium vanilla latte," he requests.

"Sure, and I think I'll get a caramel macchiato," she says, as she gets up to go tell the barista their order.

He checks his phone and sees a new message come through.

8:06 pm
Melissa: Hey ☺

Lena comes back to the table with both of their coffees. "That was pretty quick. Did you have them ready back there?" he jokingly asks.

"Of course not. So, has there been any news about your sister?" she asks, as she sat back down in her leather-cushioned high chair.

"The cops found her car abandoned by a river in Portland, but we still haven't found her," he says.

"Oh, I'm so sorry about that. How have you been doing with everything?" she asks.

"I mean, I'm as good as I can be. My family has been doing their best keeping me in the loop with everything. They found her purse and this necklace that our mom gave her, but still haven't found her," he takes a sip of his hot vanilla latte.

"I'm so sorry you're going through that. It must be rough for you right now, no?" she asks him.

"I'm doing ok. Just trying to focus on my classes and my life here in China. It's hard, you know? I'm here, but I'm not really here if you know what I mean," he responds.

Terry feels someone staring at him while he is talking to Lena. He takes a quick glance over to the counter and notices the barista looking at him with her arms folded. "She looks really familiar. Where have I seen her before?" he thinks to himself.

"I know what you mean. I felt like that when my parents got divorced." Lena says.

"I didn't know your parents were divorced. I'm sorry about that," he responds.

"It's ok. It happens. When I found out I couldn't sleep, I couldn't eat, I lost like 25 kg in less than a month. It was stressful, but I figured out ways to deal with it. Some ways were healthier than others, but I dealt with it," she wipes her left eye, as she finishes telling her story.

"I'm sorry about that. That must've been tough," he replies, as he hands her a tissue out of the brown tissue holder.

"It was, and I'm an only child, so I had to deal with it by myself. But I'm ok now, and I think my mom and dad are both happy," she states.

"So, who owns the café?" he asks.

"Well, they both kinda do. At least for now. They have found an investor and I think they will both sell their shares of the company. I will be able to get a portion, other than that I don't really know what they will do," she mentions.

"I understand. Do you believe in marriage?" he instantly asks.

She pauses, takes both of her hands, and curls her blonde and brown shoulder-length hair behind her ears.

"I do. I still believe in love. Some people shouldn't be together; unfortunately, it takes them years to accept it," she says.

"That's quite harsh," he replies.

"It's true. I love my parents, but I'm not sure if they should've been married. I mean, it was the whole filial piety," she exclaims, slamming her coffee cup on the table.

"What do you mean?" he asks.

"You've heard of it before, right?" she asks.

"Yes, but I don't know much about it," he says, wiping his mouth with a loose napkin.

Terry sits up in his chair and takes a sip of his vanilla latte. He takes another look over at the counter and the barista is still staring at him.

"So, filial piety is a Confucius philosophy, and it's based around five relationships: husband to wife is one of the relationships, and it's something we take seriously. My dad met my mom and things moved quickly. It is up to the son to pass on the family name. My grandparents said it was time for my dad to get married, have a baby, and he did. His family introduced him to my mom and here I am," she says, as she smiles and tilts her head to the left like she was taking a glamour shot.

"I see what you mean. Is it still a popular idea, or are more younger people starting to deviate away from it?" he asks.

"Of course, you still respect your parents and family. People are just doing more of what they want to do. Many young people want to explore and live life and see what the world has to offer. Others will get married and settle down. It's more about finding what works for you," she responds.

"I mean, that's no different from other cultures, right?" he proposes.

"What do you mean?" she asks, trying to catch her breath.

"Like for your culture, it's about honoring your parents and family. That's most cultures, I feel like. Cultures just have different names for it. For instance, my parents grew up in Portland during the early 1970s. My city was segregated, there was political and racial tension, and there was a hippie movement that was coming up from San Francisco. Oregon banned black people from working, living, and owning property in the state until 1926. A little over 40 years later, my mom was in Portland working as a secretary and my dad worked at a factory that built trucks. My parents met during the Portland State University student strikes. My dad had a friend who went there, and they went to join the protest," he explains.

"What were they protesting?" she asks.

"There was a lot going on in the late 60s and early 70s in America. Students were protesting the Vietnam War, Bobby Seale was put into prison, there was..."

"Who is Bobby Seale?" she interrupts and asks.

"He is a political activist, author, and co-founder of the Black Panthers," he responds.

He sees her eyebrows raise a little bit. "The Black Panthers, a political activist organization that was founded to protect black people from police brutality. Bobby Seale and Huey P. Newton helped to found the organization, and it branched out from there. My dad was in the organization and participated in a lot of marches and different programs in our community. My mom's brother had been beaten up by the police during a traffic stop, and she eventually joined the Black Panthers as well," he explains.

"Your mom and dad sound really cool," she states.
"They were very interesting people. They met during those student strikes and ended up falling in love. They were together because they loved each other, but also for survival. My grandparents had lived in poverty their whole lives and wanted my parents to be better off. Not so much filial piety, but kind of. Both of our parents were trying to honor and protect their families and move forward in the best ways they knew possible," he states.
"I understand that," she responds.

"So, why did you really want to meet me so suddenly?" he finally asks.
She looks up at the sky for a moment, and looks at Terry.
"What do you think about the new girl?" she asks.
"Who? Are you talking about Melissa?" He knew exactly who Lena was talking about.
"Are you talking about Melissa?" she mocks him.

"Yes, I'm talking about Melissa," she says, as her voice volumes up.

"I mean, she's ok. I've only had one conversation with her, and I saw her on the elevator that one day. I believe it might've been her first day at the office. She seems cool," he replies nervously.

"Do you think she's pretty?" she interrogates.

"Do I think she is pretty? I think she is ok. She's ok," he repeats himself.

"You asked me to come down here to ask me questions about Melissa?" he says.

He takes another sip of his latte, when he catches a glimpse of the barista coming over to them.

"Are you two ok over here?" the barista asks.

He tries to take a quick look at her name tag, but she turns before he could really see what it says.

"Yes, we are ok," Lena replies.

The barista and Lena take a slow glance at each other, and the barista walks back to the front counter.

"What was that all about?" he asks.

"Nothing. She's one of the new baristas here, and I think she is just getting used to things right now," she responds.

"Back to Melissa. I think she likes you," Lena states.

"Why do you think that?" Terry asks.

"Well, she just asked about you a lot. 'Where are you from? How long have you been here? Are you single?' I don't know why she asks me," she expresses.

"And what did you say to her?" he wonders.

"America, 5 months and maybe," she responds in order.

"Why maybe?" he laughs a little bit.

"I don't know what you do. You're a single and handsome guy," she states.

"I appreciate that, but I think we both know who I'm interested in," he confidently states.

"Melissa?" she quickly responds.

He takes a final sip of his latte and looks over at the barista. "That's where I saw her before," he thinks to himself.

"Wait a minute. That night I saw you on Nanjing road, were you with that barista?" he asks her.

"Her name is Rachel," he finally got a good look at her name tag.

"What are you talking about? Was I with her that night?" she restates his questions.

"That's what I'm asking. Is that her?" he confirms her question.

"Yes, we were together that night. We were just two friends hanging out that night," she states.

"Is that the girl you ghosted me for?" he asks.

"I didn't ghost you, I'm still talking to you, right?" she responds.

He knew that Rachel was the girl that he saw Lena with that night. He sees Rachel writing something down on a piece of paper, and still looking at him.

"I think your 'friend' doesn't like me. She hasn't stopped staring at me since I've been here," he says.

"Maybe she thinks that you are 'ok' and wants to have a conversation," she says, with a slight smile on her face.

"That's a good one," he says.

"Anyway, what will you wear for Halloween?" she asks.

"I'll probably wear a Jason mask from the "Friday the 13th" movies," he states.

"Oh, the horror movie series?" she responds.

"Yeah. I didn't know you were into scary movies?" he probes.

"Well, those bloody and gory movies don't really scare me. Sometimes they make me laugh," she responds, while drinking the last little bit of her macchiato.

"You're sick! But I feel the same way," he replies.

"What will you be?" he asks.

"I'm thinking either a werewolf or a pumpkin," she responds.

"Those are two totally different concepts," he tells her.

"I know, and they both have different meanings," she says.

"So, I guess it will just depend on how you are feeling that night?" he interrogates.

8:59 pm
Melissa: How is your night going?

"Yes, it will depend on my mood. I might buy both and go from there," she responds, as she moves her empty coffee cup to the side.

"That's fair. Well, I do have to go home and get something to eat. I think your 'friend' has had enough of our conversation," he says, as he quickly nods over to the counter.

"We are about to start shutting it down here anyway. We can meet tomorrow and go through everything for the event," she states.

"That sounds good to me. I'll be in around 11:30," he responds.

Lena gets up and takes the coffee cups to the trash, as Rachel comes over to the table. She hands him a neatly folded piece of receipt paper, and she quickly walks away. "What was that about? This girl is weird," he thinks to himself. He slowly opens up the folded piece of receipt paper to see in big bold letters:

SHE'S MINE!

"What in the world is going on tonight? It must be this weather?" he thinks, as he folds the piece of receipt paper back up. Lena comes back over to the table; stops in front of him and says, "What's wrong?"

"Nothing at all," he responds.

"You sure? You seem like something is wrong," she replies.

"No, I'm ok. I think I'm just tired. I'm going to go home and lay down," he explains.

Terry wasn't sure why he kept his mouth closed. He didn't think it was a big deal, but inside he was upset. "Who is this girl and why is she so protective over Lena?" he thinks.

"I'll see you tomorrow," Lena says.

She reaches out for a hug, and he hugs her back. Meanwhile, he can still see Rachel staring at them from the counter.

"I'll catch up with you tomorrow. Don't be out too late," he says to her, putting his phone in his left pant's pocket.

"I won't be late, big head," she says back.

He pushes open the doors and enters into the crisp evening air. He digs in his right pocket to feel for his phone and sees that he has a new notification.

> 9:05 pm (to Melissa)
> Terry: Hey there. My night is going well. About to go home. How was dinner with your friend? ☺

As he waits for Melissa to respond, he calls for a taxi. He could take the subway home, but he'd rather spend the extra cash for some quiet time. Terry enjoys being in the city with all the culture, nightlife, and sights; oftentimes, he would rather be in a quiet, more serene place. He opens up the app and requests a ride. His ride is 4 minutes away.

He walks over to the curb so that he can quickly get in once the car arrives. A long day, and some time spent in a confusing environment, has him exhausted. "What was the deal with Rachel?" he thinks. The moon shines through the night clouds, as it helps to illuminate the city. "It must be the crescent moon that has people acting weird," he thought to himself. Terry always felt that there was a connection between the cosmos and human behavior. Whether that was people behaving strangely during a certain moon phase, people being in a better mood when it's sunny, or people wanting to cuddle up in bed on a rainy day.

His mom always told him to listen and pay attention to mother nature and life would be a lot easier. "Nature has a way of telling you everything you need to know if you stay still," his mother would tell him. On this night, he stood still and closed his eyes for a moment. He hears cars speeding by from friends street racing each other, footsteps from people trying to get home, dogs barking from pets who are walking their owners, and winds gently blowing from mother nature's best behavior.

Honk! *Honk*! *Honk*! Terry hears the taxi driver pull up to the curb

"Duìbùqǐ," Terry says.

"It's ok," says the driver.

He gets in the car and the driver pulls off into the late-night traffic.

9:08 pm
Melissa: It was ok. Just went for hot pot with one of my girlfriends. What are you doing?

9:09 pm
Terry: On my way home. I had just met a friend for coffee. I'm exhausted though. 😔

9:10 pm
Melissa: Coffee so late? How many classes did you have today?

9:11 pm
Terry: Yes, but it's never too late for coffee. I had five classes today and a study session in the afternoon.

9:11 pm
Melissa: It actually can be too late for coffee and then you will be up all night. That does sound like a busy day.

9:12 pm
Melissa: So, you said you are on your way home? How far do you live from the center?

9:13 pm
Terry: I live in Aocheng, so not too far from the center.

9:14 pm
Melissa: Oh, I see. That's over there by the zoo and water park, right?

9:15 pm
Terry: Yup! I can see the water park from my window and I can hear the Tigers growling at night.

9:15 pm
Melissa: Are you serious? Hahaha! That doesn't scare you at night?

9:16 pm
Terry: I mean it wakes me up at night. But what can I do? Tell the tigers to be quiet? 😂

9:17 pm
Melissa: That's very true... hahaha. Are you ready for the Halloween party?

Terry notices that he is not too far from his apartment, and he gets ready to be dropped off. The driver pulls up next to his building. "Xièxiè," Terry says, as he gets out of the car. He closes the door and reaches for his phone, which he has in the back pocket of his gray pants.

9:19 pm
Terry: Yes, I think so. Me and Lena are going to meet one more time before the party, just to make sure things are in order.

9:20 pm
Melissa: Don't you mean 'Lena and I?' Your grammar is a little off...hahaha.

9:21 pm
Terry: Well, excuse me. I think you are right though...lol.

9:22 pm
Melissa: You know, we focus a lot more on grammar as ESL learners.

9:23 pm
Terry: Yeah! Yeah! 😎

9:24 pm
Melissa: Maybe we could go for hotpot after the Halloween Party. I think you would like it.

9:25 pm
Terry: Yea sure. It will be my first hotpot experience. I'm looking forward to it.

9:26 pm
Melissa: Sounds good to me! 🙂

He enters his dark apartment and runs directly into the clothes rack. "It's too dark in this apartment. I can't see shit!" he shouts out.

He drops his backpack down, turns on the heat, washes his face, and cleans the dishes. Barely making it to his bed, he passes out on top of his royal blue comforter.

XIII

She's Your Girlfriend?

"Terry! Terry! I think your mask came!" shouts Shelley.

"I'm right behind you, Shelley," Terry responds.

"I know. I just wanted to make sure that you heard me," she says.

"Yeah, I know," Terry says, opening up the package.

"Try it on. I've never seen the movie, so I'm interested to see this mask," she requests.

He takes the mask out of the bag. It's the typical hockey mask with a single strap connected to the back. He puts it around his face, as he smells the plastic.

"Roooaaarrr!" Terry turns around and says to Shelley.

She looks at him and says, "That's it? I thought there was more to it."

"There's like a janitor outfit that you could wear with it," he says.

"So, where's your janitor suit? You have the full costume, right?" she asks.

187

"No, I didn't think that far ahead. The mask is enough though. Isn't it?" he responds, while he lifts the mask off his face.

"I've never seen the movie, but that doesn't look that scary," she says, as she stares at the mask.

"What? No way! If you saw somebody coming down the street in this mask, wouldn't you be scared?" he asks. She begins to respond, as Barry walks in from his class.

"Not really. I would think that the person needs help or is a part of some sort of club," she says.

"Yeah, a murder club," says Barry.

"You guys don't know what you're talking about. This is an oldie but goodie, and now I am ready for Halloween," Terry says.

"Is Lena ready as well? You two like each other, right?" Shelley asks.

Terry turns his head sharply and is shocked by the question. Barry has a slight smile on his face and looks at Terry for a moment. Everyone in the office knows about his feelings toward Lena.

"What are you talking about? I don't know what you mean," he responds.

"I heard that you told her that you liked her and that you two have hung out outside of work," she says, staring at him.

Barry takes a glance at Terry and their eyes connect for a moment.

"There's nothing wrong with hanging out with someone after work. That's not a crime, last time I checked," he responds.

"You're right. But I do think that you two make a cute couple," she states.

"Thank you, but we are just friends. Plus, I think she has a girlfriend," he says, as he was trying to cunningly gain some information.

"That girl isn't her girlfriend. I think they are just friends, but she'll be here tomorrow for the event," she states, as she turns around and faces her computer.

Terry and Barry both turn and look at Shelley.

"Wait, she's coming?" Terry asks.

"Yes, that's what I heard. She is a photographer and I think they want her to take some pictures of the event for our website," she says, looking at her paperwork.

"Oh, I see," he says.

He knew that she was talking about Rachel. He remembers that note she gave him, before he left the coffee shop that night: SHE'S MINE.

Wait, that was too nice, it was more like: **SHE'S MINE!**

Terry looks over and sees Barry looking at him, "You alright?"

"Yeah, yeah, I'm fine." He wasn't, but he couldn't show that he wasn't. He finishes up his notes from the previous class and heads to his next class.

"Just have to finish some paperwork, and then I'm out of here. I'm starving and could go for a jiānbǐng right now," Terry says to himself, at the end of his workday.

"Almost 8:40 pm, it's time to get out of here." He packs up his things and sets his lessons aside for the next day. He sees that Kelly is still in the office, and looks like she is getting ready to leave as well.

"Hey Terry! Are you getting ready to leave?" she asks, as she packs up her company tote bag.

"Yup! I'm done for the day," he says.

"Could you wait for me? We can walk out together," she asks.

"Sure, I'll wait," he responds.

Kelly goes into the back of the center to grab her things, and then she comes out. She comes out and shouts, "Are you ready to go?"

"Yup, just waiting for you," he responds, as he hits the glances at this phone screen.

They both walk out of the center, as the āyí shuts off the lights and locks the door for the night.

"How was your day, Terry?" she asks.

"Not too bad. Just 4 classes today. How was your day today?" he inquires back.

"Pretty good, pretty good." They both step onto the elevator, and begin to lower down to the lobby.

"Are you ready for the Halloween party tomorrow?" she asks.

"Yes, I'm actually quite excited. I have my costume and everything," he explains.

"Did you go Trick-or-Treating a lot as a kid?" she wonders.

"I sure did. We used to also go out on Mischief Night. That was when I got a little older, though," he says to her.

"What is 'Mischief Night?' It sounds bad." she says, as the elevator made it to the lobby of the building.

"It's kind of exactly what it says. We would go out and throw eggs at houses. Or we would tp houses," he says, stepping off the elevator.

"What does that mean?" she asks, with her eyebrows squinted.

"It means to throw toilet paper around someone's house or lawn. First, you would throw the eggs, then throw the toilet paper at the house or tree. Makes it harder to clean up. It was all done out of good clean fun," he says, as he mimicked the motion of throwing an egg at someone's house.

"That sounds like a mess. I wouldn't be so happy if someone did that to my house. I would find them and throw toilet paper and eggs at whoever did it," she says, mimicking the motion of throwing toilet paper at someone.

"Well, I'm sure you have something like that here. Maybe not like Halloween or Mischief Night, but something similar. Isn't it called the Hungry Ghost Festival?" he assumes.

"You are exactly correct. It's also known as the Zhōng Yuán Festival 中元节 and we have our own customs around it. It's said that you should get home before nightfall during the Hungry Ghost Festival," she states.

"Why is that?" he asks.

"Well, the whole festival is about the souls of those who have passed on coming back, and roaming the Earth with the living. The festival is here to keep the souls from being mischievous. Whereas in your culture, your living souls are being mischievous with your Mischief Night. For us, this usually falls between August and September here in China. We pay honor and worship our ancestors during this time and we burn joss paper. When we burn paper money, it's done so that our ancestors will have a prosperous afterlife," she informs him.

"That's so cool! Thank you for sharing. I guess I'll get home early during the Ghost Festival," he says.

"It's already passed," she says, as she chuckles a little bit.

"Oh, well thanks for the heads-up for next time," he responds.

They both step out into the chill of the autumn evening, and he feels the wind blowing on his skin. "Speaking of a heads-up. I see Melissa has taken a liking to you," she says.

"Melissa? I mean she's…we've been chatting," he hesitantly responds.

"Since she's started, all she does is talk about you. She's always talking about how handsome she thinks you are, and she said you two are going for hot pot tomorrow," Kelly says.

"We will go after the party, but it's nothing serious," he says to her.

"Ok, I'm just saying. I know you also have a thing for Lena, so just be careful. You seem like a nice guy, even though you just told me you throw toilet paper at people's houses. We had another black male teacher from the states here before you and he was awesome, but I like you better," Kelly says.

"Ok, I don't really know what to say to that but thank you," he responds with a lot of confusion.

"Well, I'm going this way, so I will see you tomorrow," she tells him, as she makes a left and walks down the street.

Terry walks down to the metro station, takes off his book bag and walks through the security checkpoint. "What did that mean? Is she comparing all the black people she meets?" he thinks to himself.

"I wonder what Lena's doing," he says, as another strategic random thought of Lena pops into his brain. His train promptly arrives and he steps into it. As he takes his phone out of his left pocket, he sees a girl at the end of the train. She looks like the same girl from the elevator, and the gym that he has been seeing. He takes another glance at her, and sees that she has on the Eye of Horus necklace. They lock eyes with each other for a moment and the train stops. The young woman gets off of the train and smiles at him; he gets up and looks at her through the closed train doors.

"She looks exactly like Melissa," he thinks. The train starts moving, and he sees that she has a small maroon-colored luggage bag, and she has on a Real Madrid football jersey.

"Did I just see Melissa leave?" he thought to himself.

"I have to get home and just chill for the rest of the night," he thinks.

He sits back down, as he looks down at his finger-smudged phone screen. The train picks up speed, as he is thrown back into his seat by the centrifugal force.

He lays back into his seat, closes his eyes, and puts in his all-black wireless headphones that he brought with him from home. Just as he is about to set his playlist for home, he decides to text Lena.

9:20 pm
Terry: Hey there. Are you busy?

9:21 pm
Lena: What's up? I'm not busy, just got done with dinner and about to head home. What are you doing?

193

9:22 pm
Terry: I'm doing well. I'm on the metro going home.

9:23 pm
Lena: Are you ready for tomorrow?

9:24 pm
Terry: Of course I am. I have my half of a costume..lol.

9:24 pm
Lena: I think it will be fun. I had fun hosting with you the last time we did an event.

9:25 pm
Terry: I did as well, and I learned a lot about the Dragon Boat Festival. You looked great in that blue dress as well. Speaking of dress, what will be your costume for tomorrow?

9:26 pm
Lena: You will have to wait and see. 😊

9:26 pm
Terry: Keeping it a surprise, I see.

9:27 pm
Lena: What will you do after the event?

The train stops, and he looks up at the station to see how close he is to his home. "Oh, this is my stop," he gets up and runs out of the doors just before they shut. "I must've not been paying attention." Walking around the corridor to get to the escalator, he looks down at his phone.

9:28 pm
Terry: Nothing much. Probably find something to eat.

9:29 pm
Lena: We should go for hotpot tomorrow.

9:29 pm
Terry: Yeah, I'm down for that. I've never had it.

9:30 pm
Lena: Ok cool. We can leave right after the event.

9:31 pm
Terry: Sounds good to me. I'm about to eat and pass out. I'll talk to you tomorrow.

9:32 pm
Terry: Goodnight pretty lady!

9:33 pm
Lena: Goodnight handsome!

He walks to a 7-Eleven and picks up a plate of spaghetti, an ice tea, and goes to his building. Once in his room, he turns on the tv and heats up his single man's dinner. After eating, he lays down on his couch and watches some NBA highlights on his phone. His head nods off to the left and his phone falls on his chest, as he falls asleep for the night.

Bang! *Bang*! *Bang*! Three boisterous knocks at the door cause Terry to jump out of his sleep, and run into his living room table with his right foot. He looks through the eyehole and sees that it is Matt standing there.

"Hey, what's up? Why are you knocking like the police?" Terry asks, as he rubs his eyes and his foot at the same time.

"Hey, my bad brother. I know it's like 7 am, but I wanted to see what you were doing for Halloween. You're working today, aren't you?" Matt asks.

"Yeah, my job is having a Halloween event, and I'm co-hosting it," Terry responds.

"Well, what about after? Me and some buddies are getting together later," Matt states.

"I think I'm going to dinner with one of my coworkers afterward. There are some other holidays coming up. Maybe we could hang then," Terry says, as he finishes yawning.

"Well, I'll be around. If you finish dinner early just let me know and…hey man you alright?" Matt asks him.

"Yeah, I just thought I saw something by the elevator," Terry says back.

"Something like what?" Matt asks.

"It was like a shadow by the elevator. Never mind, I think I'm still tired," Terry says, putting his attention back to Matt.

"Get some more rest and message me later. If you're busy we still have Thanksgiving, Christmas, and New Year," Matt smiles and says.

"For sure, bro, I'll talk to you later." Terry closes the door and flops back onto his couch.

"I'm really seeing things now. Maybe I'm just delusional. How delusional can I be?" he thought to himself. This shadow always seems to appear when he is stressed, nervous, or upset about something. The shadow is there and then it's not. It's been like this since he lost his parents. "Let me message Naomi and see what's going on," he thinks out loud.

7:10 am (to Naomi)
Terry: Hey Nay! Any updates about C?

He lays back down for a moment, but realizes he should get up and get ready for work. He still has to teach a couple of classes and then host the event. All of his lessons are prepared for the day, he just has to deliver the content to his students. Taking a look out the window, he sees a little bit of fog roaming through the tree shaking. "It seems a little chilly outside today. I do love this fall weather," he thinks.

"Gravy, get out of the leaves, or you will get sick. And put a jacket on, because it's cold out here." He can hear his sister's words in his head, playing like his favorite song.

"I may have to go home soon. What if they never find her? Don't think bad thoughts, Terry. I'm sure the police and my family are doing everything to find her," he thinks. Guilt starts to mix into his emotions like vegetables in a pot of hot soup. He tries his best to not think about it and get ready for the day. He hurries and takes a shower, because he feels like he should get to work early today. "The early bird gets the worm. At least when there are enough worms to get," he thinks. He puts his Jason mask in his bag, and the rest of his papers; he contemplates catching a taxi to work on this day. He takes another look outside and sees the leaves radically shaking in the trees. "Let's catch a taxi," he decides.

The taxi is 5 minutes away, so he goes downstairs to wait. He takes a look at his watch: 9:30 am. Arriving at work a little before 10 am, he's the first teacher in the office. His class will start shortly, so he looks over his Halloween trivia to make sure he has all the information correct. He opens up his PowerPoint presentation and begins to scroll through the content:

1. What is the fear of Halloween called?
   Answer: Samhainophobia
2. What is the most popular Halloween candy in America?
   Answer: Skittles

"I think they will have some fun with this," he says to himself. Just as he is scrolling through the PowerPoint, he feels his phone *buzz*. He takes it out of his right pocket and sets it down on his desk.

10:10 am
Naomi: Hey there. I hope you
are well in China. No more news

yet on C. The police and search teams have been looking all over Multnomah Falls. We kinda also have another situation on our hands.

10:15 am
Terry: What other situation?

10:16 am
Naomi: We haven't heard from Jared. He went to a food pod a couple of days ago and we haven't seen or heard from him since.

10:17 am
Terry: What? He just left? Where is he?

10:18 am
Naomi: We don't know. We hope he's not back on his binge again. I know you're at work, so we can catch up later. I love you.

10:19 am
Terry: Please do, and I love you to Nay.

Putting his phone down, he sees that Danni has walked into the office. "Zǎo shàng hǎo Danni," he says. Danni turns to him and smiles.

"You can speak mandarin now, Terry?" she asks.

199

"Far from it, but I have been working on it with my YouTube and Duolingo lessons," he smiles and replies.

"That's really cool, Terry. Do you know how to say good afternoon?" she asks.

"Wǔ ān," he confidently states.

"I see your personal lessons have been paying off," she says.

"Until I have to have a conversation in Mandarin, and then I'm lost," they both laugh, as the rest of the teachers file in for the day.

Terry is getting his things together for his classes, when he hears a familiar soft voice say, "Terry, can I talk to you for a minute?" It's Lena standing in the office doorway.

"I have class in about 10 minutes," he says.

"It won't take that long. I just wanted to quickly go over the rundown for the event," she replies. He felt that something was wrong, because she seemed to be frowning. He follows her to classroom 8. She closes the door and leans up against the door, blinking furiously.

"So, you're going out with Melissa tonight?" she asks.

"We are just going out for dinner tonight. There's nothing special going on," he responds.

"So, you forgot that we were supposed to be going out tonight?" she quickly asks.

"Oh, I'm sorry. We aren't dating, and you ghosted me for months. Also, you're dating the other girl. I didn't think you were very concerned about me," he says, sitting back in his green chair.

"If I wasn't concerned about you, why would I ask you out for dinner? You two are going for hotpot, right?" she asks, as she folds her arms.

"Wait, how do you know about all of this? Did Melissa tell you?" he inquires.

"Don't worry about it," she says.

There is an awkward silence for a moment, as they both have a stare down with each other. "Why do you have to be so difficult?" she asks.

"I'm difficult? I'm difficult? I told you how I felt, and you're the one running around the city with someone else. I can't sit here and wait for you Lena!" he exclaims.

"That's fair. She's your girlfriend?" she asks.

"What? Of course not. That girl from your coffee shop, is she your girlfriend?" he asks back.

"No, of course not!" she exclaims.

"Look, can we go next weekend? Melissa and I are just friends," he pleads.

"That's fine. You better not have sex with her," Lena says, unfolding her arms, as she reaches for the door.

"You are too funny. Anyway, what is your Halloween costume for tonight?" he asks.

"I'm going to be the Queen of Hearts," she responds.

"Like from a deck of cards?" he confusingly asks.

"No, like from your life," she responds.

"That was a dumb joke," he laughs and follows her out the room.

"Anyway, have a good class. I'll see you a little bit before the event," she says.

He goes back to his desk, and she goes back to the front desk. He checks his watch: 10:29 am. He grabs his lessons for his class and leaves his desk. As he walks by the front desk, he locks eyes with Lena and winks at her. Well, it was kind of a wink because he can't wink with his eyes. It was more like a weird squint. The next few classes go well, and it's time for the Halloween event. Some of his adult students have young children, and they had brought their children with them to the event. "Witches, vampires, spider-men, batmen, and pirates," he says to himself, as he briefly scans the office.

He goes into his bag and grabs his Jason mask and a plain white t-shirt that he brought with him. Melissa comes into the office dressed as a witch.

"Are you a good witch or a bad witch?" he asks her.

"Depends on how you make me feel," she responds and winks.

"That's fair," says Terry, as he places his mask on his desk.

"So, you will be Jason?" Melissa asks.

"Yes, and I think someone has some fake blood that I can put on my shirt," he responds.

He continues to get ready and puts on some of the fake blood that one of his colleagues brought. While he is randomly putting fake blood all over his shirt, his coworkers start coming into the office. Danni is a princess, Alex is a vampire, Kelly and Shelly are both werewolves, and Barry is a drifter. Terry finishes putting on his costume and puts on his mask. Only seeing through the two holes in the mask, he steps out of the office and into the main lobby. Terry and Lena make eye contact and the show is ready to begin.

"Thank you all for coming tonight! My name is Terry and this is Lena! Good night and Happy

Halllllllooooowwwwweeennn!" Terry says. The students and their families began to leave with a ton of candy and masks that they decorated. He puts the microphone down and slowly slides off his mask from his face.

"As always, great job you two!" Danni says to them.

"Thanks for all the arts and crafts. I think they really enjoyed painting their own masks," he says, fanning a piece of paper by his face to help cool him off. Hosting always requires him to put out a lot of energy.

"I quite enjoyed that part as well. Your trivia was pretty good too! I did not know that people had a fear of Halloween or that it was a technical term for it," Lena says, as she places a cut-out red heart back onto her custom. Danni nodded her head in agreement.

"Thank you. It seemed like everybody enjoyed themselves," he responds.

He begins to help clean up the lobby of his center. Toilet paper from the mummy wrap game, candy wrappers from all the chocolate bars, and printer paper from the Halloween trivia. Terry gets Barry to help him move one of the tables back into the center of the room. Terry puts the table down and sees Melissa approaching him.

"I really liked your mask. It was scary!" Melissa proclaims.

"You think so? I'm glad someone thought it was scary. I thought Kelly's werewolf costume was scary. She had the whole fangs and makeup thing going," he states.

"I agree, but now she's back to being Kelly," she responds.

"Anyway, are you ready for some hotpot? The place isn't that far from here. It's maybe a 5-minute walk," she says.

"I'm more than ready for some hotpot. Just let me drop my stuff off at my desk, and I'll be ready," he says, taking a quick sip of lukewarm water from his plastic cup.

"That's fine with me. I will use the bathroom to change and meet you back in the lobby," she suggests.

"Ok."

Terry walks back into the teacher's office and passes by the front desk. He sees Lena at the front desk talking to Rachel. Lena had invited Rachel to come to the event to take pictures, because Rachel was a professional photographer. "At least the camera looks professional even if the person taking them isn't," he thinks to himself.

"Nice job Terry! I told Lena already that I truly enjoyed the event," Alex declares.

"I appreciate that, because Lena put it all together, I was just there to host and look good," Terry responds and laughs a little bit.

"Nobody could see you though," says Alex.

"That's true," Terry agrees.

He drops the mask into his backpack and pushes in his chair. "I'll see you all tomorrow," he says, walking out the door. Melissa is sitting in the lobby waiting for him.

"Hey, are you ready?" he asks.

"Yup!" she responds.

As they walk out the door, Terry glances at Lena, and she is looking at what appears to be Rachel's camera. He knows that she is thinking about him. He hears his phone *ding*, and he reaches for his back pocket.

7:05 pm
Lena: No sex!

Terry smiles to himself and puts his phone back into his pocket. "How did you like the event?" he asks her.

"I enjoyed it. I really liked your part with the trivia. That was really cool about the history and customs about the... about the day. It's not a holiday, right?" she asks.

"No, it's not a holiday. It's a day when people can become someone other than themselves, and it is celebrated. I liked your witch outfit," he says, as he presses the button for the elevator.

"Thank you! I found the outfit on Táobǎo," she states.

"I found my mask on Táobǎo," he agrees.

"They have so much stuff," she says, getting onto the elevator.

"Do you have a jacket? I think it's going to be chilly tonight," inquires Terry.

"Yup, It's in my bag," she responds.

They reach their elevator stop and enter the main lobby. Melissa grabs her pink gym bag and pulls a black Nike windbreaker out of it. "I like your windbreaker," he compliments.

"Thank you! You dress really well yourself!" Melissa exclaims, as they walk out of the building.

"Really?" he humbly asks.

"Yes! You always look good and put together. Your clothes are really nice, and you look good in them. Plus, I think you've lost weight since you've been here, right?" she asks.

"You calling me fat?" he chuckles.

"Yes!" she responds.

"That's funny. Actually, I did lose some weight over the past few months. Thank you for noticing," he says.

They walk onto the sidewalk, and she puts the address into her phone. "I thought you said you've been here before," he reiterates.

"I never said that. I said that it's close to the office, and it is. It's only a 5-minute walk," she says, as she starts walking down the street.

It turns out that the hotpot restaurant was a 5-minute walk down the street. They get there and are seated at the front of the restaurant. "Is this seat ok?" she asks.

"It's fine," he responds. They both take off their jackets and sit down opposite each other.

"So this is your first time eating hotpot, right?" she checks, as she moves her chopsticks and her plate closer to her.

"This is my first time here," he says, as he scoots his wooden chair closer to the table.

"We have to get some soju for you as well," she says.

"Soju? Like Korean wine?" He asks.

"That's exactly what it is. Have you had it before?" she asks, as the waiter comes back with some hot water.

"I had it once before, I believe," responds Terry.

"Ok cool. What do you want to eat?" she asks. The waiter comes and places the hotpot down on their table. The waiter puts the burner in the bottom and fills the hotpot with some water.

"Do you know the history of huǒ guō?" she asks him.

"The history of what?" he asks, confused with the Mandarin name for the dish.

"It's pronounced, Huǒ guō," she says slowly.

"That really didn't help," he confirms.

"Anyway, it's believed to have been around since the Jin Dynasty and was a big part of Mongolian dining. The more famous ones are the Chongqing or Sichuan hotpot, which are known for being quite spicy," she explains.

"I didn't know that. Thank you for explaining that to me. That's kinda similar to what we call in the black community as a cookout. At least it sounds similar," he says.

"What's that? It sounds like it's fun," she asks, as she takes a drink of her hot water.

"Well, you know what a grill is, right?" he proposes.

"Yes. You can cook meat on it. Like a barbecue?" she responds.

"Exactly! For us, we come together and have a cookout anytime. Especially in the summer, when the weather is warm. We also have them for special events: birthdays, graduations, holidays. They started becoming more popular in the southern parts of the States and then became more widespread. We also have things like Memphis BBQ and Texas BBQ. The Texas BBQ is more sweet and spicy, while the Memphis BBQ is more known for its spices and dry types of BBQ," he explains.

"That's so interesting. Well, what shall we order?" she asks.

As he takes a look at the menu, he notices the Eye of Horus necklace she is wearing. He takes a look out the window and sees this half-transparent shadow across the street. He stands up and leans forward slightly to get a deeper look.

"Is that my..." he thinks to himself. He is stuck in time and Melissa tries to get his attention.

"Hey! Terry, are you ok?" she asks.

"Yeah, I'm fine. I just thought I saw something," he says, rubbing his eyes.

"You need some water or something?" There seemed to be some concern on her face for his condition.

"I'll take some more water," he responds.

She pours him some more hot water. Then, they decide to order their food for the evening: chicken, broccoli, beef, fish, and some vegetables. The conversation and soju continue to flow during the middle period of the night, where the Earth tangos with the Sun. Terry takes a look at Melissa and wants to ask her a question.

"Can I ask you something?" he asks.

"Yes," she agrees.

"Are your mom and dad both Chinese? I hope that doesn't offend you and if it does, get over it," he says laughing.

"That's an interesting question and no. My mom is Chinese, and my dad is from Kazakhstan," she replies.

"That's why you're so pretty?" he playfully responds.

"I think so," she responds, tilting her head to the side and smiling, like she was taking a glamour shot.

"Well, I have another question for you. Are you single?" he inquires.

"Wow, getting personal I see. I am single. I was in a relationship for a couple of years, and we had a breakup. What about you? Lena, she is your girlfriend, no?" she investigates.

"No, she isn't my girlfriend," he says, quickly glancing out of the side window.

"If you say so," she says with a smirk on her face.

"What happened between you two?" he asks, as he reaches for some more hot water.

"We just grew apart, and I think he was messing around with someone else. It was tough, because I thought I loved him," she states.

"I'm sorry about that," says Terry.

"It's ok. I think the first month after the breakup was really rough. I think I was just having sex with anybody that I matched with on Tinder. But after I had sex with those random guys, I also felt bad afterward," she explains.

"What made you feel bad?" he asks, as the waiter brings out the raw meat.

"Quick question. I have to just cook this myself, right?" he asks.

"Yes! You have to pick up what you want, and put it into the water to cook. And I felt bad because I knew those guys didn't care about me, and I felt like I was giving away a piece of my soul when I had sex with them," she replies.

"Is that why you wear the Eye of Horus necklace?" he asks.

"That's part of it. Also, my sister has one as well. Having that deeper understanding of someone and using your inner strength is really important. Going beyond the physical is important," she says, putting some vegetables into the boiling water.

"I totally agree," he says.

They eat, chat, and drink until about 1 in the morning. Surprisingly, after 3 bottles of soju, Terry doesn't feel like he normally does after drinking all night. His face hasn't swollen up, his throat isn't scratchy, and his skin wasn't bumpy. He feels pretty good for the first time in a couple of months. Melissa has completely encapsulated his thoughts and attention for the evening. The evening sprints by, and he is feeling like he is on cloud nine, and wants the night with her to continue. He's not thinking about Lena, or his family situation back home. He is totally in the moment, and it's serving him well. When we can fully embrace ourselves in the here and now, we become a better version of ourselves. He takes a look at his watch: 1:20 am.

"Are you ready to leave?" he asks.
"Yes, and maybe you could show me your neighborhood," she responds with a smile on her face.
They push in their chairs and begin to head to the door. Melissa pulls out her Alipay to pay for the hotpot. "I'll send you half of the bill," he states.
"Don't worry about it. You can pay for the meal next time we go out," she insists.
The taxi comes within ten minutes and they get into the white car. By the time the taxi came, they had already been kissing for five minutes. Terry sees the driver looking at them through the rearview window, as Melissa pulls his head closer to her forehead.

He shoves his apartment door open, as she comes into his apartment and takes off her shoes. "Can I use your bathroom?" she asks.
"Yeah sure, it's right there," he points to the bathroom.
He drops his bags down and tosses his unfolded clothes into his closet. He can hear the water running in his bathroom, when he thinks he hears a knock at the door.

"Not now," he thinks. He runs over to the door with a white undershirt and blue Nike shorts on. He sees that it's Matt. "Dammit, Matt! Not now!" he thought in his mind. He slowly opens the door, so that Matt could only see his face.

"Hey, Terry. Big Terry what's going on man?" he could tell Matt was drunk.

"Hey! Actually, I have some company right now, so I can talk to you guys later," Terry responds, as he sees one of Matt's friends coming down the hall.

"You got a girl over? Hey y'all, Terry's about to get some pussy!" Matt shouts.

"Would you shut up? Look, I'll text you in the morning," Terry says.

"Is that what you're going to tell her?" Matt says, as he starts to laugh.

"Look, I'll leave you alone. You good on the rubbers?" Matt asks.

"Yeah, I'm ok. See y'all later," Terry says, as he hastily closes the door.

"Is everything ok?" Melissa says, as she comes out of the bathroom.

"Yeah, everything is ok," he says, as he still hears Matt shouting down the hallway. Terry takes a look at Melissa and notices that she has taken her necklace off. She grabs his left hand and walks him to his bed. He slightly kisses her on the left side of her neck and hears her moan in his ear. He throws the royal blue comforter off the bed; she grabs his right hand and stares at him.

"What's wrong?" he asks.

"Do you still have that Jason mask?" she softly asks.

"Yeah, it's in my bag. Why?" he responds, feeling confused by the question.

"Put it on," she demands.

Without asking questions, he jumps out of bed and runs to his bag. He grabs it and puts it on his face. In a few moments, Terry and Melissa connect with each other on a deeper level, as they both reach their pinnacles of pleasure. Sweating on each other's largest organ, they drift off into the night, asleep on different pillows.

XIV

I Have...

Terry continues to teach and go to the gym as his normal routine. They chat every so often, but still haven't really had another date together. By the time the sun reaches its lowest departure, he has only spoken with her a handful of times. He felt that if he gave her some space, then things might get better. Letting go of something or someone is challenging, but activating the will to let go is powerful. It is tough when someone doesn't respond or doesn't seem interested, but he knew that he couldn't control that situation. "I have to stay focused on myself and my goals. If Lena wants to talk, then she knows where I am. I have to stay committed to myself," he thought to himself.

"Over in America, a young woman has been found dead in the mountains right outside of Portland, Oregon. This is just another heartbreaking story of someone who has gone missing in the American Northwest. We go live to our reporter in Multnomah Falls."

Terry is resting on his couch one January afternoon, when he hears this story on the international news channel. He slowly turns his head to the left and looks at the television. Lifting his body out of its sloth, he sees the headline: "Missing Woman Found Dead in Oregon, USA." He blinks his eyes a couple of times, and opens up his mind to really listen to the story.

"Yes, I'm here outside of Multnomah Falls, about 35 minutes outside of Portland, Oregon. It appears to be a young woman who was left at the bottom of one of the trails. The woman appears to have been transferred here from another location. Police have been on the scene for the past couple of hours, as the body has been taken to the coroner's office for identification and further investigation. This area of the Pacific Northwest has unfortunately been a realm for people who have gone missing. Oregon is in the top ten states in America, which report the most missing people. Police and investigators are still working this scene to put the pieces together, and we will report more on it once we receive an update. Back to you Jim," the reporter says.

Terry rubs his eyes, as he wonders if this is Carla, and he reaches for his phone.

> **5:30 pm (to Naomi)**
> Terry: Hey cuz. I just saw a story on the news out here, about a body that was found at Multnomah Falls. I know you said that her car was found right off of Interstate 84. Any news?

He puts his phone down, and sits on the couch for a minute with his face planted in his hands. "This can't be her," he thinks to himself.

"I'll always be here for you, and I'm so proud of you, Gravy. I'm sure mom and dad are proud of you as well," he remembers Carla's words on the day of his college graduation. Standing there in his green graduation robe and his yellow academic hood, a tear rolls down his right eye. Carla, Naomi, Jared, and the rest of his family were at the graduation, and it meant the world to him.

"Do you remember what mom and dad said to us three months before the accident?" Carla asks.

"We will always be there for you, watching over you and protecting you," Carla and Terry both said simultaneously.

"Thank you so much for keeping me straight. Not only just these past couple of years, but my whole life. It's because of you, that I got that track scholarship. Remember when you made me race, James. It was in that race that I really realized I was fast. Luckily for me, it paid for my college," he says to her.

"You worked hard at it, and you deserve it. Now we can send you to Mars!" she exclaims.

"I like that idea," he says, as he hugs her.

Terry always knew that his parents wanted to see him graduate from college. His parents didn't go to college, and couldn't wait for the day they saw both of their kids graduate from college. When the accident occurred, Terry was still in school. It was determined that the driver wasn't paying attention, and ran into the front of his parents' car, killing them instantly. When unfortunate events happen in life, a response can happen in two ways: either they can become the fuel to the fire, or they can be the anchor that holds us down. Terry, with some pushing from his sister, was able to let that situation be the fuel to his fire.

Even though he hadn't reached his initial goal of working for NASA yet, he feels that his time has been well spent after college. "The engineering field is a tough field to break into. I just haven't been able to find the opportunities. Even with a name like Terry, I still can't get the job I want. I can get the interview, because the name on my resume isn't too ethnic. But after the interview, I still can't get a callback," he tells his sister, shortly after his graduation.

"Maybe you should look into teaching. You could go back and be a substitute. I mean what school doesn't need teachers?" she suggests.

"You're right. But teachers don't make any money," he responds.

"It's not about the money Gravy. Did you study engineering to make a lot of money?" she asks.

"Yes!" he emphatically says.

"Look, C, I have to do something. I feel like I'm stuck in life. Just working these part-time gigs isn't enough," he responds.

"Maybe you should really look into it," she states.

5:45 pm
Lena: Hey there 😊. How are you?

Terry checks the message from Lena, and he also sees that he missed a message from Melissa.

5:20 pm
Melissa: Hey Terry. You ok?

Melissa has recently left the company and found a job working for another organization. They haven't really spoken since the night they hooked up, other than brief cordial conversations. Recently, he hasn't been in the best mood and has stopped going to the gym. Terry knows that he needs to get back to it, but his energy hasn't been there the past couple of months. Our bodies know when our energies are off, and our minds and souls will act in ways that are unfamiliar to our bodies. It is up to our spirit and our intuition, to bring our bodies and souls back on one accord.

During his experiences, he hasn't always been totally honest about his emotions. At times, this has caused him to become more reclusive in his life.

5:50 pm (to Lena)
Terry: Hey I'm not that great, honestly.

5:51 pm (to Melissa)
Terry: Hey Mel, I'm doing ok. How are you?

5:52 pm
Lena: What's wrong? I was watching the international news and I saw that they found a missing woman in Portland. Is everything ok?

Terry gets some water and lays back down on his couch. He turns to the TV, to see if there is any more news about the woman who was found in Oregon.

> **5:59 pm (To Lena)**
> Terry: I have been having a rough time.

> **6:05 pm**
> Lena: Do you want to talk about it? I can get a bottle of wine and come over.

> **6:07 pm**
> Melissa: I'm doing ok. Just at my new job. It's a little stressful, but I'm getting to know my new coworkers. I would like to see you again soon. Is that ok?

He is patiently waiting for any message from Naomi, but instead he sees a message from everyone else.

> **6:08 pm**
> Lena: I get off in an hour. I could come to you when I'm done.

> **6:09 pm**
> Terry: I would like that. 😊

> **6:10 pm**
> Lena: Ok. I will see you shortly. Send me your address when you get a chance.

6:11 pm
Terry: Will do. Just give me a
moment.

Terry and Lena can't seem to leave each other alone. He feels that there is some connection there that is deeper than a physical attraction. Even when they aren't physically talking, he feels that she is still thinking about him. The eye contacts, the subtle smiles, the casual winks, and frequent thoughts have completely engulfed him with her aura.
"This year has gone by really quick. How have I made it so far?" he thinks to himself, as he stares up at his white ceiling.

"I'm proud of you, son. High school graduation is special, and I'm happy to see that you've made it," says Terry's dad. "Thanks pops! I couldn't have done it without you, mom, and sis. I almost didn't make it," Terry says back.
"It's ok son. Eleventh grade was so good you had to do it twice," he says to Terry. Terry looks at his dad and chuckles, "you got jokes."

High school was a rollercoaster ride for Terry. He was an all-state track and field athlete, trying to find his way. Up until tenth grade, he was this shy and very reserved kid from Albina. The summer before his eleventh-grade year, Terry had a girlfriend, and it brought out his personality. He started playing sports, had a beautiful girlfriend, and had a part-time job at his local grocery store. During that year, he emerged as a star athlete. He became a county champion in sprinting and started on the basketball team as a small forward. Also in his eleventh-grade year, he found out that his girlfriend was pregnant. Terry told his parents, as he tried to prepare himself for fatherhood. "We will be there to support you as much as possible Terry, but you will have to work more hours and give up a sport," his mom tells him.

About three months into the pregnancy, Terry's girlfriend lost their baby. By this time, he had already given up basketball, as he knew he was better at racing. "You know son, we always told you that this life was not fair and wasn't going to be easy. But you...you provide life with brass knuckles to help knock you out," says his dad, as he drank a cup of whiskey and black coffee in the morning.

"I know, pops," Terry says, as he sits down at the kitchen table. "You will have to repeat the eleventh grade. I'll always be here for you. In your darkest days and when you may feel all alone, scared, or confused. I'll still be there for you. Even when you don't notice it fully," his father says.

"I have to do better, pops," Terry says.

"You will, and I believe in you," his dad says, as he finishes his special coffee.

The last two years of high school, he was locked in and was able to score 1350 on his SATs. Between phenomenal personal statements, two outstanding references, and a great high school track & field career, Terry was able to attend the University of Oregon. "I miss running track & field. I was really good at it. Especially during the last stretch of the race, when I would turn the corner and..." before he could finish his final thought, he felt his phone *buzz*.

6:25 pm
Lena: Would you send me your address?

He was caught up in his own memories.

6:26 pm
Terry: Yes, I will send it now.

He sends her the location and walks over to his fridge to get his water bottle. Taking a couple of sips, and he sits back down on his couch. His head moves frantically between the TV and his phone for any updates. Deep in his spirit, he knows what has happened, but his mind doesn't want to accept the truth. He knows that his sister has most likely been killed and dropped off like a piece of garbage. But who could've done this?

6:31 pm (to Jared)
Terry: Yo, cuz. It's been a minute. I wanted to know if you've heard anything about Carla?

His stomach shouts at him, and he decides to order something to eat.

6:33 pm (to Lena)
Terry: Hey, are you hungry?

6:34 pm
Lena: I could go for a burger and fries from McDonald's. Pllleeeaaaasssee!!! 😇

6:35 pm
Terry: I'll order right now. I'm starving.

6:36 pm

Lena: Thanks love! ♥

Terry opens up his Alipay to place an order for Mcdonald's. As he finishes placing their order, he sees a message come back from Naomi.

6:40 pm

Naomi: Terry, I was going to call and tell you but, it's true. It's true. She's dead. The police found her burned body. The story you saw was true. I can't stop crying.

Terry's phone drops out of his hands, and his eyesight diminishes to the point where he can't see one step in front of him. Silence fills the room, until he lets out an omnipresent wail, and he curls up on his bitter cold hardwood floor.

Bang! *Bang*! *Bang*! He hears three knocks at his door, and he is still laid out on the floor sobbing. "Terry, are you ok?" he hears Lena's voice from outside his door.

"Terry, open the door. I know it was your sister that was found in Oregon. I'm so sorry. I saw it on the news earlier and figured I would text you. Can you open the door please?" requests Lena.

He slowly morphs out of his fetal position, and wipes warm tears from his left eye. Pushing himself up off the floor, and with one foot in front of the other, he walks to the door. Reaching for the lock with his right hand, he sees his handshaking. He grabs his right hand with his left and

222

slowly reaches for the door again. Slowly opening the door, he sees Lena standing there with black Nike stretch pants on and a blue Nike hoodie. They lock teary eyes, and she pulls him close to hug him.

He feels a couple of bags hit him in the back. "What is that?" says Terry.

"Oh, I saw the delivery man on the way up. I also have some wine and chocolate for you as well. I'm so sorry, Terry," she says.

"Thank you for picking up the food and the wine," he responds.

Terry closes the door and takes the food to the island in his kitchen. He takes out two pearly white plates and sets them down. Resting his arms on the counter, he puts his head down for a moment. Lena comes up behind him and puts her right hand on his back.

"Have you heard from your family?" asks Lena.

"My cousin messaged me earlier, but I haven't spoken to anybody yet," he responds. She grabs a tissue from the delivery bag and hands it to him.

"Is there anything I could do for you?" she asks

He takes the tissue and wipes his face. "Thank you so much for asking. I'm just happy you're here, and you picked up the food," he says.

"That's what we talked about earlier, right? Being able to talk and communicate with each other when we aren't feeling our best," she states, helping him to wipe the tears from his eyes.

"You're right. Let's sit down and eat, and crack open up some of this wine," he suggests.

Terry finishes his dinner and then grabs the bottle of wine. "What kind of wine is it?" he asks.

"It's a red pomegranate wine that I like," she responds.

They proceed to open the wine, when the news story comes back on.

"Do you want to turn it?" Lena asks.

"No, I want to see what happened?" he responds.

Grabbing the remote and turning up the volume on the TV:

"We are live back in America, where a young woman was found dead at the bottom of the Multnomah Falls. The victim appears to have been killed somewhere else and transported here. The victim has been identified as 34-year-old Carla Eyvette Jones of Portland, Oregon. The family has been notified, and the police are continuing their investigation. Carla has been missing since May, and it's been almost a year, but now hopefully the family can have some closure. Back to you in the studio," the reporter says.

"What a minute," he says, leaning his head forward.

"What is it?" she wonders.

"I threw up in the bushes in June, right? I found out Carla was missing the next day. The reporter just said that she was reported missing in May," he says.

"Your family didn't mention that before? That's really strange," she responds.

Terry reaches for his phone and immediately looks for Naomi's contact.

7:30 pm (to Naomi)
Terry: I just saw the news out here, and they said that she was reported missing in early June. That's a whole month before you told me! What's going on?

He puts down his phone and begins to cry in Lena's lap. She holds him tight and begins to cry with him. Some after dinner laughs and a half-bottle of wine later, Terry is in a slightly better mood.

"Be careful Gravy. Don't go over there acting like you don't have common sense," he repeats his sister's words, as he throws his third glass of wine in the back of his throat.

"Gravy?" Lena looks at him.

"Have I never told you about my nickname back home?" asks Terry.

"No, you haven't," she says, as she sits up.

"Well, it was a nickname that my sister gave me," he says.

"Gravy? Why Gravy?" she asks.

"I'm going to tell you. When I was a kid, I always loved gravy. You know you can put it over biscuits or whatever you want, right? Well, for whatever reason, I could just drink gravy straight, and I could put it on anything. My parents would have to hide it from me, and my sister would sneak out of her room at night to bring me some. And ever since I was a little kid, she and the rest of my family always called me, Gravy," he says.

"That is like the best nickname ever. Can I call you Gravy?" she wonders.

Terry takes a pause and says, "Sure, you can call me Gravy."

They finish the bottle of wine and order another bottle. The bottle comes and they continue to share life experiences and stories.

"I have to go home," he says.

"Well, I want to come with you," she quickly responds.

"Really?" He's surprised by her response.

"Yes! Li-Na wants to come with you," she says, enunciating her first name.

"Wait, your Chinese name is Lena too?" he asks.

"Yes, but not L-E-N-A, but L-I-N-A. 'Li' means beautiful and 'Na' means elegant in Chinese," she responds.

"Why did your parents name you L-I-N-A?" asks Terry.

"Well, I had a baby sister before, but she died when she was a 1-month-old," she says.

"I'm sorry," he responds.

"Thank you. When my mom got pregnant again, she said that she felt elegant and beautiful. That's where my name came from. I must say that she was right to give me that name," she smiles, as she looks at him.

"Thanks for sharing and she was right to name you that," he says.

He takes another sip of his wine and begins to tear up again. She takes his glass and puts it on the table and says, "I know it's tough." He keeps his head down and allows his heart and spirit to speak up for him.

"It's just been a long year. Things have just been out of sorts lately," he puts his head in his hands, and begins to softly cry.

"You know I'm here for you, right? I care about you, Terry, and I want to be there for you. You're one of the best men I've ever met," she says.

"Really? You think that highly of me?" he asks

She puts both of her soft hands on his cheeks and pulls him in closer. He slightly misses her lips and kisses the side of her mouth. He chuckles in his mind, because he doesn't want to spoil the moment.

"Can I kiss you?" he asks. They begin to kiss, and he opens his eyes, and sees her eyes are open too.

"What are you staring at?" she belts out.

"What are you looking at?" his best rebuttal falls short, as they both start to laugh. She stands up and reaches back with her right hand, to help guide him to the bed. She sits down on the right edge of his bed and pulls his hips closer. Lena helps him take off his t-shirt, and pulls him by his gray undershirt. They continue to kiss, and he strokes her short brown hair, as she slightly moans in his left ear.

"I want you so bad, Terry. I want you to fuck me," she says. He slides his left hand slowly up her right thigh, as his fingertips start to get a little wet. They both slide off her red panties, and she puts her short brown hair in a tight bun. He grabs her by her hips and helps her to straddle him. He reaches for his wallet to look for a condom, and she pushes his wallet away.

"I want it badly," she whispers in his left ear.

He sits up to kiss her, as his body goes limp. He tries to move his arms and legs, but everything has gone stiff.

The two of them are connected, and his body has completely gone limp for a moment. After moments of desire, they both reach the pinnacle of their passions. She curls up next to him, and they both sleep the rest of the night away.

7:40 am

Naomi: Terry, there's been so much going on, and I've been so afraid of telling you. Yes, she's been missing since May, and we haven't heard much from Jared. I have to be honest, because I didn't want you to worry. Especially, with you being all the way over there in China. You're the first one in the family to take a giant step like this, and I wanted you to be focused on your life there. Now, the police think Jared is a person of interest and they are looking for him. Apparently, they have camera footage of C's car at Jared's apartment 2 days before she was reported missing. I'm so sorry Terry, please message me when you get a chance. I love you!

Terry wakes up before Lena and checks his phone; he notices the lengthy message from Naomi. He lifts his head and feels his head banging and realizes that he has a knocking hangover. "Ahhhh, my head hurts," he says, rubbing his right temple. He takes a look at his phone to see the time: 9:00 am. Looking over to the left side of his bed, he sees Lena sleeping on her side. Her arms are folded, and she seems to be in a deep sleep.

He quietly walks to the refrigerator, and picks up his charger along the way. His battery is at 6%. He grabs some water and looks in his cabinet for some aspirin. The phone charger is twisted a little, so he slightly bent it and placed it standing up on the couch cushion to charge. He reads through Naomi's message and becomes upset.

9:05 am

Terry: Hey cuz, I understand, but you still need to tell me. I know you wanted to keep my mind off of things, but I'm still family. What's going on with Jared? That's really strange. Let's talk soon!. I will go to work later today, so I can talk with you before I go. I care about you guys and I just want to know what's going on. I will be home soon. I will be waiting for your message.

He has a couple more sips of water and takes a pill for his hangover. Laying his head back on the couch, he feels his phone vibrating. He notices that it's Naomi calling, so he sits up and swipes for the green accept button.

"Yo Nay! What is going on?" he says to her.

"What's up Gravy? I'm making it the best I can," she says.

Terry can see that Naomi isn't home, but that she is walking around her neighborhood.

"Why aren't you home?" he asks.

"I'm going home soon," she responds, as she appears out from a streetlight.

"Terry, there's been so much going on without you here." She puts her head in her left hand and unleashes some information to him.

"She went missing in May and that's when we officially reported it. We thought that she was just with that guy and that's why she was MIA, but when it went over a month without us hearing from her, I took it upon myself to ring the alarm. This whole time, Jared has been acting so weird and his communication has been sporadic. Her body is currently at the coroner's office, and we are waiting to hear from them. From what I understand, it looks like her body was taken to the Falls, and she may have been killed elsewhere. Jared and his friend Rick have been scaring me lately. I think they are into some other things, but Terry I miss you so much, and I just didn't want to burden you with this. You're the first person in the family to ever do anything like this. Majority of us have never left the area, let alone go across the world to work and live. I just wanted you to focus," she says, as she starts to cry.

Before he can respond, he sees Lena get out of bed with nothing on. Only in her birthday suit, she gets up and walks to the bathroom. Momentarily distracting him, he gets back to his conversation.

"I understand that Nay, but I can't remain focused if you guys are hiding things from me, right? Now, our worst fears are confirmed because she is really dead. And what is going on with Jared? I remember when he missed like 80 days from school because he was always with Rick. I told him about hanging out with Rick because I always thought Rick's uncle was into human trafficking. My pops used to tell me stories about Rick and his connections. But you gotta keep me informed, Nay. I will talk to my boss today and let her know I need to leave within the next couple of weeks. I love you guys, and I just want to be there during the times that we need each other the most. At the end of the day, all we have is family," he says, as he looks at Lena wobble back to his bed.

"Do you need anything?" she mouths as she sits on his bed and lays back down.

He slowly shakes his head side-to-side, and looks back at his phone.

"I'm so sorry, Terry. This is not what I wanted. I just wanted things to be perfect for you," Naomi says.

"I'm not only doing this for me, but I'm also doing this for the whole family. I have to work today, but I'm going to ask my boss for bereavement leave to come home," he says.

"Ok, Gravy. I love you and the family appreciates what you are doing. Did I hear a noise in the background?" she asks. She always knew when he was preoccupied.

"No. What are you talking about? he asks.

"Let me see her?" she says.

"See who? There's nobody here," he responds quickly. He tries to convince her that Lena isn't in his bed.

"Hi, whoever is there!" Naomi shouts over the phone, as she walks into her house.

"She's probably naked. Did you two have sex? You better have wrapped up," she says.

"Look, nobody is here, and I need to get ready for work, so I'll talk to you tomorrow," he states.

"Suuurrree! Well, I will call you when we hear from the coroner and if we hear from Jared. I love you, Gravy," she says.

"I love you too, Nay," he states.

He slides the red button across his phone screen and places his phone down for a moment to gather his thoughts. Questions are sprinting through his mind: "Where is Jared? Why did she really wait to tell me?" Terry can't help but develop a thriving migraine at this point. He gets up to grab some more aspirin and water; he looks over to his bed.

"Hey are you ok?" he asked her.

"I'm ok. How are you? Come here," she demanded, as she turned over to her right side. This movement exposed her upper body a little bit.

"You're truly beautiful. And I'm not just saying that because we had sex last night," he says, as he made his way over to the bed with some aspirin in his hands.

"I'm ok. I just have to talk to Danni today and let her know that I have to go back to the states," he tells her.

"Does she know what's going on?" Lena asked.

"Yeah, well she doesn't know everything. She knows that my sister has been having some issues, but she doesn't know about her missing or dying. I didn't want her to think I couldn't perform my job if I had problems back home. I didn't want to create any excuses," he tells her, throwing the aspirin to the back of his mouth.

"That makes sense. I still want to come back with you. Whenever the official day for the funeral is, I want to come meet your family and be there for you," she says, sitting up as the covers fall down exposing her front side.

"Uhhhh yeah. Sorry, I got distracted for a moment. But if you really want to come with me, I would love that," he says, as he is still looking at her exposed front.

"Just let me know. I think my parents are going to hand the business over to me at some point," she states.

"Really? So, they are finally going to give you the coffee shop?" he responds.

"I think so. In the meantime, I think you should get back in bed and have some fun before you have to go to work," she says.

Terry throws his water on the floor and hops back into bed with Lena. They go for another hour, and he realizes that it's time to go to work. They jump into the shower together, and get cleaned up. Lena lives across the street from the office, so they both catch a taxi downtown.

During the ride, she is gripping his hands, and they are kissing the entire time. Terry notices the glances from the driver. Arriving downtown, they remain attached to the soul from the previous night as they get out of the car. The northeastern winds continue to attack their winter clothes: Lena with her blue jacket and Terry with his black bomber jacket.

"I have to run upstairs and get ready for my classes. I already told Danni that I would need to talk to her about something important. We will meet after my second class, I believe," he says.

"Ok, text me when you are done talking to her. Also, let me know when you know more information about going home, because I'm coming with you. I'm going to nap and then go to the gym," she says.

"Ok pretty lady! I'll text you in a few," he responds.

They share a warm embrace in the bitter coldness of winter. She kisses him for what seems like an eternity. She tries and walks off, but he pulls her back into his chest with his right hand.

"You know I have to go, handsome," she says, kissing him quickly on his icy lips.

"I know. I just didn't want to let you go yet," he says.

Embracing for one more hug, she stands up on her toes and throws her arms around his neck. She comes right up to his chin; she has to stretch out for a full hug. Momentarily disconnecting, she walks across the busy interaction towards her high-rise apartment. He heads into the office and scans his code to enter into the main lobby of the building. Walking into his center, he sees Danni sitting at the front desk, and their eyes attach when he walks in.

"Hey Terry, how are you today?" she asks.

"I'm doing ok for the most part. Are you still able to talk this afternoon?" he asks, as he gets some water from the cooler.

"Yeah sure. Just let me know when you are done with class, and we can go to classroom 3 to chat," she says to him.

He agrees and walks into the teacher's office. "Hey guys," he says in a very low energetic voice.

"Hey, what's going on, Terry? How are you?" Barry wonders.

"I'm making it, I guess," Terry says.

"You guess? Everything alright mate?" Barry responds.

"Yea. Well, I'll talk to you about it later," Terry states.

Terry sits down and turns on his computer to get the day started. His head is cloudy with grief, agony, sadness, confusion, and lots of regret. "Was it the right move to leave my family? If I was still home my sister would still be alive. I have to go home and stay home. I wonder if...I wonder if.." his thoughts fade out.

"Hey, Terry, I was wondering if we could plan the next center event together. I really like the job you and Lena did with the Halloween event," Barry interrupts Terry's personal grief report.

"I'm sorry. What did you say, Barry?" he asks.

"Something wrong mate? I hope you can talk about it later. What I was saying is that I would like to host an event with you soon. I really think you and Lena did a great job with the Halloween event. It was bloody brilliant, mate, and I think everybody enjoyed it," Barry explains.

"Oh, I appreciate that and sure. We can talk about it later when we get off work," Terry suggests.

Barry agrees and goes back to printing out his lesson plans for the day. Terry looks at his watch on his left wrist: 11:25 am. Just enough time to print out some papers and make some coffee. Getting up to walk to the coffee machine, he feels his phone vibrate. He puts his right hand in his pants pocket to grab his phone.

11:25 am

Melissa: Hi Terry! Are you working today?

Since the time they connected, he hasn't really been interested in speaking with her. Especially when the one he wants, Lena, is showing him the attention he wants.

> **11:26 am**
> Terry: Yeah, I'm at work now. What do you want or need?

> **11:27 am**
> Melissa: Oh ok. I want and need to talk with you soon?

> **11:27 am**
> Terry: I don't know. I'm going back home soon.

> **11:28 am**
> Melissa: Like, back to America?

> **11:28 am**
> Terry: Yea. The police just found my sister dead in the mountains.

> **11:29 am**
> Melissa: I'm so sorry, Terry. I thought I saw that on the international news yesterday. Do you need anything?

> **11:29 am**
> Terry: I'm ok. Thanks.

11:29 am
Melissa: I still would like to talk to you. I think you need to know something before you leave.

11:30 am
Terry: Maybe next week. I have to teach now.

11:31 am
Melissa: Ok. I'll keep taking care of myself.

He takes his coffee and cream and goes back to his desk. He mixes his coffee together, grabs his papers, and then heads into classroom 3 for his group lesson.

The afternoon quickly approaches and Danni approaches Terry at his desk.

"Hey Terry, do you have about 5 minutes?" she asks.

"Yes, I'm free," he responds. They head out of the office and walk towards the classrooms.

"We can go into classroom 3," she instructs.

They walk into classroom 3, and he closes the door behind them. They both sit down across from each other.

"So, what's going on, Terry?" she asks.

"Well, I have some things going on back home. I know we spoke earlier about my sister missing," he pauses, and bits down on his bottom lip.

"Oh no Terry! Is she dead?" Danni asks, slowly cupping her mouth with both hands.

He slowly nods his head up and down.

"Yes, she is. They just found her at the bottom of a mountain not too far from where I grew up," he says.

"I'm so sorry, Terry. How are you doing? What can we do to help?" she asks.

Terry is taken aback by Danni's genuine concern and empathy.

"I will have to go home soon. My family is going to let me know the details about funeral arrangements, then I will have a more concrete date," he explains.

"I think I can understand how you feel. When I was studying in the UK, my cousin was taken and sold," she responds.

"Sold?" Terry asks.

"Yes, she was taken by some guy she was dating and sold into human trafficking. We haven't seen her since, and this was almost 5 years ago," she says.

"That's intense Danielle. What did you do?" he asks.

"My semester was almost over, so I came back to Hebei Province when I was done," she responds.

"It's such a wild experience. It was one of my biggest fears about moving over here. What if something happened to my family or friends? I wouldn't be there to help," he says.

Although Danni was a couple of years younger than Terry and his manager, they had a genuine understanding and respect for each other. Danni was wise and reflective, and Terry appreciated that. Not only from a manager, but also as a person. Being wise isn't always attained by someone who is older.

"I understand that. It can be a difficult decision to make a move like what you did. But I must tell you that we love having you here. The students adore you, and the staff admires your work ethic. Personally, I just really enjoy having you on the team. I don't want you to leave, but I understand. We do have bereavement leave that you can use. Would you want to come back to China?" she asks.

"Thanks Danni. Honestly, I am not sure at the moment. I think I need to be with my family for a little bit," he responds.

"Totally understood mate," her British lingo appears at times.

"I will keep you updated on what is going on, but I think I will have to leave within the next couple of weeks," he says.

"Keep me updated, and I will work with you to get you home," she says.

They both stand up and Danni comes over to give Terry a hug.

"We are here for you, Terry," she says.

"Thank you, Danni," he says, as a single tear falls from his right eye.

He wipes his eye, and opens up the door. They both walk out of the classroom and go on with the rest of their day.

XV

What Are Your Intentions?

That night after work, Barry and Terry go to the bar for what Terry knows will be the last time they will hang out. Terry walks into the bar and sees the same bartender, Bobby, from the night that he passed out.

"Hey, Barry. And it's...uhhhh...Timmy, right?" Bobby guesses wrong.

"Close, it's Terry. And Bobby, right?" Terry guesses right.

"Yeah, that's right man. I see you're doing much better from the last time I saw you," Bobby says, grabbing two menus from behind the bar.

"Much better. Thanks again for helping this Měi guó rén out," Terry says.

"No problem, man! You're my favorite American. Well, you and Tom Hanks. Anyway, what will you two have? Last time, I believe you got the Dark and Stormy," Bobby states.

"Yes, let me get just one. I think that will do me right for the night," Terry says.

"And I'll just have a Tsingtao," Barry says.

While Barry is talking to Bobby, Terry takes out his phone. Still perplexed by the situation with his sister, he decides to look at his sister's Instagram, to see if there are any recent posts.

"So, what's going on, Terry?" Barry says, looking at Terry.

"The police found my sister's dead body at the bottom of a mountain yesterday. They don't know what happened, and I'll be leaving China soon," he says.

"I'm so sorry mate. I couldn't imagine that type of pain. If you need anything, please let me know," Barry says.

"I appreciate that man. I think I just really need to be home with my family," Terry responds.

"I understand that. Have you talked with Danni already?" Barry says, as his beer is placed in front of him.

"I spoke with her today. She told me to let her know when I would need to leave," Terry says, as his Dark and Stormy arrives.

Bobby wipes down the space next to Terry, as the guests leave the bar. Terry looks across the street, and sees a transparent silhouette outside the bar window. Terry jumps out of his seat and runs out of the bar, but when he gets outside, the figure is gone. "What was that? That looked like someone I know," as Terry was finishing his thoughts, Barry came out after him.

"Hey mate, you ok? You bloody scared us half to death," Barry says, trying to catch his breath.

"I'm fine. I just thought I saw..." Terry stutters.

"You saw what?" Barry asks.

"Look, it's nothing. Let's just go back inside," Terry demands.

"Hey Terry, I'm not sure what you are seeing, but I wanted to tell you to trust your gut feeling. When our spirit is trying to guide us, we need to take the back seat. Don't second guess yourself and what you are feeling or seeing. The things we want are in plain sight, but we are looking at everything else. We are too distracted, but when the world wants to connect with you, it will find a way. Many people will run from or ignore these feelings and intuitions; therefore, remaining in a willful state of ignorance. You owe it to your future self and family to listen and relinquish," Barry says.

"I know, but what if I don't know how to listen and relinquish? What if I don't know how to do that stuff?" Terry asks.

"Be quiet and listen. Stop moving so fast. You're too quick to react hastily and not to hastily think," Barry responds.

Terry looks up at the sky and sees that it is a crescent moon tonight. "You gotta let things go, Terry," he tells himself.

They both begin to walk back to the bar, as Bobby comes running outside.

"Hey, you guys ok?" Bobby said.

"Yes, we are ok. And you're about thirty seconds too late. Come on, let's go back inside," Barry suggested.

Back inside the bar, the three acquaintances toast and take a quick sip of their individual drinks. Terry goes back to his phone momentarily and looks at Carla's old pictures. There were some pictures of her with family at different events: birthday parties, weddings, and a graduation. Some pictures of Carla traveling around the Northwest: Seattle, Portland, and Tacoma. "Nothing seems strange or out of the ordinary," he tells himself. She was smiling and was usually next to Naomi or Jared in the photos. In many of the pictures, Carla was pointing at Naomi and Naomi was pointing back with big smiles on their faces.

As he continues to quickly swipe through the pictures, he notices one picture from early January. About 4 months before she was actually reported missing. He notices that Naomi and Carla both had the same necklace. A silver apple necklace hanging around both of their necks. The necklace that Carla had, was bought by their mom and dad. "So, Naomi bought a silver apple necklace too?" he thinks to himself.

"How are you feeling?" Barry asks, as Terry's thoughts come back into focus.

"Honestly, I'm sad, frustrated, angry, confused. All the above, I guess. I just want to continue teaching and focus on that. Everybody has their different ways of grieving, and I do it by working. Keeps my mind off of things," Terry explains.

"That's totally understandable. Will Lena go with you when you go back to the states?" Barry asks.

Terry pauses for a moment and looks at Barry. Barry smiles and tilts his head to the right, as he raises up his eyebrows. "Lena said that she wants to come, but she may have to arrive after me," Terry states.

"What are your intentions with her?" Barry asks.

"My intentions?" Terry answers a question with a question.

"Yes, your intentions. What are your intentions with Lena? I know you two already hooked up," Barry says.

"How do you know all of this stuff?" Terry asks.

"I listen to what the universe is telling me," Barry responds.

"Intentions? I've never thought about it. I like her and want her to be my girlfriend, but I think she is still seeing that girl. I have to go home, and would like her to join me," Terry says.

Terry takes another sip of his Dark and Stormy; he looks up at the television screen and sees some basketball highlights. "I can't wait to go home and go to a Blazers game," Terry thinks to himself.

"You're bewildered mate! It doesn't sound like you have much of a plan for you and Lena. Or even for yourself," Barry says, taking a final sip of his beer and putting the glass on the mahogany bar top.

"I mean, I can't jump steps. She would have to be my friend first, right?" Terry responds.

As Terry reaches for his drink, he sees a familiar face walk into the bar. He notices the same pink shoes, long black hair down to her waist, sun-kissed skin, and has those same raspberry lips. "Is that Melissa or the girl from the elevator?" he thinks to himself.

"There should be some type of intentions, Terry. If you really like her, you don't have to jump to marriage and kids. Make that the ultimate goal, but break it down into smaller goals. I think she likes you as well, and it seems like you two have a good friendship. I would argue that it is more important that you have a good relationship with yourself," Barry says.

"What do you mean?" Terry asks.

"You two like each other and want to be with each other. That's great! Part of your turmoil is that neither one of you seem to have a good relationship with yourself. Look, we all need and want relationships with other people, right? But we often neglect the one relationship that sets the prospects for every other relationship in our lives: the relationship with self," Barry says.

"That's a really good point. I guess I never really thought that much about intentions and knowing myself. I like her and want to see where things could go. I'm still talking to other women, and I'm sure she is still talking to other people. We haven't made anything official. At least not yet," Terry explains.

"Make your intentions clear when dating or trying to date. It saves you a lot of pain and agony in the end. If it's fun and very casual that you are looking for, then state it. If it's serious and a relationship you are looking for, then state it. Don't have people in limbo, because that makes you a bad person. And most importantly: know thyself, Terry," Barry says.

"You got some good points," Terry says.

"Some points?" Barry asks and laughs.

"All your points are good," Terry laughs back, as he takes another look at the young woman who walked in the bar. Just as he goes to order another Dark and Stormy, he feels his phone vibrate.

9:45 pm

Melissa: So you don't want to speak?

"Ahh no," Terry says out loud.

"What's wrong mate? Hey, is that Melissa?" Barry asks.

"I think so," Terry says, as he sees Melissa get out of her seat. Terry sees that there is another guy sitting down at the table Melissa just left.

"Hey, guys! How are you?" she says, as she gives both of them hugs.

"We are doing alright. How's the new job going?" Barry asks.

"It's going ok I guess. How are things at the center?" she replies with a follow-up question.

"She's still hot," Terry thinks to himself. Just as he finishes his thought, he sees the guy she came in with stand up.

"Things are going ok, but we miss you," Barry says.

The guy starts walking over to the bar, and he appears to be breathing quite heavily. Terry knows this guy is trouble, and puts his phone in his pocket. Terry directs his attention to the guy walking over, and sees that his fists are balled up.

"It's so good to see you two. How are you, Terry?" she says, turning her attention to Terry.

"I'm doing ok," Terry says, as he sees the gentlemen come up to him shouting in Mandarin.

Terry stands up and clutches his fists, as Melissa and Barry try to jump in between them. Before they could jump in between them, the man took a swing at Terry's face. Terry goes under the punch and grabs the man's t-shirt and pulls him close. Terry pushes him back and the man throws another punch. This time, the punch connects with the left side of Terry's face. Terry throws a counterpunch with his right hand, but the man dives under it. Barry steps in front of Terry, as Melissa pushes the man to the back of the bar. Bobby runs from behind the bar, but the battle has concluded.

Barry pushes Terry outside the bar and rushes him away from the front door. They escape to a side corner about 20-feet from the bar.

"What the hell was that, mate? Did you even know that lad?" Barry says, trying to catch his breath.
"I don't know who that was. He sucker-punched me! Son of bitch!" Terry says, as he touches his left cheek.
"Hey, we gotta get outta here. Let's leg it to my place and get away from this," Barry suggests.
"Sounds good," Terry responds.
They both take simultaneous peaks down the street and briskly walk back to Barry's apartment.

"Bobby wants to know if you are ok. He apologizes and says that the guy was Melissa's cousin, but he didn't say what was wrong with him," Barry says, still trying to catch his breath.
"Tell him I'm ok. It's not his fault. I just want to know who that guy was," Terry says.
"Bobby says that he is not calling the cops and says he will talk to us later," Barry responds.

They finally arrive at Barry's high-rise building and get to his room. The left side of Terry's face has started to turn black and blue, and it looks like he has a golf ball hidden in his cheeks. Barry gives Terry a pack of ice from his freezer. "That's what I mean about intentions. His intention was to punch you in the face and he did it," Barry says.

Terry takes off the pack of ice and raises his eyebrows at Barry.

"Intentions can hit hard, I guess. I'm kinda in the relationship purgatory. Sometimes I want to be in a relationship, and sometimes I want to be a hoe," Terry says, putting the ice pack back on his face.

They both chuckle, and Terry winces as the cold seeps into his bruise. Terry has no idea who this guy was, and he wants to text Melissa.

"Don't send a mad message, especially when you are mad at the person. It will cause more problems. Wait until you have a clear mind and thought process. Right now, your thoughts are filled with anger and revenge. It never ends well," Barry says, pushing Terry's hand closer to his bruise.

Terry looks down at his phone for a moment and realizes that Barry is absolutely right. He still doesn't want to put his phone down because he is angry. Terry knows that clearer minds must prevail, and it's better to control his emotions than to let them run wild like a gazelle.

"I'll put the phone down and just chill. I'll have to go home soon. I guess I didn't make my intentions clear with Melissa. Why do we always have to make our intentions clear and know thyself? Let's just have fun," Terry says, as he flares his right arm up and down to help him visually make his point.

"I get what you mean. You know, when you don't make intentions clear, and you don't know yourself, you can end up punched in the face. It's just a bad mix. Learn to turn your lead into gold, Terry," Barry says.

"Who are you, an Alchemist? Terry responds.

"Learn to turn those raw emotions and desires into an illuminated or spiritual being," Barry explains. Terry hears his phone vibrate.

10:15 pm
Melissa: Terry, I'm so sorry about tonight. My cousin apologizes as well. But I do need to talk to you before you go back to America.

Terry looks at Barry, and he puts the phone down on the wooden dining room table. Terry sits down in a metal dining room chair, and he continues to assist the relationship between the ice pack and his face.

"I won't respond tonight," Terry says.

"Good," says Barry, "go home and get some rest."

10:19 pm
Lena: Hey are you ok?

"I think I might do that. I don't want to get in any more trouble tonight," Terry says, still slightly wincing, as he gently touches his bruise.

"That's a good idea, mate. And you can take the ice pack with you!" Barry exclaims.

10:21 pm (to Lena)
Terry: Yea. I'm ok.

Terry continues to press the ice against his cheek, as he gets ready to leave Barry's apartment. "I will keep you updated, bro. You know, relationships are just so complicated. They shouldn't have to be," Terry says.

"That's because you complicated the most important relationship," Barry says, looking at Terry.

"I know. I get it, you are all spiritual and deep," Terry responds back with a slight laugh.

"I'm going to guess that you shagged her and the intentions weren't clear," Barry says.

"The intentions were clear, we shagged it and that was it. These are your slang words I'm using of course," Terry responds.

"Are you sure? Did you even look at each other?" Barry asks.

Terry thinks for a moment; he remembers putting on the Jason mask and Melissa taking off her necklace. "Why did she want me to put on that mask? Why did she take off her necklace?" he quickly thinks to himself.

"You seem like a bright lad, Terry. You don't need to be going through this drama and madness. Think about your relationships and what you want out of them. Think about what you want from yourself," Barry suggests.

"I see what you mean. I think I just need to go to sleep tonight," Terry responds.

10:33 pm
Lena: I heard you got into a fight?

"You get some rest. Sleep and recover and go at it again in the morning, mate. I will keep you and your family in my

251

spirit. Remember to think Terry! Think!" Barry says, as he taps the left side of his head.

> **10:34 pm**
> Terry: How did you know? News in this city travels fast.

"Alright man, well let me leave. I'll text you when I get home. Thanks for everything man, I really do appreciate it! I know sometimes it may seem like I don't. Just...thank you," Terry says, as he reaches out his left hand. Barry stands up and looks at Terry. He shakes Terry's hand with his left hand and reaches out to give him a hug. They hug for a quick breath; Terry grabs his phone and leaves out the door.

His mind is racing, and he can't figure out why this guy would punch him. "What is going on with Melissa?" He reaches for his phone to message Melissa, but he hears Barry's voice in his head, "Don't send a mad message, especially when you are mad at the person. It will cause more problems. Wait until you have a clear mind and thought process. Right now, your thoughts are filled with anger and revenge. It never ends well."
Terry realizes that Barry is right, and he decides not to text Melissa. He decides to text Lena instead.

> **10:35 pm**
> Lena: You know, this is the expat area. News gets around fast. Are you ok? Where are you?

He heads to the elevator and Barry's words continue to bounce off the fences of his mind. "Remember to think, Terry!" Terry gets into the elevator and descends to the lobby of the building.

> **10:37 pm**
> Terry: I'm doing ok. My face is a little swollen but I'm fine. 😔
> I'm just leaving Barry's. What are you doing?

Ding! The elevator reaches the bottom floor, and he steps off. Every breath seems to puncture the left side of his face. "He got me good," Terry says to himself. The Crescent Moon's focus is on Terry, as he enters into the unknown of the night. His breathing becomes normal, and his anger descends back down into his soul. Letting go is a skill that has to be learned over time. The freedom of letting go, allows the opportunity for more self-discovery. He knows that letting go of this situation is the best option, and he should speak with Melissa in the morning. "Maybe I didn't make my intentions clear? Maybe I truly don't know who I am," he thinks to himself.

> **10:39 pm**
> Lena: I'm so sorry. Some people are just jerks. I can give you some sports cream to help with the swelling. If you feel like it, you can walk over.

> **10:41 pm**
> Terry: I'll come over. Give me five minutes to walk over.

10:42 pm

Lena:

He starts walking to Lena's apartment, as he has become more familiar with the city after months of living there. He now has his favorite local bar, favorite local coffee shop, his gym, and his favorite place to get gravy with his dinner. There's a restaurant that serves gravy with western food, and he was ecstatic when he found it. Just like he was ecstatic when he first got off the plane in Beijing, when he took his first trip on the speed train to Tianjin, when he could finally understand five words in Mandarin, when he first asked Lena out, and many others. Now, he will have to pass on many more first, in order to go back home.

Making his way to Lena's, he zips up his jacket a little tighter and picks up his pace. Remembering that he had some gloves in his bag, he reaches for them and puts on his blue woolen gloves. Even though Terry is from Portland where it gets cold in the winter, his bones still freeze as he gently walks down the street.

10:45 pm
Lena: Can you pick up some water from the store before you come over? And some Chocolate?

10:46 pm
Terry: Yes, of course. What kind of chocolate?

10:46 pm
Lena: Doesn't matter. Thank
you. 😍

The message stops Terry in his tracks, as he quickly turns around and goes into the store. He walks into a 7-Eleven and picks up a bottle of water and some chocolate-covered peanuts. "You know I'm allergic to peanuts, Gravy? But thank you anyway. Why do you always give me stuff that you know I can't eat? And I wouldn't eat them if I could, you know I've been back in the gym with Nay," Carla says. "I'm sorry. I'll guess I'll just eat all the chocolate-covered peanuts myself," he responds.

"You do that on purpose," she states.

"Things don't happen on purpose, we all have intentions whether we acknowledge them or not," he says, as he walks away eating the chocolate-covered peanuts.

"You suck! Well, I want you to stay safe on purpose when you go overseas. I don't know when I'll see you again," she says, getting up from the glass kitchen table.

"Let's see: Thanksgiving, Christmas, New Year's Eve and so on. Look C this isn't 'goodbye,' it's 'see you later,' just remember that," he says.

"It better be," she responds, walking out of the cold kitchen.

Terry feels something coming down the left side of his face, as he looks up at the night sky. "I think it's snowing," he says to himself. He puts the water and chocolate covered peanuts in his bag and shuffles a couple of blocks to Lena's apartment. He is still shivering, as he pulls off his gloves and pushes the button to get the elevator's attention.

"I had no idea it was going to snow tonight. My first time experiencing snow in China. Maybe I'll have a snowball fight," he thinks to himself, as the elevator reaches Lena's floor.

He gets to the front of her door, and she opens it before he could even knock. "How did you know it was me?" he asks, shaking some early snow off of his face.

"I heard you coming because you were stomping your feet," she says.

"Oh, I thought it was the special connection we share," he replies.

"Not at all," she playfully states.

"Hey, I didn't know it was supposed to snow tonight. Will it snow a lot?" he wonders.

"Do I look like your personal weather girl?" she says.

"Yes," he answers, as he grabs her waist and pulls her close.

They kiss and his heart goes into a full sprint, as she puts her arms around his neck. He gently lifts her by her waist and quickly puts her back down.

"Oh, what happened to your face? That guy must've really sucker-punched you," she says, looking at his swollen left cheek.

"I really don't know what happened tonight," he says, as he gives her the water and chocolate-covered peanuts.

"Oh, my favorite! Start from the beginning?" she demands, as she sits on her black suede couch, and he follows behind her. "Me and Barry…" she cuts him off and says, "You mean Barry and I. You're an English teacher, and you should know this," she explains.

"Can I tell my story?" he asks. "Sorry," she responds before drinking some of the water.

"Anyway, Barry and I were at the bar tonight just having a quick drink, when I saw Melissa come in with some guy. I didn't pay it no mind. I'm talking to Barry and the bartender, minding my business, when she comes up to us. I thought she was just coming to quickly speak, which she did at first. I asked her about her new job. While we were talking, I noticed that the guy had stood and started walking over to us. I saw that his walk was almost a sprint, and when he came up to me, he was shouting in Mandarin. Before Barry, Melissa, or the bartender could jump in between us, he took a swing at me and I ducked it. I grabbed him and pushed him back. Then, he took another swing, and it connected with the left side of my face. I threw a counterpunch but he went under it. After that, people had jumped in and Barry pulled me out of the bar, and we ran away. What was all that about?" Terry says, as he is acting out the entire fight. Lena is sitting there eating her snack, like she was watching a new movie.

She smirks at him, shakes her head, and rests her chin in the palm of her right hand.

"Nothing to say? It was so random. The bartender didn't call the cops, and we went to Barry's apartment," Terry says.

He hears Lena take a deep breath before she says, "I know you had sex with her."

Terry is puzzled for a moment and sits down on the couch. "What are you talking about, Lena?" he asks.

"I know you and Melissa had sex. It's ok, I just know that you two had something going on," she states.

He sits there for a second before he speaks, as he is trying to think of a way to deny what she just told him. "What are you talking about?" he asks.

"Seriously?. I knew she had her eyes on you from the moment she started asking questions about you. It's ok, she's really cute. Did you enjoy it?" she asks, popping a chocolate-covered peanut in her mouth.

"How did you find out?" he confusingly responds.

She just stares at him.

"We did hook up, but it was only once," he explains.

"It's ok. We weren't boyfriend and girlfriend, and I kinda ghosted you for a little while there," she says.

"You really did. Well, I knew you slept with the other girl. Rachel is her name, right?" he responds.

She pauses for a minute and puts one more peanut in her mouth. "I did. I was just exploring my options at the time," she says, chewing the remains of the peanut.

"Seems like we were both out there trying to get some," he jokingly says.

She throws a peanut at him, as they both laugh, and he puts his phone down on the table. "Hey, where's Riley?" he asks.

"Awww, do you miss her? She is with my parents. They wanted her to stay with them for a little while," she responds.

"I thought Riley was pretty cool," he states.

He takes a moment to look outside her window, and he sees the ground protected by the snow. The light from the moon bounces off of the snow and gives the city an extra sparkle to it.

"If it keeps snowing like this, I'll have to stay here tonight," he says.

"That's fine. You might have to take out the trash," she demands.

"I'm not your boyfriend, and I'm not doing chores," he smiles, as he looks at Lena.

"What are we?" she asks.

"What do you mean?" he responds.

"When you introduce me to your family in America, what will you tell them? 'This is a local Chinese girl I met, who has flown across the world to support me in my time of need. Oh, and we are just friends.' That sounds strange to me," she explains.

"She has a good point there," he thinks to himself.

He knew that he wanted to be with her, but he also enjoyed being on his own in a new country. The feelings he had for her didn't fade, they were just different. Best practices would include them being friends before lovers. But they already had sex, and they know that they've had sex with other people. At this point in their situationship, it's hard to go in reverse. Growing and being open with each other is the best way forward. One can't undo what's already been done.

"Is it impossible to work on our friendship and date at the same time? I think we've learned quite a lot about each other in these past few months, even if we weren't talking," he says.

"I would like that. So, are we dating other people?" she asks.

"I don't want anybody but you. Since I've come to China and you walked through those doors at work, you've consumed my soul. Every night, every week, every month, and everything in between has been finding ways to make you pay attention to me. Even if it involved trying to make you jealous. I feel like you…I feel like you..I feel like you see me Lena," he says, sitting down next to her on her black suede couch.

Terry has never really opened up in a relationship or friendship, quite like he has with Lena. His parents cared for him and his sister, but they had their own problems. For a good portion of his childhood, his parents were separated. Only getting back together shortly before he graduated from high school. They still lived in the same house, but his mom would often stay with some of his cousins. It was difficult for him to recognize and understand what a successful relationship looked like. Dating for him as a young man was a turbulent occasion, because he was trying to figure things out on his own.

He decided to stay closed up and emotionally unavailable for most of his dating life, which caused his heart to break and caused him to break hearts. No one is immune from heartbreak, it is a part of life and he understood this. After his ex-girlfriend lost their baby, he performed emotional reconnaissance to his relational brick wall. He stayed that way through the rest of his 20s and when he decided to move to China, he hoped for new relationships and friendships. He wasn't expecting to meet someone who would break down his relational brick wall.

Those times when we are not expecting to meet someone special, are the same times when special comes knocking on the door. Or, in Terry's case, walking into an office. Lena has gotten through to Terry, to the point where he is trying and putting in an effort to be a better man. Not necessarily for her, but for himself. If he could be a better person for himself, he knows that everybody else connected to his life would benefit.

Lena looks at him and grabs his cheeks. "I'm sorry for not being clear about my intentions at the beginning. You have opened up my eyes to things I've never even thought of. Growing up, there was no way that I thought I would date a foreigner. You've changed my perspective on life and allowed me to be myself around you. Being with you gives me a sense of ease and understanding I've never felt before. And I don't care how you introduce me to your family, as long as I'm there," she says.

They lean in for a brief kiss, then sit there holding each other. The wind starts to pick up, as it knocks on the panoramic windows of her apartment. She unravels out of their embrace; looks out the window and sees that the snow has gotten taller over the past few moments.

"I think you will be staying the night. I'm pretty sure the subways are closed, and I think it may be tough getting a taxi or DiDi right now," she says with a smile on her face.

"It sounds like a sleep over to me. I may need a change of clothes," he assumes.

"I think you will be fine," she responds to him. Terry heads to the bathroom, as Lena finishes her sentence. The drinks from earlier have finally caught up to him, as he starts to feel tired. Coming out of the bathroom, he sees that she is curled up on the couch playing on her phone. He sits down next to her and gently rubs her lower back and her feet.

"I may have to meet you in America. I told you that my parents are handing the business over to me. Well, they are going to transfer it over to me quite soon," she explains.

"Wait. What is happening?" he asks.

"My parents still have co-ownership of the shop, but they have been intending to give it to me. They've been fighting over it for the past few years, and it's caused a lot of anger in my family," she tells him.

He is a little stunned, and any sense of word cohesion has left his brain.

"You don't seem to be too upset about it," he notices.

"Not really, because I knew that this was going to happen one day. I knew when I was a teenager that my parents weren't really happy. Every couple argues and has disagreements, but my parents were consistent with it. My parents were from a small village, and my dad's family knew my mom's family. My dad's family gave a strong suggestion to my mom's family that they should date and eventually get married," she says.

"A strong suggestion?" he repeats.

She shakes her head up and down slowly.

"Since I'm an only child, I'm stuck in the middle. I still love my mom and dad, but I think they both have stepped out on each other. I just can't confirm it. Anyway, they did the 9 yuan divorce but are still debating over assets," she says.

"What is the 9 yuan divorce?" Terry is totally confused.

"Well, you can go down to the same bureau that gives you your marriage certificate, and they can issue you a divorce certificate for about 9 yuan. It's like rapid or instant divorce, and many people choose this option. It gets more complicated if there are kids, or businesses, or a lot of money involved. I think my parents just wanted to divorce, and think about the business later," she says, as she continues to play with her phone.

"I did not know all of that," he says.

"It's fine. Like I said, I knew it was going to come down to me getting the business. So, I will have to stay for a couple of days, then I will fly out to meet you. How long do you plan on staying home?" she asks.

"I intend on staying for at least a month. Then, I'll make a decision on whether to come back or not. Danni said that they can hold my position for a month. I really would like you to come with me," he responds.

"I really want you to stay here, Terry. Why do you have to leave?" she says.

"Are you serious? They just found my sister dead in the mountains. I have to go home," he says, as he rubs his left cheek.

"Ok, then do what you need to do," she starkly says.

"I will, he starkly responds.

"Do you know when her funeral will be?" she asks.

"Not yet. Hopefully, my cousin will tell me more tonight, and I can make my travel plans," he states.

"Could you take some clothes over for me?" she asks.

"I'm not your chauffeur? You better pay me extra for this," he jokingly says.

"Oh, I'll pay you extra," she smiles and winks at him.
"I only want cash!" he exclaims.

He takes a look outside of the window and is unable to see the Ferris wheel, Tianjin Eye, which is a staple of the city skyline. Instead, he sees that the snow has picked up and is now blanketing the entire downtown. They stay up for a little while, watching movies and talking. Eventually, around 12:30 am, they both fall asleep on the couch. At 1:30 am, he slowly separated himself from her to use the bathroom. He gently wakes her up by tapping her shoulder and whispering in her ear, "Wake up, pretty lady." She slowly gets up and walks to her bed, where they both pass out on top of her covers.

XVI

I Just Wanted to See You Naked

2:04 am

Naomi: Hey Gravy, I'm sure that you are sleeping, but I wanted to keep you updated about C. They did the autopsy and found that she didn't have soot in her lungs. Meaning, she was already dead when her body was burned. The funeral might be in 2 weeks if that's ok with you. We thought it would give you enough time to get home. I still haven't heard from Jared, and the police are still investigating. Message me when you wake up. I love you, Gravy!

The sun has risen and is walking on the pond next to Lena's house. Birds are singing the morning away, as Terry stretches out his left arm and wraps it around Lena. She cuddles up next to him, and he assumes that she can still smell the cologne that he put on the day before. The swelling on his face has slightly gone down, but the swelling is still the size of a cherry. He takes his arm off her and gently touches the left side of his face.

"Ahhh," he grunts.

"Don't touch it, babe," she says.

"I can't help it," he responds.

"Help yourself and put your arm back around me," she insists.

"Speaking of arms, I got up in the middle of the night to use the bathroom and when I got back in bed I noticed something about you. Did you know that you sleep with your arms folded? Like you're mad at someone in your dreams," he playfully says.

"Shut up. I've always done that. I don't know what I do when I'm sleeping. I could just throw my arms all over the place, but I don't do that," she says back, while throwing her arms in the air to show him.

He kisses her on her forehead, and then she guides him to her lips. They lay in bed for another 10 minutes before he checks the time on his watch: 9:05am. "I have to go home and take a shower before I go in," he says.

"Just take a shower here. You can borrow some of my boyfriend's clothes," she laughs and smiles.

"You think you're funny, don't you?" he asks back.

"I can quickly buy you a pair of underwear and a t-shirt. I can literally order them for you right now, and they will be here before you go to work," she offers.

"That sounds good. I still need to take a shower," he states.

"Ok cool. What's your shirt size?" she asks.

As he tells her his sizes, she walks into the bathroom to grab a clean towel and washcloth for him. He checks his phone and sees the message from Nay. He doesn't tell Lena right away, because he is enjoying his time with her. Although he knows that their time will quickly come to an end in China, he is hopeful that she will make it to America.

"Are you off today?" he asks.

"Yes, I took off so I could talk with my parents. Here is your towel and your washcloth. You can hop in when you're ready; I turned the water on. I'm going to come in and brush my teeth," she responds.

He plugs his phone into the charger and heads for the bathroom. He takes off his clothes and gets into the hot shower. She goes to the kitchen for a moment and quickly returns to the bathroom. Lena takes out her toothbrush, but doesn't put any toothpaste on it. She just puts the toothbrush in her mouth and plays with it.

"What are you staring at?" he smiles and says.

"You and all that sexiness," she says.

"Oh, yeah? Maybe you should join me," he suggests.

She throws the toothbrush in the sink, and throws her black t-shirt and black panties on the bathroom floor. She jumps into his arms, as he picks her up and she wraps her arms around his neck. The water continues to pound their bodies, and he turns her around to face the bathroom wall. She sticks her ass out and he grabs it. She gently moans, and he grabs her by the waist. He speeds up the pace and water splashes all over the bathroom tub. He continues as he is standing at full attention, and she lets out her pleasure and splashes her wet hair in his face. She turns around and continues to kiss him, as they both are dripping wet. The warm water wraps them in a steamed embrace, and her legs continue to shake momentarily. Just as they begin to kiss again, there's a knock on the door.

"I think that's the delivery person," she says, bouncing out of the shower.

"That was really quick," he responds.

"I told you they wouldn't take long. I have to get out and get your stuff. You continue to shower," she insists.

He pulls her close for one more kiss, and she falls into him. They disconnect for a moment, and she takes the dry blue towel and quickly wipes down her dripping body. She grabs her black tank top and black panties and puts them back on her body.

"You better put on some shorts too, girl. Out here showing the neighborhood all your goodies and stuff," he says.

"I'll show them all my goodies if I want to," she says, smiling and walking out the bathroom door.

He can hear her talking to who he assumes is the delivery person. He turns off the hot water and grabs his dry pink towel. She comes back into the bathroom with a package.

"That came really quick. Let me try them on to make sure they fit," he says.

"Sure, I just got a basic white shirt and some underwear. They should fit," she replies, as she hands him the clothes.

He takes the clothes from her, as she takes his towel and continues to dry off his body. She rubs down his chest and goes down to his abs; she kisses him gently on his bruised cheek. He tears open the clothes and starts with the underwear first. They are a plain pair of blue underwear.

"These don't look like they are going to fit me. They look a little too small for me," he says.

"Just try them on," she demands.

He lifts his left leg and puts it through the sleeve of the underwear. He follows with his right leg, and he already feels the circulation in his legs stop.

"These are really tight," he says, gasping for air.

They both pull the underwear up to his waist, as he holds his breath for a moment. The underwear hugged him, and every imprint below his waist can be seen.

"I think it's sexy," she says, as she pulls his head close to her. She slowly kisses him and bites his bottom lip.

"You're so sexy, you know that, right?" he states.

"I did. Now, hurry up and get dressed with your tight underwear," she jokingly says.

"What if the shirt is tight too? I feel like you did this on purpose, Lena," he responds, as he opens up the shirt. Luckily for him, the white button-up shirt wasn't tight, and fits comfortably.

He finishes getting dressed and checks the time: 10:40. He goes over to the bathroom sink and shouts to her, "Do you have an extra toothbrush I can use?"

She walks into the bathroom and hands him an extra toothbrush and some mouthwash.

"Are you trying to say that my breath stinks?" he asks.

She slowly nods her head and exits out of the bathroom.

He continues to get himself ready for work, and he can hear her cleaning up her apartment. He comes out of the bathroom and there's some deodorant on the living room table.

"Is this non-stick and dry?" he asks.

"I don't know. Just use it," she smiles and says back to him.

"Whatever," he says under his breath.

"What did you say?" she instantly asks.

"Nothing," he responds softly.

They both smile at each other, and she playfully tosses a yellow throw pillow at him. Being the athlete that he is, he was able to dodge it and avoid the darting pillow. He puts the deodorant on and goes to check his phone.

"85%. I have to get a new phone soon. It takes this thing hours to fully charge, and then it's down to 50% in like 10 minutes," he thinks to himself. He walks into the living room and sees her putting some paperwork together.

"Everything ok?" he asks.

"Yes, I'm fine. There's some paperwork I have to get together before I meet with my parents," she responds.

"Ok, I have to get going. Thank you for the tight underwear and the scented deodorant," he says with a smile.

"You are going to work smelling like..." she pauses and picks up the deodorant bottle, "smelling like wild lavender," she raises her eyebrows at him.

"Well, thank you. It looks like the sidewalks and roads are clear," he says to her.

"Sounds good babe. Don't forget to let me know the exact day of the funeral and when you plan on leaving," she responds.

"Will do," he confirms.

He grabs his book bag, his phone and walks over to the door. Before he could get another word out of his mouth, she jumped in his arms. She puts her arms around his neck, as they share a quick embrace. He can't believe that this is his reality, but he knows that he will have to leave one reality and go back to another. She puts her legs on her brown hardwood floor, but keeps her arms wrapped around him.

"I really like you. Like, I really, really like you," she whispers in his left ear.

"I like you more," he says back to her.

They eventually release and he walks out the door. He feels a pat on his butt and hears, "You got a nice butt," as he continues to walk.

He walks down to the elevator, and he zips up his jacket. He takes his phone out of his pocket to respond to Naomi. "They are acting way too strange with my sister's death. Why did Carla and Nay have on the same necklace in the picture? Where is Jared? Who would burn her body, and what are they trying to hide?" he wondered.

The elevator comes up to Lena's floor just as he is about to respond to Naomi's earlier message.

11:05 am
Terry: Hey Nay, call me!

271

He sends the message and gets onto the elevator. He goes to the back of the elevator and rests his head against the window. Next to him, is an advertisement for wedding services. The walk to the office won't take long, but it is cold outside after the night's snowfall. The elevator crunches down to the lobby, and he gets off the elevator. As he is getting off, another gentleman gets on the elevator. Terry holds the door open for the gentlemen. "Xièxiè," says the gentleman. Terry turns to him and says, "bú kèqì."

He feels his phone vibrate and puts his attention on his phone.

11:06 am
Naomi: I'll call you now.

He puts his headphones in, so that he can talk with Naomi. Luckily, the wind isn't upset today, so he can talk on the phone without much interference. He sees Naomi calling him; he turns up his volume and swipes green to answer the video call.

"Hey Gravy. How are you doing?" she asks.

"I'm good Nay. Just walking to work right now," he responds.

"Are you leaving some girl's house?" she interrogates.

"I'll tell you about that later. What's going on with my sis?" he promptly asks.

He hears Naomi take a deep breath and swallow before she speaks.

"So, they did the autopsy and found out that her body was burned after she was killed. They are saying that it was blunt force trauma to her head and abdominal area. They believe that someone is trying to cover up their tracks, and they are still looking for the suspect," she explains.

"So, somebody beat my sister to her death, then burned her body to cover it up, right?" he asks.

"That's what seems to have happened," she responds.

He takes a deep breath, as he waits for the pedestrian light to turn green.

"How did they find her body? Who found her body?" he asks, as his voice tightens up a little.

"A police officer found her body. The police said it appeared she had been dragged from a higher place in the mountains down to the bottom," she says.

"Like somebody wanted her to be found," he responds.

"All of this is so crazy, and we still have no idea where Jared is. All of the family is here like: Uncle Rick, Uncle Jeremy, Uncle Will, and Aunt Pam and all of their kids. We are thinking of having the funeral in 2 weeks. Do you think you could make it home by then?" she asks.

"I will book my ticket either tonight or tomorrow. I'm bringing someone with me," he responds.

Naomi's eyebrows slightly raise a little bit, as she appears to be surprised. "Is this the one you were telling me about from before?" she wonders.

"Yes, that's her. She will most likely meet me in the states. She has some business to handle in China first," he responds.

Naomi pauses for a moment and tilts her head to the side.

"What?" he replies.

"Are you sure this girl is going to come? It sounds like she just said that, but you don't know if she's actually coming. Are you sure you want to leave her?" she interrogates.

At this point, his frustration and confusion with her and the current family situation have peaked.

"I think she will come. We've already talked about it, and she will come after she handles some business with her family. I have to make a decision for myself and I have to leave. I need you guys, and I think you guys need me too. Anyway, thanks for the update. I will let you know when I book my ticket home. I'm almost at my office, but I wanted to know something. Saw an old picture of you and C with the same apple necklaces on. Our parents bought those necklaces, but I didn't know you had the same one," he says.

"Oh, Jared bought me one for my birthday, a couple years back. I was excited, and I took a picture with C, because her necklace was similar, and I thought it was cute," she responds.

"Oh, ok." he quickly says.

"Wait, do you think I had something to do with this? Really, Terry, she was my best friend. What the hell is wrong with you?" she says, as her nostrils rapidly move up and down.

"I didn't say that. Look, I'm sorry. We're all stressing and grieving right now, and I'm grieving from another country, and it's tough," he explains.

"I know Gravy. You know I would never do something to C, and you should know that. We can hear each other, even if we can't be here for each other. We love you and can't wait until we can see you again. I know it's only been less than a year, but it's felt like forever. Get to work safely, and we will chat later," she says with a warm smile, as she sits up from her brown suede couch.

"You're right, Nay, and I love you too! Speak to you soon. Bye," he states.

She hangs up just, as he is walking into the lobby of his building. When one can't physically be there, those are the times when our connections reach a deeper point. He knew that Naomi had a valid point, "We can hear each other, even if we can't be here for each other," he repeats in his mind. He feels that something fishy is going on back home, and is really beginning to feel anxious about going back. He was starting to enjoy his expat lifestyle, but family business is calling. The fabric of his family has changed, and he will have to find his way back into the mesh. Life doesn't get easier, one has to become stronger. Especially when that strength comes through someone showing weakness. This journey has changed him in many ways, even if it's only been for less than one year. He has found a confidence and comfort in himself that he didn't know existed. Those times when we step out into the most unfeasible journeys, are when we get the most invaluable experiences.

"Hello Terry," Kelly says to him, as he walks through the center doors.

"Hi Kelly. How's it going today?" he asks.

"Not bad. I heard you are leaving," she says, with a frown on her face.

"Wow, word travels fast in this place, huh?" he responds, with a sense of surprise in his voice.

"Yes, we are a small center. Danni has already informed us. Is everything ok back home?" she asks.

"Not really. I had a death in the family, so I need to be with them," he responds.

"Oh, my goodness, Terry! I'm so sorry," she says, as she comes around the desk to give him a hug.

"I appreciate that, Kelly," he responds to her comfort.

"How have you been feeling?" she asks.

"Up and down for the most part. I've been talking about my feelings, and when I get home I'm going to talk with a counselor to work through some things," he says.

"Why wait? I'm sure you could do some teleconferences now," she suggests.

"That's very true. I didn't think about that," he admits.

"I want to make sure you're doing your best to take care of yourself. I know talking about this stuff may be hard, so thank you for being open," she says.

"No problem Kelly. I will miss all of you," he says.

"We will miss you too. I love seeing you and Lena host events together. Will she go with you?" her question shocks him.

"Come on Terry. We know you two have had the hots for each other, since the second she came into the office," she says to him. Then she grabs his right ear and pulls it down to her mouth,

"I think you two make a beautiful and happy couple. Marry that girl, no matter what people say," she states.

He is silent for a moment, then whispers in Kelly's ear, "Those are my intentions, Kelly." He goes into the office and sees Danni sitting at her desk.

"Hi Terry, good morning!" she exclaims.

"Hey Danni, how are you today?" he asks.

"I'm doing ok. How about yourself?" she responds.

"I'm doing the best I can. Hey, where is everybody else?" He looks around the office and notices that the staff is nowhere to be seen.

"I think they are setting up a room for an activity. Any word on when you will have to depart?" she asks.

"The funeral will most likely be in two weeks, so I will probably leave next Monday," he responds.

"Ok, that's fine. I will make a note that your last day will be Sunday," she says.

"That's fine with me. Can we still meet later?" he requests.

"Sure! I will be free in the afternoon," she says to him.

He pulls his roller chair to his desk and turns on his computer screen and monitor. He prints out the materials for his classes and takes some quick notes for his lesson. For this class, he wants to add something to his lecture. He stands up, pushes in his chair, and goes to his first class of the day.

"Good morning!" he says to his class.

"Good morning, teacher!" the class responds to him.

"Before we get started today, I would..." his speech is interrupted by a student coming in late.

"Sorry teacher," the late student says.

"It's ok John," says Terry, as he grips the podium.

"Before we get started today, I would like to inform you all that I will be returning home in two weeks due to a family emergency. I want to take this time to thank you all for these wonderful classes over the past year. You all have made an impact on my life, and made me enjoy my teaching experience. Thank you and I really hope all of you do well in your future endeavors," he says, as he starts to feel his emotions rise to his face.

"We will miss you, teacher. It's hard for us to keep good international teachers," one student says.

"It's hard to keep them here for more than a year. We understand that you have a family emergency. How long will it take you to get home?" another student asks.

"Well, like I told you guys earlier, I'm from the Northwestern part of America. I'm from Portland, Oregon, and it will take me about 19 hours to get back home," he says.

"What do you do for 19 hours on the plane?" someone asks.

"Just watch movies and listen to music, but I mostly sleep. It's a good time to catch up on some movies and some music. I've watched <u>Spider-Man: Into the Spider-Verse</u> and <u>Creed II</u>, my first time coming over," he says to his students.

"Oh my goodness, I love both of those movies," says one student.

"Did you see that movie, Cherry?" Terry asks.

"Of course! My friends and I have watched it quite a lot," Cherry says.

"Hey, good use of the present perfect tense there, Cherry," he smiles and says.

"Thank you, teacher," she replies.

"You welcome, Cherry. As you continue to navigate through your young careers, I am only an email away. I will do my best to help you with your English questions," Terry says, as he begins his lesson for the day.

His lesson ends, and he walks back into the office and sees Danni sitting at her desk. She stands up and turns to him, "Are you free, Terry?"

"Yes, I'm free now," he says, as he follows her out of the door. They walk down to classroom 1 and head in for a quick chat.

"So, you said that the funeral will be in a couple of weeks, right?" she asks.

"Yes, and I would need to have time to spend with my family and get ready to bury my sister," he responds.

"I totally understand, and I'm so sorry again. Will you need help getting all your stuff home? If you need, we can ship some stuff for you," she offers.

"That's so kind of you, but I think I should be ok. I will just have one big suitcase. I'm going to book my ticket tonight," he states.

"Well, you take as much time as you need, Terry. If you need, we could transfer you to a position in the states. We definitely want to keep you, and we will do what we can to help you in your time of need," she responds.

"I appreciate that so much, Danni. You guys mean so much to me, and I wish that I didn't have to leave so suddenly," he says.

"It's ok Terry. It's time for you to be with your family now," she says to him.

They finish talking and they both walk out of classroom 1. He goes back into the office to prepare for his evening classes, and Danni walks down the hall. There are designated times for things in life. A time to be alone, a time to be with friends, a time to laugh, and a time to cry. There are times to curl up in a ball and be afraid, and there are times to stand tall and be brave. Sometimes all of these can happen in a matter of moments, and Terry is doing his best to be ready for what may come. As the day runs by, he knows that it's time to go home. Tonight, he is the last teacher left in the office. He gets to the lobby of his building and checks his phone before leaving the building. Once outside, he doesn't want to take his hand out of his gloves.

> **9:37 pm (to Melissa)**
> **Terry: Hey there, I hope you are well.**

He feels better after the incident in the bar with Melissa and her cousin. His face isn't as swollen anymore, and he has calmed down. He touches his bruise and feels that the swelling has gone down. No longer does it feel like a hungry mosquito had a feast on his face. The cold weather and wind continue to wrestle with his body, as he makes his way to the metro station. Getting home, he makes one of his favorite meals: frozen pizza. The four-cheese pizza that he gets from the international grocery store is his favorite. Usually, it takes about 10-15 minutes to unfreeze, then he heats it in his oven.

He makes some green tea and goes to his living room. He turns on the news, but only as background noise while he searches for a flight back home. "Let's see what I can find?" he says to himself, pulling his small dining table close to him.

He goes through a couple websites, and he finds a flight that will take him to Portland through Vancouver. "A 20-hour trip isn't that bad. The layover isn't too bad either. I'll just be sleeping the whole time," he thinks.

While he's eating his four-cheese pizza that is awkwardly cut in half, he hears a knock at his door. "I totally forgot I was supposed to meet up with Matt and his friends at some point," he thinks out loud. He walks over to the door and reaches down to unlock the deadbolt.

"Hey bro, I'm so sorry that I've been hard to meet up with. I'm not avoiding you bro, I promise," Terry says.
"It's ok man. I understand that you just don't like Mexicans," Matt laughs and gives Terry a handshake.
"You know it's not like that, bro. I just got a lot going on," Terry responds.
"I'm joking with you. I understand man, and I'm sorry about your sister," Matt says.

Terry doesn't know how to respond, because he never told Matt that his sister had passed away. "How does he know?" Terry thinks to himself.
"How did you know my sister passed away?" Terry asks Matt, with a hint of wonder in his voice.

"I watched the news and put things together. I know you said that your sister was missing, and I saw on the news that they found a dead woman at Multnomah Falls. I'm so sorry, bro," Matt says, as he gives Terry a brief hug.

10:20 pm
Melissa: Hey Terry, I'm doing ok.
How is your face?

"Hey man, do you need to grab your phone?" Matt asks, as Terry's phone vibrates.

"It's ok," Terry says, leaning on the side of his door.

"Do you guys know what happened to her?" Matt asks.

"Not yet," he responds.

"That area is getting really bad with people disappearing in the woods and mountains. Especially with women being trafficked," Matt says back.

"You sure know how to brighten up someone's day," Terry's sarcasm spills out.

"Listen, over the past 30 years, people have been disappearing a lot in the Pacific Northwest. There's always been a lot of human trafficking cases, especially up and down the I-5 corridor. There was a similar case a couple years back, where a woman's dead body was found burned at the bottom of Multnomah Falls. It turned out that she was being trafficked, and was trying to run away to get help. It might be something to look into. It's just sad, and if you need anything, let me know," Matt says, with his eyelids almost closed and his face slightly frowned.

"Thanks man, I really appreciate that," Terry says.

"That was an odd sequence of random facts," Terry thinks to himself.

"Are you going to go home soon?" Matt asks.

"I'm leaving next week," Terry quickly answers.

"Well, if you want to meet up before you leave and get a quick drink, let me know. Or if you need help with your luggage, let me know." Matt says, as he reaches out to give Terry a handshake.

"I will. Thank you, Matt," Terry says, as he embraces Matt's handshake.

Terry slowly closes the door, as Matt turns and walks to his apartment at the end of the hallway. He goes back over to his couch, sits down, and grabs his phone. He sees the message from Melissa and that he had a missed call from her on WeChat.

10:23 pm
Terry: Hey Melissa, I'm doing ok.
My face is feeling much better.
How are you?

He continues to look for flights on his phone. Returning home will be a challenge, because he has acclimated to his life in another country. He liked living internationally. The wonder of traveling and sightseeing, the adventure of just everyday living, and the journey of finding one's true self. He didn't want to give it up, but he has grown a lot during his travels. Growth takes time, and it happens in different ways for everyone. Living internationally and truly becoming a global citizen, has made him more aware of his individuality.

It is possible to go to another place and do quite well. Whether one is catching a taxi internationally, signing a gym contract in another language, or simply ordering food in a foreign place. You have to celebrate the little victories in life. Every baby step leads to a grown-up goal, and each step is important and shouldn't be skipped. He knows that he is becoming a better man right before his eyes.

10:25 pm
Melissa: I'm ok. Do you have a moment to talk?

10:26 pm
Terry: Could you give me 5 minutes?

10:27 pm

Melissa:

He finds a flight for the following Monday at 7:30 pm, with a layover in Tokyo, then reaching Portland, Oregon at 6:00 am. "I'll be traveling back to the future and living Monday all over again. That's like a movie or something," he thinks.

Terry bought his ticket home. This flight will take him from Tianjin Binhai International Airport back to Portland. He receives a text with his flight confirmation number in it. He finishes up his last slice of pizza, and he inadvertently transfers some grease from his fingers to his phone. Grabbing a napkin, he looks up at the TV and sees a news story about wildfires in California.

"How did Nay know that C's body was burned? The news never said anything about the body being burned." He sees that Melissa is video calling him.

He swipes right to answer the call.

"Hey, Terry. How are you?" she asks.

"Hey, Melissa. I'm doing ok. Just booked my ticket to go home next week to be with my family," Terry says.

"I'm sorry again about your sister," she responds.

"Thank you," he responds to her.

"I wish you the best, Terry and I wanted to tell you that I'm not pregnant," she states.

Terry chuckles and feels a sense of confusion come over him. "What are you talking about?" he asks.

"I've been trying to talk to you after we hooked up. And I thought you were avoiding me, because you thought I was pregnant," she says.

Terry laughs for a moment, and then gathers himself to begin his thought.

"I never thought that. And I had a condom on that night. So, I'm not really sure what you're talking about," he explains.

He can hear Melissa take a deep breath and say, "I think we were really drunk that night."

"I mean, we did have a lot to drink, but I still had a condom," he tries to remind her.

"That was a fun night. Honestly, I just wanted to see you naked! You have a really nice body, Terry," she says.

He laughs and says, "I appreciate that. I work hard for this body," he jokingly says.

"Oh, do you?" she sarcastically responds.

"Of course I do. I do it by eating mooncakes," he says.

They both share a laugh, and then silence encompasses their conversation. He hears Melissa breathing on the other end. Suddenly, she starts the conversation again.

"I know you're going back to America, and I wanted to know if you could do me a favor." Terry feels that there is a hint of desperation in her voice.

"What's...what's wrong?" he hesitantly asks.

"I'm not sure if I told you that I have an identical twin sister. Well, we haven't seen her for weeks. We aren't sure where she went. My family is split between Kazakhstan and China. She has some friends in New York and Seattle, I think. I know you are from Portland, but if you hear anything or see anything, let me know. Her friends are not the nicest people," she explains, as she looks down for a moment. Her long black hair hangs over her face.

He takes a deep breath and responds with, "What do you mean they aren't the nicest people?"

"I think they are involved in some sort of organ theft or something," she states.

"Harvesting?" he answers.

"Yes, that's it. We just aren't sure, and we have been very worried. If you hear anything, you can just call me. I'll still be here in Tianjin," she says.

He squints his eyes, as his brain starts to run. "What is happening here?" he thinks to himself.

"I will keep my eyes open, and if I hear anything, I'll let you know. I have some friends living in New York that I went to college with. I may take a trip there, once I get back. What's her name?" he asks.

"Her name is Melody. I really appreciate it, Terry. Text me sometimes, you still have my WeChat. I wish you a safe flight back to America," she tells him.

"Thanks so much, Melissa. I wish you well in the future, and I will keep you updated if I hear or see your twin," he responds.

"Goodnight," she replies.

"Goodnight Melissa."

He checks his emails and sees the confirmation number for his flight and realizes that he has to pack. The one thing he hates about traveling is the packing that comes with it. "There has to be a company that could ship my clothes back home. I also have to ship home the gifts I have for my family," he thinks.

He does a quick search on WeChat and the Tianjin Expat group and finds a moving company. It was at this moment that he realized, "I'm going home." Before he falls asleep on his couch, he sends Naomi a message.

> **10:35 pm (to Naomi)**
> Terry: Hey Nay, I booked my ticket home. I wanted to talk to you, so let me know when you are free.

"I should also text Lena, before she starts asking questions," he proposes.

> **10:36 pm (to Lena)**
> Terry: Hey there. I hope you had a good day. I booked my ticket home for Tuesday morning. Maybe you could come the following

week. I'm about to go to bed.
Goodnight.

Terry plugs up his phone, sets his alarm for 9:30 am, and steadily drifts off into recuperation.

XVII

I Want You Here With Me

12:45 am

Lena: I know you're probably sleeping, but I'm glad that you were able to book your ticket. I may not be able to come until the week after, so I don't think I will make the funeral. Let's meet by the Tianjin Eye tomorrow to talk and chill. Goodnight big head!

12:40 am

Naomi: Hey Gravy, let me know when you are up, and I can call you. Talk to you later, Goodnight.

The next morning, he is up before his alarm goes off. It's a good feeling to not need an alarm and wake up well-rested. He rolls over and almost falls off of his small couch. He liked sleeping on the couch, even as a young child. When he would go visit family in Seattle, he always slept on the couch. Carla would take the extra bed, and he would sleep on the couch. Something about curling up on a couch with limited space, made him feel safe and secure.

He slowly rolls over, unplugs his phone charger, and puts his thumbprint on the screen. The typical routine for him, as he gives himself a long morning stretch. The sun is peeking through the curtains and the winter wind whistles through the morning sky. He sees that he has a few missed messages. He checks the time on his phone: 9:00am. "I still have some time before work," he thinks. Nay has messaged him, and he wants to talk to her right away.

9:03 am
Terry: Hey Nay, I'm up now if you're free to talk.

Putting his phone down, he gets up to use the bathroom and splashes some warm water on his face. *Ding.* He quickly grabs the towel from his bathroom sink and wipes his face off. He goes back to the couch, and picks up his phone to check the messages.

9:05 am
Melissa: Thank you for talking to me last night. I really did have a good time with you when we were together.

9:06 am (to Melissa)
Terry: No prob.

"I need some water," he goes over to grab a small clear plastic cup from the kitchen. Terry pours himself some warm water from his water cooler and walks back to his couch. *Ding*. He hears his phone go off.

9:09 am
Naomi: I'm free now.

Terry instantly puts the cup down, and he goes into his WeChat app to give Naomi a video call. He video calls her, and it rings once, twice, three, four times, as he gets frustrated. "What is she doing?" Terry thinks to himself. He tries doing a voice call, and she finally picks up.

"Ter...can...hear...me," Naomi mumbles.
"Nay? Nay, I can't hear you, it sounds like there is a lot of noise in the background," he responds, tilting the phone up, so he could see the screen better.
"Can you hear me now?" she says.
"Yes, I can hear you. Where are you? It sounds like a party in the background with loud music," he wonders.
"No, I was just over at a friend's house," she stutters a little to get her words out.
"Are you drunk?" he asks.
"I'm fine, Terry," she swiftly responds.

"What is going on with her?" he thinks to himself.
"Anyhow, I booked my ticket for next Tuesday at 6 am. I need someone to pick me up from the airport. Either you or Uncle Jeremy could pick me up," he requests.
"I got it. I think me and Jar..." she stops herself immediately.
"What did you say?' he asks.

"Nothing," she responds.

He is confused and getting frustrated with her. "Why is she acting so strange? I know everybody handles grief differently, but she is acting really strange," he thinks to himself.

"Hey, Nay, how did you know that her body was burned?" he asks.

"What are you talking about, Terry?" she responds with a rhetorical question.

"Earlier you said that they found her burned body at the Falls, but the news out here never said that her body was burned," he quickly answers.

There is a moment of silence, as it seems that Naomi is trying to gather her thoughts. Finally, she took a deep breath and began to speak.

"On the news in Portland, it said that she was burned. Maybe they didn't tell the whole story where you are," she says.

"I guess. It's just strange that you said what the news and police didn't even seem to report. I've checked online and there are no reports of her body being burned. Not even one comment," he responds.

"I think your mind is a little off today, Terry," she insists.

In a slightly distinct voice, he could hear some familiarity.

"Hey, Nay, get over here!" This voice sounds like someone that Terry knows.

"Is that Jared?" he asks.

"No, it's not. Remember, we haven't seen him in months. That's just one of my friends. If you need someone to pick you up at the airport Tuesday morning, Uncle Jeremy and I will be there. I have to go. Have a good day, Gravy," she says, as the call quickly ends.

"What is going on there?" he says out loud.

He stays on the couch for a moment, as his thumb and index finger gently rub his forehead. *Ding*. The phone rings once again.

"What now?" Terry thinks to himself. He gathers his thoughts momentarily and looks at his phone. As soon as he sees who the message is from, the endorphins in his body begin to perform jumping jacks.

9:24 am
Lena: Hey handsome! Good
Morning. 😙

It's amazing how a 'good morning,' message from someone special can bring immediate joy. The hair on his arms stood up a little, his heartbeat sped up and his pupils sparkled. "Just the person I want to talk to this morning," he thinks.

9:27 am
Terry: Good morning, beautiful. I
just had the weirdest conversation
with my cousin.

After he hits the send button, he sees that Lena is trying to video chat with him. He quickly answers.

"Hey there," she says, as her big brown eyes pierce through the phone screen.

"Hi beautiful," he responds.

"At the coffee shop before I head into the center. What happened with your cousin?" she asks.

"She's just been acting very strange. She really hasn't given me an answer for how she knew that my sister's body was burned, especially when the news didn't say anything like that. Then, I think I heard Jared's voice in the background, but she said it wasn't him and hung up the phone. Anyway, I booked my flight home for next Monday," he says.

Lena looks down at something for a moment and then lifts her head and looks at him.

"Ok, like I said I will probably miss the funeral, but I can fly out the following week. I just have to finish some stuff for the shop," she says, looking down at something again.

"That's fine. I can't wait for you to meet my family. I think they will love you," he says with excitement.

"I can't wait to meet them either," she says with a low voice.

"Hey, are you ok?" he asks.

"Can we meet at the Tianjin Eye tonight?" she responds.

"Sure. You're working today, right? We can just go over together," he states.

"I'm going to leave early, but we can meet there," she hastily responds.

"Sounds good. Blow me a kiss," he says to her, as he is attempting to flirt a little.

"Blow yourself a kiss," she says with a smile on her face.

"Don't be like that," he jokingly states.

"Anyway, I will see you in the center, go brush your teeth," she responds.

"Whatever, I never have morning breath. I think I will brush my teeth and I guess I'll see you later, pretty lady," he says, as he gets up off the couch.

"Bye handsome," she says, as she blows him a kiss.

Terry gets ready for work and picks out his outfit; a plain white button-up with gray slacks and a brown pair of dress shoes.

He gets to his office around 10:50 am. As soon as he walks in, he sees some balloons on the floor and a banner that says: "We Will Miss You Terry!"

His office put together a going-away party for him. He feels a tear start to come down his right eye.

"You guys didn't have to do this," he says.

"We know, but we wanted to. We know that this has been a tough time for you, and we just wanted to say thank you. Thank you for coming to Tianjin and coming to our center to teach our students. We wish you all the best in the future, and we hope that you can return to China in the future," Danni says, as she hands him a card.

"We will miss you, mate," Barry says.

"I'll miss you," Alex says, as he gives Terry a hug.

Terry has another tear falling down his right eye. Sometimes the people who have the most impact in our lives, are only present in our lives for a short time. The staff in the center have truly become his friends, as he has spent most of his time in Tianjin with his coworkers. It's been quite the journey for him, but he knows that it's just beginning. This was a risk for Terry, but he wanted it. To develop and find our true selves, we have to be in situations where we are uncomfortable. Growth can't come from comfortability, and he knew that he had to take a risk for himself. Strategically placing himself in a place where he didn't know anybody, didn't know the language, and where he stuck out like a sore thumb.

"I'm still here for a few days, so I'll still be working. Thank you for your hospitality and help throughout my year in China. I will never forget you all, and I hope that I can return in the near future," Terry says, as he wipes a tear from his face. He goes into the office to put down his card. In the office, he sees that they also bought a cake for him.

"What kind of cake is it?" Terry asks Danni.
"It is your favorite," she says to him.
"How did you know my favorite kind of cake?" he asks, with a sense of confusion in his voice.
"Remember the survey you filled out when you first got here? It was on the survey, and we knew that your favorite flavor was red velvet," she responds.
Terry turns to the staff and says, "Thank you so much."

He sits down at his desk and prepares his first lesson. He checks his watch: 11:20 am. Grabbing his lesson plans, he walks out of the office and into classroom 1. Another day speeds by, and he is ready to go and meet Lena. She has already left the office. He saw her a couple of times at the office on this day, the typical passing by each other in the hallway. Reaching for his phone, he texts her to find out her location.

8:32 pm
Terry: Hey there! Hope your day went well. Are we still meeting at the Eye?

He puts the phone down, as Barry walks into the office and says, "Hey mate, how are you feeling?"

"I'm doing ok. Just trying to feel my emotions and not feel guilty for leaving. I'm also excited to go home and see my family and friends. It feels like it's been longer than a year or whatever it's been," he says, as he loses track of time.

"Don't feel guilty. Be happy you still have a family to go home to. I'm sure they're excited to see you," Barry responds. Just as he is about to respond to Barry, he feels his phone vibrate in his hand.

8: 36 pm
Lena: My day was ok. Give me like 20 minutes, and I'll meet you over there. Can't wait to see you. 😊

He looks up from his phone, with a smile planted on his face.

"Lena?" Barry asks.

"Yes, it's her," Terry responds.

"You two are really good together. But I don't think you should feel guilty. Not too many people have the wherewithal to do what you did. I mean, correct me if I'm wrong, but I'm sure you've grown from this experience," Barry states.

"Barry, I found a power and spirit inside me that I didn't know I had. I think I truly found something greater within me, by putting myself in unfamiliar situations and finding ways to thrive," Terry explains.

"That's great, mate. Well, I have to finish some paperwork now. I'm sure I will see you this week." Barry turns and looks at his glaring desktop screen.

8:40 pm

Terry: I can't wait to see you either. I'm leaving the office now. 😶

Terry shuts down his computer and tosses his bag over his shoulders. The winter solstice has subsided tonight, as it is not too cold. With a slight breeze in the air, he steps outside and zips up his all-black bomber jacket. He decides to order a DiDi, so that he can get there faster. Within 20 minutes, he can see the Tianjin Eye. The Ferris wheel is gleaming a regal purple and luminescent white, giving light over the Hai River. He feels his phone buzz and an instant smile comes across his face.

9:04 pm
Lena: Be there in 3 minutes.

9:05 pm
Terry: I will see you shortly.

The DiDi stops on the Yongle Bridge and Terry enters the night air. There is a path that leads down to a riverwalk, where people can enjoy the sights of the city. He decided to stay underneath the bright Ferris wheel, so that Lena could easily find him. The previous week had been quite breezy, but on this night the air was calm. He takes a deep breath and the cold air swims up his nose and into his eyes. He sits there, closes his eyes, listens to the world and enjoys just being. Terry looks down the illuminated riverwalk and sees her walking towards him.

"Hey," Lena says, as she walks over.

"Hi," Terry says.

As soon as he reaches out his arms, she jumps into them. He spins her around, while tightly holding her waist. Putting her down, she fixes her blue overcoat. Quickly, they share a cold-lipped kiss, and look at each other.

"I missed you today," he says.

"I missed you too. How was your surprise going-away party?" she asks.

"It was a nice surprise. I wasn't expecting that, and the red velvet cake was really good. I'm going to miss all of them," he responds.

She stops walking and raises her eyebrows at him.

"I'm going to miss you too," he says, kissing her on her left cheek.

"Terry, I...I...I don't know if I'm going to make it now," she stutters through her sentence.

He stops walking and drops his jaw.

"What do you mean?" he asks.

"My parents need me to be here for the next couple of months. This is getting messy, and I'm kinda stuck in the middle. Trying to be there for my mom and dad isn't easy, but I don't think I could leave them right now for someone they've never met," she replies to him.

"So, what will I say to my family? You said that you would be there for me. I don't want to sound needy, but you've helped me throughout this whole process of dealing with my sister's death. Even if you don't come to the funeral, it would be nice to have you there," he responds.

Before she starts to talk, her phone begins to ring. She quickly answers the phone and turns her head. He can't understand what she is saying.

"Look, I'm sorry, but I can't leave right now," she says, as she puts her phone back in her coat pocket.

"Is that her? Is that your girlfriend?" he demands.

"What are you talking about?" she states.

She walks over to a cold-wooden bench by the water and sits down. The lights from The Tianjin Eye continue to dance with the stars in the sky. He comes over to sit on the cold-wooden bench, puts his face in his hand for a moment, and takes a deep breath.

"Ever since the first day you walked in that office and said, 'Hi, I'm Lena,' I knew there was something special about you. Immediately, I'm thinking, 'Can I have your WeChat?' Then, logic starts to set in, and I think that I should be careful with you. There's no way that she would even look my way. Every second that goes by, I realize how much I miss you. I start missing you, and I just want to see your smiling face every day," he says, as he uses his hands to act out his feelings.

"I think I'm going to cry," she says, as it seems that she has a strong case of the emotional sniffles.

"I told my friends and family that, 'I'm really into her,' and that 'I just want to take a chance and see where it goes.' Honestly, I denied my feelings for you at first. Then, we finally went out on a date. I spent days thinking about what to wear and how to perfectly coordinate my outfit. I think I looked pretty good that night. I got drunk and completely missed your mouth after I asked, 'Can I kiss you?' I don't get enough pain, though. I started talking to Melissa, after I knew you were with Rachel. You and I were just friends. A few missed messages from you, and I realized that I'm still growing up in the relationship department. I'm trying to find out who I am. I just wanted you to talk to me before and after the Halloween party, but my pride stopped me from reaching out to you," he says, as he slowly slides his cold left hand under her warm right hand.

"I like you, Terry," she says.

"I've fallen for you, Lena. I just want to be able to say, 'She's mine.' I want people to ask me, 'She's your girlfriend?' I want to proudly shout, 'yes!' That's what I want," he explains.

"I have to go home, but I wish I could stay. I think it's during our toughest times, there's always someone who shows us that people still care about people," he says to her.

"What are your intentions, Terry?" she asks.

"I just wanted to see you naked," he says, as she softly punches him in his left arm.

He takes a moment and looks up at the sky. Everything is still and calm. The wind, the water, the night is calm. "What is the world trying to tell me?" he thinks to himself.

Then he looks into her big brown eyes, points to his heart, and says, "I want you here with me."

She grabs his cheeks and pulls him in close. The coldness of the night is subsided by the warmth of their embrace. They separate, but continue to look into each other's eyes. He wipes a tear slowly falling down her right eye.

After 10 seconds, she looks at him and says, "I see that the swelling has gone down. It doesn't even look like you were sucker-punched," she says.
He slightly touches the place where the bruise is and says, "Thanks for that feedback. I was hoping it wouldn't be that noticeable, but you noticed," he replies.
"You know I'll always tell you the truth," she explains.

They spend the next few minutes on the bench, enjoying the winter night underneath the luminescent Eye. At this point, he is no longer cold, but feels that everything in his body is warm. She lays her head on his shoulder, and he leans back on the bench. The walkway has a few stragglers, but there isn't a crowd in sight. They can enjoy being one with the universe tonight. There's no need to rush, no need to disagree, no need to stress, just the need to relax and enjoy each other's company.

"Could she be the one? Will she really come to America soon?" He tries to shut off his mind, but turning off the mind is hard when the world is always turned on. Terry turns to Lena and kisses her on her forehead.

"I will come to you, just as sure as the sun rises, Terry. I just have to stay with my parents for a little bit. Also, I have to tell you something," she says.

"Do you hear me, Terry?" she says, as she lightly shakes his face.

"Yeah, I'm ok," he quickly wipes his face.

"What happened? Whenever someone has something to tell me, it's always a bad thing," he says.

Certain phrases or thoughts remind him of bad times, but new opportunities can allow for old connotations to ebb away and positive ones to flow in. Terry is trying to do this, but his past continuously creeps in and says, "I'm still here." Growing from the past can be a treacherous journey, but he must find the sanctity in himself to allow him to confidently approach new journeys.

"I'm leaving the office to work full-time at the coffee shop as the owner," she says.

"That's really good," he says, his voice trembling slightly.

He sits up and looks at her and says, "Whatever you do, I will support you. I want to be there for you, and I know that we will not be in the same country. I want to love you if you will allow me to, but I need to love myself first."

She looks at him and says, "Thank you for being so patient and kind to me. I promise you that I will make it over to see you and meet your family. I understand that you need to do what you need to do for you," she proclaims.

"You handle your business here and make sure your parents are good. I can come back with you to China and meet your family if you would like," he replies.

She looks up at the night sky and at the Eye and says, "I would really like that."

They connect for a final kiss, and then she says, "Can we leave? I'm starting to not be able to feel my face."

He agrees and says, "Yes, we can go. Do you want to come back to my place?"

"Yes, I would like that," she responds, her hands gripping his.

They both leave the cold-wooden bench, and he calls for a taxi. The ride comes within the next 10 minutes. They reach his apartment and their clothes hit the ground, as soon as he closes the door. The next morning, he wakes up with her body still draped on top of his. Her head is resting upon his chest. Gently waking her up, so she could roll over, he goes to use the bathroom. He checks the time on his watch: 10:30 am.

"I'm going to be late for work," he says, rushing back to his bed and calling out her name.

"Lena! Hey, I'm going to be late. I'm going to shower and leave. You can chill here for a little while," he says, grabbing his clothes for the day.

She slowly rolls over and mumbles something back to him. "What?" he says.

She rolls over again and says, "I'll stay here."

"There's an extra key on top of my microwave. Just lock the door and put the key under the door. Or you can take it with you," he says, sprinting into the bathroom.

"Sure," she says, wrapping the royal-blue comforter around her body.

He makes it to work, just before his first class of the day. During his lunch break, he feels his phone vibrate and sees a notification flash on his screen:

> 12:35 pm
> Naomi: Hey Gravy, we are all set and ready for you to come home. Uncle Jeremy is going to pick you up from the airport. I won't be there, but I'll see you when you get to the house. I love you, Gravy!

A sense of joy and excitement washes over his face, like a child's face on Christmas morning. Through all the miscommunication and secrecy, they are his family, and he loves them. "I've been gone for almost a year and I feel like I've been gone longer. My family is different now," he says to himself. He puts down his chopsticks and his pork dumplings, and responds to Nay's message.

> 12:40 pm
> Terry: Hey Nay, I'm excited to see everyone. I think I told you about the airline I'm flying on. Best part is that the ticket wasn't spendy. I love you and I will see you soon!

XVIII

Home

Terry's last week in China goes by in a flash. He gets some goodbye wishes from his coworkers and students, organizes his final classes, and packs up his belongings. The night before his flight, he is in his apartment staring at the ceiling, "Am I making the right decision? Do I need to go home? What if my life will be better here? What really happened to my sister? What will happen between Lena and I?" he thinks to himself.

"I have to stop overthinking before I lose any logic I have left," he says out loud. Everything is quiet, and he is ready to leave his apartment. He has been advised to lock the door and slide the key underneath before he leaves for good. His rental agent will come the next day, because his landlord, Mr. Chen, is out of town. He was able to develop a cordial relationship with his landlord, even though he's only seen him three times since he's been in China.

"You look very thin, Terry. When you first came to China you were very fat," Mr. Chen said, when he came to look at Terry's leaking water filter.

"Well, thank you for that brutal honesty, Mr. Chen. I have been going to the gym, and thank you for noticing," Terry responds back.

Mr. Chen was always brutally honest whenever he did see Terry. It was scary and intimidating looking for housing in another country, especially, when Terry didn't speak the language. Mr. Chen made Terry feel comfortable and accommodated from the moment they met. From a nice handshake to a warm, "Welcome to China, Terry!"

The apartment came with a washer and television, which Terry wasn't used to. He just wanted to find a place where he could relax after work. Although he is leaving a little early, Mr. Chen was understanding and empathic towards his current situation.

"This short journey is only the beginning," Terry says out loud. Traveling overseas, living, and working abroad has completely opened up his mind to the world. Things were never what they seemed on television. "I'll go home for 2 years, then I'm off to the next journey. I think it's what C would encourage me to do. It was scary, nerve-racking, exciting, adventurous, frustrating, and rewarding all at the same time; it has to come to an end," he thinks to himself. Stepping out of his comfort zone was the best way to push himself forward. He did this and will never forget this experience.

He takes a look at his watch: 11:30 pm.

11:30 pm (to Lena)
Terry: Hey there, I'm about to go to sleep. I know you have to be with your family tomorrow, so I will call you when I'm past the security check. Good night, beautiful! 😘

11:31 pm
Lena: That sounds good to me. If you need any help tomorrow just call me. I can help you to translate anything. I miss you! Good night handsome! 😘

The next morning, his room feels like an icebox, because he didn't turn the heat on. The wind's whining, the sun's shining, and Terry's trying to get out of bed. He takes a look at this watch: 7:30 am. Grabbing his phone, he notices that he has an unread message. Since he's left America, he doesn't really get text messages anymore. Everyone that he talks to has WeChat, even his family and friends back home. Most of the text messages that he receives are mostly advertisements. "This message has my phone number in it, but the words are all in Chinese," he notices.

He takes a screenshot of the message, and he opens his WeChat app to use the translation feature. As the green line runs down the text, he can't help but think that the message was an error. The green line runs through the message four times, but it finally translates. "Hello, this message is to let you know that your package is outside your door and was delivered at 7:04 am."

He sits up out of bed and touches the cold floor with his naked feet. Opening the door, he sees a small brown rectangular package on the ground, with the last four digits of his phone number on it. "What is this?" he says loudly. He lightly kicks it, as he thinks it's a gag gift from a coworker or Matt. Nothing happens after he kicks it. He picks up the package and brings it into his apartment.

Grabbing a pair of scissors, he begins to cut the clear tape off the box. Shaking the box a little, there is a sound of chain links inside, "Did someone buy me a necklace?" he wonders. Opening the box up slowly and moving his head back, he can see a glimmer inside the box.

Inside the box, he picks up what seems to be a gold necklace. "She bought me a gold necklace. That is really nice," he thinks out loud. "It's a gold Eye of Horus necklace," he notices. "She must not know that I already have this necklace. I could use another one," walking back to his bed, he picks up his phone.

7:45 am

Terry: Hey, brown eyes. Thank you so much for the gift! You know I already have one, but I will proudly wear the one you just bought me. Anyway, thank you, and I'll talk to you later.

Terry goes to the bathroom and tries on the necklace. "This looks really good on me," he admires the necklace that he is now supporting. At 10:30 am, he is all packed up and ready to go, but still has a couple of hours before he has to be at the airport. With his flight leaving at 7:30 pm, he figures he will leave for the airport at 2 pm.

"The airport is about an hour away, and with traffic, it could be a little longer. If I get to the airport around 3, I should have enough time to go through security, check-in, and relax before the flight," he decides.

Just as he sits down, he hears a knock at the door. He opens the door, and sees the rental agent standing there. He passes the final check, and the rental agent leaves within five minutes of being there. Plopping down on the couch, he takes one more look at his watch: 10:45 am. He decides to lay down for a moment. His eyes began to weigh heavily, as his phone vibrated; he instantly grabbed it.

> **10:46 am**
> Lena: Hey handsome! I hope that you slept well and are excited to go home. And uhh...I didn't buy you a gold necklace. I don't know what other hoe you got that is buying you jewelry. 😂

He can't believe what he just read. "If she didn't buy this for me, who did?" he wonders. He puts his phone down, and he falls asleep before he can message back.

> **11:56 am**
> Lena: Hey, did you check the package? Maybe you can have a look at that, because I know you already have a necklace like that.

12:03 pm
Lena: Are you ok?

The howling wind wakes him up, as he slowly opens his eyes. He sits up quickly and looks at his watch: 1:58 pm. "Oh shit, I gotta go!" He jumps off the couch and rushes into the bathroom. Within 20 minutes, he has bags ready, checks the apartment for any belongings, turns off the television, and calls for a taxi. He puts his big suitcase and his book bag outside his apartment. Looking around one more time, he doesn't have much time to reminisce, and he is content with his decision.

The taxi will be at the front entrance in 3 minutes; he rushes onto the elevator with his luggage. He takes the necklace off, and puts it in his pocket. He hustles out the front door and runs to the taxi. Terry puts his big suitcase into the trunk and quickly gets into the back seat. Taking a sigh of relief, he checks his watch: 2:30 pm. "I should have enough time to do what I need to do," he reminds himself.

Traffic is its usual self on this day, and everything is at a standstill. He reaches for his phone, so he can message Lena back.

2:35 pm
Terry: Hey there, I'm sorry. I fell asleep and almost didn't get up in time. I didn't look for a return address on the package, and I threw the package away. 😬

Traffic begins to pick up, but he is still 35 minutes away from Tianjin Binhai International Airport.

> **2:37 pm**
> Lena: I'm glad that you were able to get up. But I don't know who sent it to you, and you will never know either. Maybe it was one of your other hoes. 😉

> **2:38 pm**
> Terry: Whatever, there are no other hoes. You're the only hoe in my life! 😉

Traffic slowly clears up, and the driver is able to pick up the speed. Terry lays his head back on the seat and closes his eyes for a moment. He rolls down the window to take in the sounds and smells of the city one last time: cars honking and changing lanes, the bǎo'ān giving someone directions in Chinese, delivery drivers whizzing through the streets and the sound of a local radio station blaring in the taxi.

"I'm gonna miss this," he thinks to himself.

Completely emerging in another's culture, is the truest way to understanding someone's DNA. Even when you may not know the language, there's always a way to understand someone. Terry allows the wind to bounce off of his face, as the taxi reaches the airport. "These things don't get easier," he reminds himself.

3:15 pm
Terry: I just got to the airport.
I'm going to call you once I get
to my gate.

3:20 pm
Lena: Ok handsome. Let me know
if you need any help.

3:21 pm
Terry: Will do!

It takes him about an hour to go through his passport check, security check and luggage check. This is the only international airport in the city and it gets quite busy. He ends up at Gate 1 at 4:15 pm. "That was an intense process, and I was still able to make it with some time to spare."

He video calls Lena, and he sees a blurry screen before it clears up.

"Hey there, pretty lady. Let me put my headphones in really quick," he says, as he wrestles to untangle the wires to his headphones.

"Ok, I think I'm good now. How are you?" he asks.

"I'm ok handsome! Just here at the shop going over some paperwork. How are you feeling? How did you almost oversleep?" she responds.

"I think I was really tired, because I got up so early. The package came at 7 this morning. After I brought it inside and opened it, I just fell back to sleep," he explains.

He looks up at the flight information board and sees that his flight is on time: "Tianjin, China (TSN) to Portland, Oregon (PDX) on schedule for departure at 7:30 pm."

"It's good that you woke up. Did you have an alarm set?" she asks.

"No, it was the wind blowing that woke me up. I guess nature was telling me to get up and catch this plane. I'm so confused about this necklace," he responds, as he takes the necklace out of his right pants pocket and waves it in front of the phone.

"Wow, that looks like real gold too. Maybe one of your friends or coworkers bought it for you. I would hold onto it for memories," she suggests.

"I mean, it's coming back with me. Maybe I'll give it to my new girlfriend," he says and chuckles.

"I don't want it," she replies and smiles at him.

He puts the necklace back in his pocket and says, "Do you know when you will come to America?"

"Not sure. We can talk more about it later," she states.

"Let me know, I'm sure we'll talk once I'm back," he responds.

"This isn't 'goodbye,' it's 'see you soon,' right? she asks.

"That's right," he confirms.

Terry pauses for a minute and looks at the sunsetting on the city; then, turns to look at Lena. "I think I've truly found myself," he thinks. A tear starts to roll down his left eye as he stutters, "I'm...I'm...I'm going to miss you."

"I'm going to miss you too, but we will talk once you get back to the States," she assures him.

"That sounds like a plan to me," he responds.

He clears the blur from his eyes, and he sees that Lena is now crying.

They spend the next 10 seconds looking at each other, and he says, "I think I'm going to get some coffee before they open the gates. I love you, Lena," he says.

Lena looks at him and smiles, "I love you too, Terry. I hope you have a safe flight and message me when you get home," she requests. They both blow kisses to each other and hang up the call. An hour later, the flight begins to board, and he gets onto the plane. As he straps on his seat belt, he looks out at the early night sky and feels his phone vibrate.

7:25 pm
Lena: Hey cutie!

7:26 pm
Terry: Hey pretty lady!

7:27 pm
Lena: Can I kiss you?

-The End-

Printed in the United States
by Baker & Taylor Publisher Services